AN OCEAN
WITHOUT A SHORE

ALSO BY SCOTT SPENCER

Last Night at the Brain Thieves Ball (1975)

Preservation Hall (1976)

Endless Love (1979)

Waking the Dead (1986)

Secret Anniversaries (1990)

Men in Black (1995)

Rich Man's Table (1998)

A Ship Made of Paper (2003)

Willing (2008)

Man in the Woods (2010)

River Under the Road (2017)

AN
OCEAN
WITHOUT
A SHORE

A Novel

SCOTT
SPENCER

ecco

An Imprint of HarperCollinsPublishers

AN OCEAN WITHOUT A SHORE. Copyright © 2020 by Scott Spencer. All rights reserved. Printed in the United States of America. No part of this book may be used or reproduced in any manner whatsoever without written permission except in the case of brief quotations embodied in critical articles and reviews. For information, address HarperCollins Publishers, 195 Broadway, New York, NY 10007.

HarperCollins books may be purchased for educational, business, or sales promotional use. For information, please email the Special Markets Department at SPsales@harpercollins.com.

FIRST EDITION

Designed by Renata De Oliveira

Library of Congress Cataloging-in-Publication Data has been applied for.

ISBN 978-0-06-285162-8

20 21 22 23 24 LSC 10 9 8 7 6 5 4 3 2 1

To Miro & Isa
and to Alice Quinn

He who cannot howl
Will not find his pack.
—CHARLES SIMIC. "AX"

Money destroys human roots wherever it is able to
penetrate. . . . It easily manages to outweigh all
other motives, because the effort it demands of the
mind is so very much less. Nothing is so clear and
so simple as a row of figures.
—SIMONE WEIL. *THE NEED FOR ROOTS*

CHAPTER I

Mornings Were Difficult

My name is Christopher Woods, but just about everyone calls me Kip.
Soon, I'm going to be finding out what the judge has decided
to "give me," though it's really what will be taken away, such
as the right to sleep in my own bed, retire and rise on my
own schedule, go to the movies, take walks, drink wine, and
just about every other of life's pleasures, heretofore taken for
granted. It would have been less stressful if sentencing had
come immediately on the heels of the verdict, but it might be
a good sign that it wasn't. Despite the encouraging words of
counsel, I knew from the start that a not guilty verdict was a
pipe dream, and, while the lawyers continue to be insistently,
almost *insanely* optimistic, it's quite likely there's a lot more
than a slap on the wrist in store for me.

I recently read a report written by an Israeli novelist about
his six months in a coma following a head injury in the Six
Days War, a dreamy, often phantasmagoric record of the visions he had while hovering between life and death. I am certainly not comatose, and instead of visions I am beset with
piercing and exact memories, but I do feel as if I am hovering

between two distinct states of being—my life in New York City and my impending incarceration. It must be said, however, that in the ways it matters most, I've been something of a prisoner my entire life.

But being a prisoner in a cell of your own design and acting as your own warden and parole board is at a considerable remove from a real penitentiary, and as I await my sentence I have decided my life took its first turn toward the present disaster on March 12, 1997. I had been out late the night before with a woman named Laurie Kaplan, whose father was a client at Adler Associates, the small investment firm where I worked. Laurie was an actress, currently in a Sam Shepard play, though in real life she was sunny, endlessly optimistic. She was my date for an AIDS benefit held at the St. Regis hotel, a dinner followed by an art auction. I spent $22,500 on a small Kiki Smith sculpture, after which the entire ballroom applauded, a sure sign I'd spent too much. I didn't mind; it was a nice piece and a good cause—I wasn't making huge amounts of money, but I gave regularly to that particular AIDS organization, tithing myself in accordance to the precepts of the only church to which I belonged, the Church of Not Acting Like a Selfish Jerk. I got Laurie home to her sublet on Ludlow Street about midnight and was back in my place on Charles shortly after that, read for a while, and was asleep by one thirty.

Only to be awakened four and a half hours later by a phone call. Mornings were difficult for me, increasingly so as I aged. Running out of time and all that. The rising sun a blow to the heart. Another night has passed, with kisses unkissed, confidences unspoken and left to wane, wilt, wither, and die. You do your best to perk yourself up. You remind yourself that things could be a great deal worse. You are living well, you enjoy your own company, still holding at your college weight, season tickets to the Met, so many consolations. But sadness can be sneaky, and sometimes upon waking you feel a certain degree of devastation. Wallflower's lament, unrequited love, etcetera etcetera. You get used to it. It's like living through a war. Or waking up every morning horribly overweight, which I'm not, or waking up homely, which I am, sort of. However, on the morning this story begins, I didn't have time for my usual longing, and my rituals of unrequited love began to change, as if the Twelve Stations of the Cross had been suddenly supplemented with a thirteenth.

I should mention that a phone ringing in the dark did not come as a total shock to me. I was a good and grateful employee of Adler Associates, and part of what you agree to when you are overpaid by an investment firm is your boundless availability. It was wearing me out, the lack of proper rest. I was not alone in this. We were all of us old before our time. Not worn-out like lumberjacks or ironworkers. Our aging was subtler, the kind that goes with doing work that is essentially meaningless. Usually, upon waking and tending to my bodily needs, I gazed at myself curiously in the mirror over the sink, like a hypochondriac taking his own temperature or checking his blood pressure, feeling his pulse, listening to his heartbeat. I wondered if, as Orwell had warned, I had acquired the face I deserved.

My father was blessed with good looks, but I favor my grandfather—my eyes are too close together, and nothing about me is in quite the right proportion. No one has ever directly told me I was ugly, but I personally would never be attracted to someone who looks like me. Okay, we won't call it ugliness. Lack of beauty. And it has had an effect, though I'll never know how much of an effect, never know what my life would have been as a handsome man. I did the usual things to improve my appearance once I started making money. I ate well and kept thin. Exercised. What I couldn't do was sleep eight hours a night, and I looked older than my years.

I picked up the phone. "Kip Woods here," I said, as if I were on my third espresso, tracking the London Stock Exchange on my laptop.

"I figured you'd be awake," Thaddeus said.

I checked my watch: 6:13 in New York, 11:13 London, 19:13 in Singapore.

"Are you all right?" I asked.

"No. No. I'm half out of my mind. I'm sorry. I know it's early."

"It's fine. What's going on?"

"It's this house. I'm going to lose it." His voice, usually so smooth, aged in the cask of his own nature, was this morning strident, harsh. "It's what's holding us together up here. I can't cover the taxes and the place needs a ton of work. Roof, chimneys, fireplaces, grounds, you name it. This house is goddamned *historic* and when I bought it I assumed a responsibility. I was going to be the one to *keep* it up, not *screw* it up."

I have known Thaddeus Kaufman since college in Michigan. I was the editor of a fairly nutty lit magazine called *My Heart Belongs to Dada,* which the University of Michigan's English Department blindly and benevolently funded, and Thaddeus had submitted a couple of conventional short stories to me, stories that had no place in my magazine, which existed primarily to celebrate experimental writing. I was far more drawn to Thaddeus than to his stories and I took and published whatever he gave me. He was tall, graceful, and casually seductive.

The University of Michigan is vast and most of the people you go to school with you never really get to know, but even there in overpopulated Ann Arbor, Thaddeus managed to give hundreds of people the impression that he held them in the very highest regard. Whether he did or didn't actually feel that way remains a mystery to me, but one thing I am sure of is that Thaddeus courted approval and affection as if he were amassing it for some impending future of solitary confinement. You'd see him on campus with his arm around some woman, or draped over the shoulder of a male friend. With his floppy long hair and sly smile, you didn't know what to make of him. He greeted people with kisses on the left cheek and the right, like some French general or a socialite. At any rate, I took his lousy stories and we've been friends ever since, though the friendship has never been played out on a level field. It would have been ridiculous of me to even dream he could ever give me as much thought as I give to him.

"Sell the house," I said. "It's just an asset. Dump it. Move to the city." I was more than hasty. I was unkind. He didn't really like the city, and his wife basically detested it. Add in children, dogs and cats, and the half million wild birds Thaddeus fed throughout the year. Some of the birds seemed to recognize him, landed on his shoulders, ate out of his hand. He thought they came to the windows and glared at him if the feeders were running low. Who doesn't want to feel like St. Francis from time to time? That house had become the center of his life, and as his career faltered (to say the least) and his hold upon the house became more and more tenuous, his attachment to it became more intense, just as a lover will crank up the heat of his own ardor if he senses his partner's passion beginning to cool.

The house was in Windsor County, about one hundred miles north of the city. Thaddeus and Grace had owned it since he'd sold a screenplay for a great deal of money back in 1980, when his ambition to write stories and novels was on life support, and he tried his hand on a movie script, a thriller about students in a made-up Middle Eastern country who take over the U.S. embassy. As luck would have it, by the time Thaddeus's screenplay went out, Iranian students had occupied our embassy in Tehran, and four studios competed for the rights to *Hostages*. The occupation of the embassy went on for 444 days, but the auction of Thaddeus's screenplay was concluded in a matter of hours.

That house! Houses like that are like dope habits—they only get more and more expensive. Thaddeus's and Grace's names were on the deed, but you'd have to say that the tables had turned and now the house owned them. I don't think Grace cared as much as he did; she had different priorities, different secrets. I warned him from the beginning not to buy that place—for reasons that were both selfish and sensible. I didn't want him to move out of the city, but I also believed that the house was a poor investment—150 years old, in lurching disrepair, fourteen rooms, a few inhabited by creatures ranging from the meekest mice to masked, marauding raccoons, plus seventy acres, where the mice and the raccoons summered, along with deer, coyotes, wily red foxes, and the occasional bobcat. The house had a name: Orkney. Out of Walter Scott. "Writers don't live in houses that have names," I warned him, but my tone was probably too casual, too jokey. And there was no changing his mind, no magic words, no stunning insight that would bring him to his senses. He was determined.

The New York City he and Grace had come to know was a city up for grabs, teetering on bankruptcy. But it was also a hell of a lot of fun for those willing to take risks. Which they were not. Whatever seductiveness and open-door policy Thaddeus had pursued in Ann Arbor was nowhere to be seen in New York. Tiny apartment, no view, no light, not even a color TV. He and Grace spent their lives in isolation. They could just as well have been living in a cabin in the woods, except they rode the subway to work every morning. It was love at its worst, in many ways. The city pulsated around them but their eyes were locked on each other. Oh, and what a little Crock-Pot of frustrated ambitions they kept at a steady simmer. No one liked his writing and no one liked her painting. Did I forget to mention Grace thought of herself as a painter? Well, I wasn't the only one who failed to take that into account. Anyhow, there they were in their union of failure and resentment and suddenly Thaddeus had his weird success. I wondered if they moved out of the city so they could ignore the fact that he was on the rise and she was going nowhere.

When I learned that the name Orkney came from *The Pirate,* an all but forgotten novel by Walter Scott—oh, excuse me, *Sir* Walter Scott—I tried to use the ridiculousness of that to dissuade Thaddeus, but the Sir Walter Scott–ness of the old place was hardly a drawback for him. It was a plus. Could have been early imprinting. His parents owned a bookshop in Chicago, where a complete set of the Scott novels was perpetually for sale, somehow symbolizing culture and the finer things in life, with leather covers, marbleized endpapers, and gold leaf on the spines' raised bands.

Orkney's version of leather bindings and raised gold bands was Tudor roses and fleur-de-lis, a cavalcade of sconces, a minstrel's gallery, and lancet windows, many with stained glass. Three staircases, one to the north bedrooms, one to the south, and the third to yet another staircase, this to the third floor, a mean little warren of cramped rooms, meant for domestic staff. Thaddeus, whose idea of happiness had once been to have a story accepted by *The New Yorker*, now sought joy in a house full of people he could feed and entertain. I realized that his avoidance of social life in Manhattan had come from his feelings of failure. But now, he could give more because he had more and he liked that more to be seen. A little tacky, perhaps, but as suspect motives go, quite easy to forgive.

At Orkney, he could be a kind of upstate Gatsby without the terrible longing, a contented Gatsby who actually has married his Daisy. But there was something else—a vision of a new kind of life that Orkney would give them, the land, the fresh air, the Hudson River. They would have a spiritual life, something deep and lasting. Nature would imbue their lives not only with beauty but with something deep and renewing, as if their souls could thrive on photosynthesis. He'd already abandoned literature—or perhaps he thought he was just putting it aside for the time being, while the money was coming in—and he thought: If I can't write like Tolstoy, who's to say I can't take a stab at living like him? What an idea! Thaddeus would be like Levin on his many acres—but a new, hipper Levin, one with the exuberant appetites of Vronsky. How did he ever think that would work out?

Orkney didn't have serfs, but the house had come with a caretaker, who had been living for fifty years in a yellow clapboard house on the property, hidden behind a swell in the land and thirty oak trees. The caretaker's name was Phillip Stratton, but everybody called him Hat. That caretaker was Thaddeus's undoing. When Stratton was injured preparing the grounds for one of Thaddeus's parties by stringing up lights high in a tree, Thaddeus, compassionately, egomaniacally, sawed off a piece of his property and gave it to the old guy.

The gesture had its ludicrous side, but if you loved Thaddeus this would only make you love him more. Wanting to be liked can bring out the best in you. No? Now the caretaker was buried in a nearby cemetery, and Jennings Stratton, Hat Stratton's son, lived in the yellow house with a wife and two children. Even if I were to convince Thaddeus that the best—the only!—thing for him to do was unload Orkney, it would not be as easy as it ought to have been. He had complicated it in a moment of stricken largesse, and now another family was living in the center of the property, sharing the driveway, having visitors of their own, and sometimes enormous parties that rumbled on for forty-eight hours, with tents pitched and bonfires lit, horseshoe tosses, pig roasts, sing-alongs, and dancing.

Grace often attended the caretaker's parties, but Thaddeus never did. He'd stay at his desk, tucked into one of Orkney's seldom used north-facing rooms, as far from the sounds of the festivities as he could get, working furiously on screenplays that suddenly no one wanted to pay for, trying his best not to think about Hemingway's line about how people go broke, gradually and then suddenly.

After the Mimosa

That morning on the phone, it seemed the futility of hanging on to Orkney might be sinking in and Thaddeus was finally ready to sell the place. He said as much. "I should put this place on the market," he said. "I should have done it a long time ago."

"Where are you? Are you home?" For all I knew, he was in town, maybe on my corner, on his way over. I was in my boxers and T-shirt. Phone to ear, I walked to the windows, opened the blackout shades, and let what there was of a wintry Manhattan morning speak for itself. Mottled black and gray, the sky looked like a wet *Wall Street Journal*. My view was mainly my building's back garden—the dormant dogwood, the wrought-iron patio furniture upholstered in snow. Wouldn't it have been the most marvelous thing if then and there the dogwood would have burst into full bloom, its white petals with that little rusted tinge at the tip? In my position I had to at least allow for the possibility of miracles—reality itself was just not going to pull me through.

"So last night," Thaddeus was saying, "our so-called weekend guests were *still* around and I invited a few other people.

More the merrier, I guess. I kept on bringing out my best wines. Bought when I was stupid enough to think the money would never end. And I'm going 'I spent so much money on glorified grape juice. I really needed to be beaten with the peoples' scythes for sure.'"

"Where are you, Thaddeus? Right now."

"Home," he said. "Grace is sleeping. Guests still sleeping. So are the kids. The cats and dogs. I can't remember the last time I had a real night's sleep." He paused. I heard a long intake of breath. "I feel so alone," he said, in barely a whisper.

I couldn't say it, but I thought it: You've got a houseful. You've been mounting your ceaseless charm offensive. So sweet to everyone, so solicitous. And by the way: you've also got a wife and two children. And oh yes, one other thing: your body probably carries the smell of sex from last night.

Thaddeus asked, "Are you there?"

"Yes, sure, always." For a moment, my habitual and well-honed reserve was about to fail and I was close to saying, You need to come over here right now. Not that it would have thrown twenty years of laughs and denial into some suddenly revealing light, but it would have changed things. Lives are shaped by words and deeds, but what we don't say might be just as powerful as what we do. Our silence works like a lathe, giving us our final form.

"Is your mortgage being foreclosed?" I asked.

"Not yet. Don't worry, Kip, I am not asking you for a loan."

Really? There was a touch of formality in his tone, as if he was now getting to the part of the conversation he'd rehearsed. Thaddeus had always been so of the moment, off the cuff, captain of the Good Ship Spontaneous, and those things had served him well, until, of course, the very instincts that brought him success plunged him into ignominy. A shocking development, to be sure, as if your left hand had become your right foot, or your carriage had turned into a pumpkin. He'd derailed his movie career in a burst of perverse inspiration—a Sunday brunch at a producer's Coldwater Canyon house at which he threw his drink in the face of the host's twenty-seven-year-old son. Who knows why Thaddeus would do something so foolish? Trouble at home? Hating himself for auditioning for an assignment he didn't even want? What an outburst! Thaddeus always maintained that he didn't even quite remember tossing that glass of California orange juice and California champagne, even going so far as to wonder if a dybbuk or some other fanciful, malign spirit had momentarily taken control of his actions.

But it was fatal, whatever the motivation, whatever the cause. One flick of the wrist and his career vaporized. Maybe he was already on the fade at that point, but after the Coldwater Canyon brunch he was poison. Of course, if he'd been on the top of the heap, the transgression would have eventually become an anecdote. But he was in the middle of the heap. Maybe low-middle.

He continued to try, putting together pitches and spec scripts, waiting for the phone to ring, and working his charm as if he could quip and grin his way back into contention on those occasions when someone in the business agreed to meet him for a drink. As the weeks of unemployment turned into months and then a year, and when his savings were drained and his pension fund (not under Adler management, by the way) made that doomed pilgrimage from nest egg to piggy bank, he began to denounce all of the people with whom he had once happily worked, all those friends who turned out to be acquaintances, and who seemed to have stumbled into a kind of collective amnesia, forgetting all of the favors Thaddeus had so willingly bestowed when he was able to—the introductions to agents and producers, the encouraging readings, the pep talks, the Ritalin, the loans of money and Final Draft software. A small number of the people Thaddeus had hoped would rally around him when trouble came did in fact check in with calls, notes, invitations to parties. But even those semi-loyalists drifted off—the currents in the waters in which they all swam were swift and pitiless. People just went away. And what was the point of their loyalty anyhow, those decent few? All they could offer was sympathy. No one could help.

Except for me. For this morning's call to a rich friend, there had likely been a buildup, maybe over the course of a week. Notes scribbled. Grace might have had a hand in it, too, or she might have instigated the whole thing. "Ask Kip," she might have said. "He's got money and nothing to spend it on. He's obviously in love with you and he'll do whatever you ask." It was something she could have said. From the moment we met, she was watching me, not sure enough to actually say anything, or maybe she had. Maybe the financial emergency had loosened her tongue. Maybe she said, Call your boyfriend and get him to buy some land from us. Grace was a scrapper; she'd never go down without a fight.

"What would you think about buying some land from us?" Thaddeus said.

He overestimated my income, my wealth. They both did. I was overpaid but I was not personally rich, just a handmaiden to the rich. The people I dealt with made donations to the Southampton SPCA that were larger than my yearly take, but to Thaddeus and Grace I was loaded. There was no getting around it: I was the rich friend.

"You've got a price in mind?" I asked, in my sober, global-strategist voice. Orkney was not quite a white elephant, but the upkeep was ruinous. Thaddeus's career was gone, and Grace was, strictly speaking, an expense, not an asset. Throw in two children, two tuitions, all those meals, all those teeth.

"You mean that, Kip? Really. You would consider that?"

"Can I pick my own spot? There's some beautiful land up there."

"Of course. We can do a subdivision." There was a catch in his throat. Was he tearing up?

"Hey, we'll be neighbors," I said, in an offhand way, as if that added benefit had just occurred to me.

Silence. I could hear him thinking: Oh no, don't build on our beautiful pristine acres. Use this land for bird watching or picnics. Be prepared to sell it back to me when my ship comes in. Write it off your taxes. He knew nothing of the tax code, by the way.

"Here's what I can do," I said. "Figure out what you need and that's what I'll pay for it. Within reason, though. Remember—I'm not as rich as the people I work for!"

"Need? We need a lot, Kip. I won't lie to you."

I felt a twinge of annoyance. I knew I didn't really have the right to ask what I was about to ask, but really there was no getting around it.

"How's work going?" I asked, suppressing any hint of disapproval. He had gotten rich by a fluke and he was waiting for the next fluke. I couldn't really blame him. And he was up there in Windsor County, surrounded by people who didn't do normal days' work—some painted, some took photos of wildlife and sunsets, some dabbled in botanical experiments, growing hybrid strains of cabbage and apples, some made occasional forays into the city to bring family heirlooms to auction, all of them living off the fumes of old fortunes. You could almost despise them, but really in the larger scheme of things they were just irrelevant. As most of us are.

"I'm at my desk day and night, no days off, no holidays," Thaddeus said. "I'm Scrooge to my own Bob Cratchit."

"That script you were talking about . . ."

"Which one?" he asked. "Anyhow the answer was no, pass, Pasadena, which covers everything I've written in the past three years. I keep on thinking I should get a regular job somewhere. But you know what? I can't afford to get a normal job. I need more than a regular job can pay me. And anyhow I know I'm close to writing my way back into the business. And if I walk away now and get some other kind of work—not that I'm qualified to do anything in particular—then my chances of writing myself back into the movie business are pretty much wrecked. For a while, I was hoping for something at the college but you know Avon College's film department is a hundred percent experimental and the kind of movies I worked on are really of no interest. I know this guy at Random House who thinks there's a chance I might find some ghostwriting gig that I might be able to do fairly quickly and make a few bucks, but for the most part I'm here in front of the slot machine yanking away at it and afraid to move on because maybe the next pull is going to be the jackpot. You've known me forever, Kip, and you know I'm not . . ."

His voice was suddenly muffled, his hand over the mouthpiece. I heard other people coming into the room. A man's voice, another man's voice, a woman's, laughter.

"Hello?" I said.

"Sorry," he murmured. "I can't believe these people are up and around already. It's barely light."

"Who are they?"

"Look, man. I better get some breakfast going here. But I have to tell you. The money. We actually need . . . It's a lot."

That unit of measurement—a lot—no longer had meaning to me, when it came to money. I knew too many rich people, and to them a lot could mean one hundred million dollars if they were talking about a profit shortfall, and a lot could also mean five dollars if they were talking about the tip they'd given the attendant at a parking garage.

"I'm sorry, Kip," he said.

"No, no, it's okay, it's fine. These things happen." He could be hard on himself, very hard, he could actually be brutal. I didn't want him to suffer any further.

"I plan to buy that land back from you. You'll get your money back and more. You'll see."

"Oh please. Stop."

"I feel ashamed."

"In front of me?"

"In front of myself."

"It's just money."

"Money's just money when you have it. When you don't, it's everything."

Even over the phone, I felt the blunt physical fact of him. All the details that made him irreducibly himself. The almost-broken nose. The space between the front teeth. The shins worn bare and shiny by a lifetime of Levi's. The thick black hair, which he still let grow long, now no longer floppy but combed back, like a Latin American diplomat. His skin was pale but his cheeks bloomed with a permanent blush. Indoors, outdoors, winter, summer, spring, and fall, he had the cheeks of a ten-year-old boy stomping snow off his boots after an hour of sledding. Everything about him pleased me and made me want to touch him. Maybe there is always one person who finds everything about one other person alluring. Maybe somewhere there is a person who feels that way about me, or you.

Every morning I thought of him. Which often meant imagining him with his wife. The imagination must play some vital evolutionary role in the survival of the species, but the imagination can be cruel. When you imagine people waking together, you don't picture discord, or icy stares; you don't imagine boredom, anxiety, mistrust. No one needs to rinse their mouth, no one carries a secret within them like an unexploded bomb. You imagine two people enjoying everything you long for. The imagination can be merciless, and it's shameless, as shameless as time.

Once, in college, Thaddeus and I were in my apartment getting high and having a friendly argument about music— Rolling Stones versus Beatles. I was going on and on, my passion for winning the argument far outstripping my passion for Charlie Watts, who I insisted was ten times better than Ringo Starr. Thaddeus listened, which he was so good at. It was part of what people loved about him, his eloquent, gracious, encouraging silence. Henry James describes a woman as having a face that, in speech, was like a lighted window in the dark, but when you spoke to her the curtain was immediately drawn. Thaddeus was the opposite of that. He seemed more animated when he was listening, always leaning forward, nodding encouragingly. But as I went on about Charlie Watts, ratcheting up my admiration with each go-round, he finally said, "Oh, blow me," not in a sexual way, but just as a way of expressing his disagreement.

I don't know where I got the courage. A once-in-a-lifetime thing. A lightning strike. A prison cell door the jailer forgot to lock. A staircase suddenly appearing on the side of a glass mountain. He said, "Oh, blow me" and I said, "All right, I will." He laughed, but I didn't back down. I looked at him with as much boldness as I could muster. At last Thaddeus shrugged and said, "Hey, if you want to, go for it. I've never turned down a blowjob in my life." He started to undo his faded button-fly Levi's and stopped, rather theatrically. "Is this more or less your thing? Like, you know, are you gay?" he asked. I looked at him as if half confused, half amused, and said, "Uh . . . no. What about you?" And Thaddeus said, "Well, if you're not, then neither am I."

In Ann Arbor, he had a reputation and it had been earned. You wouldn't call him *needy* because he generally got what he wanted, though he seemed always to want something more, something else. And you wouldn't call him *insatiable* because, well, his manner was soft, considerate, he didn't have that vulpine look in his eyes. He *was* carnal, perhaps even lustful; he trusted nothing more than human touch, which he believed to be more truthful than words, and who could argue with that? Mainly, he wanted to be loved, he wanted to be admired, and he metabolized love and admiration the way some people can metabolize food and remain thin. He ought to have been an actor or a singer—he needed the applause. A writer of ho-hum, derivative short stories could never garner the praise he craved.

I'd seen him with so many different girls that once I asked him, Are you actually *with* anyone? To which he answered, "Any port in a storm, right?" But what did that mean? Men as well as women? Pansexuality? At the time we called it polymorphous perversity. Hands, feet, mouths, anuses, vaginas—the point was pleasure, the goal was the tingle, the surge, maybe even a kind of love, delicate, frail, with the life span of a moth.

His jeans were unbuttoned and he fished himself out. I heard the scrape of something being dragged across the floor coming from the apartment above, lived in by a guy who we referred to as Professor Plum. His wife had died and the poor soul was always rearranging his furniture. Outside, the wind had picked up; a night storm was coming in and my windows shook in their frames. The walls of my room were painted white and I kept them bare, not wanting any images or posters or sayings or symbols to somehow define me in the eyes of others. The floors were bare, too. At one point I'd had a five-by-seven Persian carpet I'd bought from a thrift shop, but soon after bringing it home I rolled it up and stored it. I thought it said something about me, though I wasn't sure what.

I took him in. The world as I had known it began to give way and it was terrifying, like crossing a frozen lake and hearing the pings and groans of the ice. I had no idea what I was doing. I had but once been inside of someone's mouth and I'd been too frozen with self-consciousness to feel pleasure. A sophomore girl I'd been dating grew restless and uncertain with our movie and study dates and thought she might change the nature of our chummy relationship via oral sex, perhaps in the same spirit that Professor Plum tried to lessen his grief by moving the sofa from the west wall to the east. We were in her dorm room and as she went at me I scanned the spines of her books—Spinoza, Kant, Russell, Schopenhauer. She told me not to finish in her mouth, and to tap her on the head when

I was close. She had ground rules. It comforted me to know that someone in the room knew what we were doing. Soon, very very soon, I tapped. She continued to grip me but moved her head, as you would lean away from a sparkler to avoid the sulfuric spit. She gave me a considerate little tidying shake and then playfully plopped down beside me and said, "My turn?" And even though she said it as if it was a question, I was in a virtual panic. The idea of orally pleasuring her was deeply disturbing to me—and somewhat mysterious, too. Thanks to porn I knew what position to take and had a general idea of the choreography. She still had her clothes on but now she was wriggling out of them, gleefully, as if preparing to jump into a cool lake on a hot afternoon. Her nakedness was not a welcome sight, but I did not flinch, any more than you would allow yourself to recoil at the bedside of a badly injured friend. My technique was absurd. I kissed her opening as if it were her mouth, one faux-passionate kiss after another, in the general vicinity of her clitoris—or so I hoped. Youth, excitement, and trust carried the day and her orgasm came quickly, a kind of vaginal sneeze. She pulled my hair, beckoning me to lie beside, which I did, and we held each other and before I could stop myself or even become fully aware of the meteor shower of emotions going through me, I began to cry. "Shh," she said, rubbing my shoulder. "I know, I know. . . ." And to this day I can't say with any certainty what she meant, what she knew, or thought she knew. She could have meant I know how intense that was, how wonderful. She could have meant I know you never did that before. She could have meant I know that's not what you wanted. I really don't know. I do know that people see you a lot more clearly than you want them to.

And here I was again, an unexpected visitor on Planet Sex.

And the main thing I remembered from my first time was to ask him to tap me before he came. "Check," Thaddeus said, which was rather flippant, but at the same time he traced my lips with the head of his penis, which I found quite romantic. I embraced him with my lips, my tongue, the roof of my mouth. But really it was my nerves, my blood, that ineffable mist that rolls silently through everyone, the thing some people call the self, and others say is the soul. I must have been gripping him too tightly; he said, Whoa. The fernlike curls of his secret hair, the brush of it against my nose, was more vivid than war and peace and the price of oil. It was somewhere between 10 P.M. and midnight. I have revisited and redone and reimagined that night countless times in my solitude. I have behaved in these imagined encounters in ways that my inexperience and shyness and fear would not permit at the time. In my imagination, I have ravished him. In my altered memories, I have made promises even a saint could not keep.

He was good enough to give me the warning tap but I didn't heed it. I drank him in as if knowing I would be walking across a desert for the next twenty years. When he stepped away, he looked at me with what I took to be admiration.

"That was intense," he said. "If I went over to the University Gay Freedom Alliance and let them know about your skills there'd be a line around the block."

"There's a University Gay Freedom Alliance?" I asked, though I was of course aware of its existence.

"Sure. But don't worry. Everything here is on the q.t. I don't tell and you don't tell."

"Of course."

"So now what do we do? Your turn?"

"Oh no," I quickly said. "Maybe some other time. I made

it with Cindy King this afternoon and my downtown is sort of shuttered up for the rest of the day."

"Okay, then. But it's now or never."

"Well, maybe a rain check."

"We'll see about that," he said with a laugh.

CHAPTER 3

Uncle Morris

Fourteen hours after ending my phone call with Thaddeus I was expected at Morris Posner's apartment for dinner. Morris was Thaddeus's uncle, his mother's younger brother. I first met Morris years before at Thaddeus's parents' apartment in Chicago when Thaddeus and I had driven in from Ann Arbor to attend a Stevie Wonder concert at McCormick Place. I often reflect back on Thaddeus's mother's expression when we appeared unannounced. You'd have thought that Thaddeus was a Jehovah's Witness and not her son by the look Libby gave him—something between blank and beleaguered. Two long moments of silence until she said, "Well, come in, come in, Morris is visiting and we're just sitting down to dinner." Thaddeus waggled his brows up and down, hoping to assure me that this was all somehow comic, but I felt sick to my stomach as we followed Libby into the dining area, watching her long graying braid go back and forth like a windshield wiper between her bony shoulder blades.

Morris was happy to see his nephew. He looked secure, playful, and prosperous with his graying hair as long as Leonard

Bernstein's, a striped shirt, suspenders, a bow tie. When he learned we were in town to hear Stevie Wonder, his immediate response was "Oh, I wish that was what I was doing. Stevie Wonder is our Beethoven. He thinks in music, he breathes music, he is music."

Somewhere along the way I mentioned my plan of moving to New York after graduation, and right before Thaddeus and I left for McCormick Place, Morris tore out a sheet from his prescription pad, circled his phone number, and wrote *Call Me* on it. "I am not known for idle invitations," he said. He saw me and I saw him and his forwardness frightened me.

Morris ran his Upper West Side pediatrics practice as if he lived in Grover's Corners, without an office staff, or an assistant, answering his own phone. He didn't send out bills but took cash or a check right after the appointment, and he'd sooner accept seashells than run a credit card. He saw children whose parents could not afford to pay, as well as cossetted children whose parents lived nearby on Central Park West, some of whom he had taken care of when they were children. His office was in an apartment building on West Sixty-Seventh Street, and his apartment, a six-room duplex, was in the same building. He'd been living alone when we first started our monthly dinners, but now his boyfriend, a Jamaican orthopedic surgeon named Robinson Kingsford, was there most nights. Robbie owned an apartment near Roosevelt Hospital, but I think he rarely slept there. Morris was tall, lanky, pale like Thaddeus, but without the contrasting rosy cheeks. He had a soothing voice and he spoke slowly, with the cadence of those who are rarely interrupted. Robbie, on the other hand, vibrated with nervous energy, like a doctor making his rounds, his eyes and his body radiating his anxiety over being detained. He was a full foot shorter than Morris, fleshy, round faced, with a light reedy voice.

The two of them, engaged in the joint project of dragging me out of the closet, really gayed it up on the evenings I was invited over. They did everything short of wearing kimonos and putting Streisand on the stereo, while they brought up matters pertaining to same-sexing at every turn. Naturally, many of them health and death related, but they both envisioned a time when civil unions between a man and a man or a woman and a woman would be legal. They thought New York City would soon have an openly gay mayor, and Morris insisted the city had already had a few mayors in the closet. They also teased each other with a lot of name-calling—Miss Thing, Nurse Ratched, Baby Cakes, you old queen you. I found it outrageous, and to calm myself, I tried to believe that this name-calling was actually evidence of how free Morris and Robbie were with each other, and how content they were with their own human nature. Yet I could not help but wonder if that nasty talk was really a way of releasing the pressure of self-doubt and shame—maybe they were not so different from me and they, too, felt the wound of the straight world's contempt.

Occasionally, Morris and Robbie invited some eligible bachelor to join us for dinner. The awkwardness and pointlessness was horribly embarrassing, being on display, having to think of a stranger as a possible partner, and, most of all, having to fear that tonight's prospect might be someone who worked in my business, or knew, even vaguely, someone I knew.

Over the last couple of years Morris and Robbie had introduced me to several men—an anthropologist with a nervous laugh, a Taiwanese with an eye patch, the owner of a wine store who refused to drink what they served him, and an athletic-looking schoolteacher who I found really interesting and funny and who I even once called but who had no interest in me.

Morris and Robbie were strictly doctor-knows-best when it came to my monkish personal life. Once, I asked them to stop trying to pair me off with someone, and my tone was sharper than I'd meant it to be.

"If you want us to stop trying to fix you, then stop being broken," Robbie said. "Choose someone, come alive, be a part of it."

"And forget about my lousy nephew," Morris had added. "Why fixate on a married man? Who is AC/DC at most, and even if he is would never admit to it."

"Not everything is a choice," I said. "Some things just are."

"He's in a whole different world, Kip. He may as well be dead."

"Would you tell a Christian that about Jesus?"

"Are you kidding me?" Morris exclaimed. "Can you even hear yourself? And by the way, I do think our Christian friends are making a huge mistake."

"And I'm not saying he's Jesus or anything," I said.

Morris made a show of wiping the imaginary sweat off his brow and flicking it off his fingers.

"But I am saying that just because something you desire might not be easy, or convenient, or even possible, that doesn't stop you from wanting it."

"At a certain point it should," said Robbie. "It's not surrender. It's recalibration."

"Well, I guess I'm not very scientific."

Morris puffed up his cheeks and slowly let the air out. We were sitting in the front room of the apartment, which had recently been painted, and the smell of the fresh latex was in the air. Robbie had brought in three dozen roses to counteract the odor but the roses made matters worse. The TV was on without the sound, tuned to Comedy Central. Al Franken was hosting satirical coverage of the Democratic Party's nominating convention. He was pointing at an overhead screen that showed Bill and Hillary Clinton and Al and Tipper Gore, the four of them linking arms while patriotic confetti swirled around them, looking pleased and groomed and profoundly well adjusted. Delegates danced in the aisles, their campaign placards going up and down like the pistons in an engine.

"You can change your mind," I said to Morris and Robbie. "But feelings are stubborn. They're not to be figured out. They have their way with you. They're bigger than the mind."

"Romantic poison," Morris declared. "Feelings can be examined. They can be analyzed and they can shift." He was, as Thaddeus had said, argumentative. Thaddeus saw little of Morris, and Morris had Thaddeus pigeonholed, calling Thaddeus Poor Thaddeus, or Our Poor Thaddeus, or Mr. Howyadoin'. He and Robbie had been up to visit Orkney just once, and Morris thought the place was pure folly, noticing every water-stained ceiling, every sputtering sconce. As far as Morris was concerned, the profusion of birds drawn to Thaddeus's beloved feeders was a health hazard.

My plea for them to stop trying to find someone for me had no effect, and now, fourteen hours after Thaddeus's early morning phone call, Morris and Robbie brought in an Israeli named David Beytenu, a molecular biologist in the middle of a two-year appointment at NYU. Beytenu commandeered the conversation. He had a long curly beard and a thick voice that made you want to clear your throat so he would clear his. He wanted to talk about determinism versus free will and argued vehemently against determination, as if he somehow knew that this was a worldview to which Morris, Robbie, and I adhered.

"If we believe in determinism we will have to revamp our vocabulary, a total top-to-bottom renovation. We can say someone is great because they have beautiful eyes or some other form of beauty. But they did not will these things, this is just how they are. So. Here's the rub. Can we use the same judgment when we praise a man for risking his life for another? For determinists—and this, I must tell you, is determinism's fatal flaw—being truthful or brave is like being beautiful or tall. It is not a matter of choice, it is just a function of being, just something we are born with." At that, Beytenu folded his arms across his chest and sat deeper in his chair, prepared to enjoy the looks on our faces as we realized the scaffolding to our belief system had just been dismantled and now everything we had once held to be true was crashing down around us.

Beytenu must have been disappointed by what amounted to our collective shrug, and he left rather early. The three of us sat in silence for a while, and then Robbie began to clear the table.

"Can someone please tell me where this guy got the idea that we were determinists?" Robbie asked, genuinely confused.

When our laughter finally subsided, Morris and I joined Robbie in clearing the table and cleaning the kitchen. They kept a small radio over the sink and Mozart wafted from the speaker. Morris and Robbie always made me feel that human happiness was not really exotic or difficult. It was a natural thing, and it was a daily pleasure to protect and maintain your domestic tranquility. You were polite, you put yourself second, and you were nice—a word I had not yet given its due.

After we'd put the kitchen back in order, the three of us returned to the dining table, where a bowl of Concord grapes had somehow appeared, their skin that dusty dark purple. Morris and Robbie were mindful about their alcohol intake and as we'd gone through two bottles of wine with dinner Robbie brought out a bottle of fizzy water, and a little plate of lemon wedges.

"So you didn't like Mr. Determinism because . . ." Morris began.

"Did you like him?" I asked. "He was tedious."

"Yes, he was tedious. But he was also quite smart, and a decent person. But really, does it even matter?"

"I guess not," I said.

"We don't understand you," Robbie said. "Nobody can live the way you do. You're going to go bonkers."

"Nobody says bonkers anymore, Robbie," Morris said.

"Yes, they do," said Robbie. "I hear that word used frequently. But really, Kip, look around you. The world is changing. It's already changed. Stonewall was a long time ago."

"Yes, and AIDS is now."

"All the more reason to speak up and be heard. You're young. You have all the energy in the world. There is a movement and you should be part of it."

"Robbie, history isn't for everybody," I said. "Most people just stand by and try not to be harmed."

"Do you ever wonder if you're using him as an excuse not to live your life?" Morris asked.

"I'm living my life. In my own way. Don't I have that right? I'm not someone who jumps up and down and says Look at me. I'm private. I don't actually want people to know anything about my goddamned sex life. People are mean, Morris. Mean,

small, and dirty. In my business anyhow. They're always looking for something to make fun of or use against you."

"You're so alone, Kip," Morris said. "It pains us."

"He called," I said. "Today."

"Here we go," said Robbie.

When I explained why Thaddeus had called, Robbie
seemed to withdraw into himself, his normally lively eyes suddenly flat and his expression vague. Morris's elbows banged
onto the table, and his forehead came to rest in his palm. He
looked like someone who had just finished his income taxes.

"Well, that's a very strange situation," he said. "The whole
thing is strange. The way he threw away his career. You adore
him so you probably think he's screwed up his Hollywood
career because he's—what? Too good for movies? Too prin-
cipled? But I'm telling you, he courts failure. Failure is what
he recognizes. And why? Because he was raised to be a failure.
I'm no Freudian—and Freud was probably gay, by the way, he
was totally obsessed with Carl Jung, way beyond reason—but
here's what Freud was right about: no man who is unloved as
a child can ever be a success. Not here." Morris pointed to his
head, where, presumably, consciousness resided. And then to
his heart, presumably the domain of our emotions. "I see it
all the time. People say what they say about pediatrics, but I
can tell you this—it's just the opposite. Pediatrics is about as
stressful a field of medicine as there is. Beyond brain surgery,
beyond oncology. Every appointment lives are in the balance.
It's always an emergency. And that's because childhood itself
is an emergency.

"So now he comes to you because he can't afford to stay in
his house. But why would he continue to live in a house he can't
afford? Why would someone do that? And why would he make

it someone else's problem?" Morris sensed his voice was rising, and he folded his hands, reassuming his favorite self, good old Doc Posner, the kindly, commonsense country doctor out of Norman Rockwell. "Honestly, Kip. There's something off here. Something strange. And that house of theirs is really strange."

"In the right hands it could be very special," said Robbie.

"It's a white elephant," said Morris. "Look, I am not as close to my nephew as I'd like to be. For some reason, or reasons, he has chosen not to be close with me. And Libby thinks 'sexual perversion' is a form of bourgeois selfishness. Sam figured out a long time ago that the best he can hope for is a peaceful household so he's never going to cross her. Sam is not overly bright. Two years at Case Reserve, over and out. So whatever. Maybe they warned Thaddeus to stay away from me. I hate to think they'd stoop so low, but you never know in these matters." He closed his eyes for a moment and gently massaged their crepey lids with his thumb and forefinger.

"Sam is a good person, with a big heart, but it's a big broken heart. With Libby it's different. She's stern, and she was as a child, too. It's in her eyes, and her jaw. Their lives have had terrible losses—all that socialism turned to dreck, that was a real kick in the ass for both of them. That bookshop has been teetering on the edge of bankruptcy for as long as I know. But think of it, think of what happened to them. Their child. Their little girl. Dead at six months. Life's most hideous catastrophe. They blamed everyone. The doctors, the hospital. Libby actually blamed me, even though I'm a thousand miles away, still I should have done something. Anything. And they both blamed Thaddeus because he was a smiley-faced four-year-old little boy who committed the cardinal sin of surviving. Shame on him for surviving, shame on him for cracking jokes and doing little dances to make them happy. So what does it leave for our Thaddeus? A life of trying to please people who can never be pleased? That's his legacy. Our parents tell us who we are. That's what they do, even if they don't know they're doing it. They tell us who we are."

"I think it's sad," said Robbie.

"Of course it's sad," said Morris. "But that kind of damage can create dangerous people. I see this in my practice all the time. I have watched so many people grow up. I see them from the very beginning. I know how it works. It's not a theory, it's observation. I see them bleed and I see them heal. And then a little later I see the scar tissue. Scar tissue. And what is it that distinguishes scar tissue from undamaged skin? Lack of feeling, lack of nerve cells. It's just a covering."

"I don't think of Thaddeus as a person with no feelings," I said. "I know what he feels. I can feel it myself. Every bit of it."

"Of course he has feelings," Morris said. "Deep feelings. Wonderful, marvelous feelings. But you ignore the scar tissue at your own peril. The fact is these scars are the dead zones. Zones where he feels nothing, or very little. And that's the danger."

"I've never known anyone who goes so far out of his way to make people feel good," I said. "Happy or noticed."

"And that's marvelous," said Morris, with cheerful confidence. "I see that part of him, too. I know he's been generous, and he signs all the worthy petitions. But the question is—why? Is it a way of keeping people in their place, so they don't get to see the real person? Sometimes all that niceness is a way of making sure nobody quite sees you."

At last, Robbie said, "I think Thaddeus really likes his uncle Morris." He was using small silver scissors to cut away the stems that were now without grapes, each showing a little teardrop of pulp. "When we went to that Easter party at his house? He took me aside and he thanked me. It was very sweet. He said it made him rest easy to know his uncle was with someone who cared so much about him and would always look after him."

"I don't need looking after, Robbie. I find it quite condescending."

"I don't think he meant it that way," said Robbie.

"Well, I'm not so sure," Morris said. "That's the thing about Thaddeus—you never know exactly what he means. He says things for effect. And when you say things for effect, it means in a way you are lying. I feel sorry for him, I do. He was a tender kid who was not treated at all tenderly. Not beaten or starved, but tolerated. It was appalling. And now we see the result."

He looked at me searchingly, until I said, "Not really. I don't see what you see. I see to the very bottom of him. I've never known anyone so completely, and I never will."

"He loves him, Morris," said Robbie. "I mean, come on. What are you trying to do?"

"I am trying to get Kip to see him for who he is."

"I see him," I said. "But you don't add up a person's qualities like something on a balance sheet. We don't know why we love the people we love, not if we really love them. That's the whole purpose of love, to take us out of the rational, binary, up or down, in or out, black or white, good or bad, profit or loss, to take us out of all those everyday things into something sacred."

"What nonsense," Morris said. "Love isn't some form of blind man's bluff. And it's not some cockeyed prayer. Ask me why I love Robbie."

"No. It's fine."

"Go ahead, ask, I want you to."

"Well, I don't really want to."

"I love him because he's a brilliant doctor who would go to any lengths to relieve the suffering of his patients."

I shrugged. Robbie's specialty was sports medicine—he did knees, rotator cuffs.

"Secondly, he is a marvelous, attentive lover. Thirdly, he is protective of me. Four? I hear music more clearly, with more texture and detail, when he is in the room. Five? I find him insightful. He's smart."

"Thaddeus is smart. And quick. His mind is so alive."

"Really? Don't you think his focus is rather narrow? You two have known each other since college, isn't that right?"

"Proceed," I said.

"Well, then how is it that he doesn't know you're gay? What kind of attention has he been paying?"

"He sees me with a lot of women. I don't know. I really don't. Maybe he does."

"He's colluding with you to keep everything secret and shameful. He is a drug you take to keep yourself stuck in whatever realm of protracted adolescence or self-hatred you were in when you met him."

"I don't agree. I bonded with him. I can't help it."

"You're a gay man in love with a married man who has two children. Wake the fuck up."

"He's many things, Morris. Not just a married father of two. And I'm many things, too, by the way. I don't see myself as a category."

"Here's what I know about my nephew. Who I love, by the way, don't get me wrong."

"Oh, I can tell."

"I do. But"—he put up a heed-this finger—"his intelligence, all of his emotional energy, his desire for success, his friendliness, his jokiness—it's all in the service of one thing, and one thing only. And that is his overwhelming, crippling desire to be liked."

"Worse things could be said about a person," I said.

"There's always something worse," Morris said. "Nevertheless, it makes him unreliable. And desperate. He will disappoint you. He will hurt you. And if you create enough space for him—he might not even mean to do this—but he will."

"Will what?"

"He will destroy you, Kip. He will."

"Oh, come on. At the very least, we're friends."

"He might not want to. But he will. He will destroy you."

CHAPTER 4

Due Diligence

I told Thaddeus I wanted to see the land I was buying before we went through with the transaction. Nothing more than due diligence, a formality, force of professional habit. "We can walk the acres together, that would be a manly thing," said Thaddeus, cleverly or cluelessly. But a resurgence of winter intervened, storms that made the national news: I would have seemed like a lunatic coming up for a walk in the woods in that weather, or its aftermath.

Ken Adler wanted me to do on-site research on a company called Tawk, which owned about four hundred stores across the country exclusively devoted to the sale of mobile phones. Adler was a very conservative stock picker, something of a tortoise in a world of hyped-up hares, and, just as he had been basically unmoved by the go-go, coke-snorting eighties, he worried about missing the entire tech boom as well. Normally, he was old-school at heart, content to continue investing in railroad bonds, tankers, and T-bills. He did not have nerves of steel, and he did not have that gambler's appetite for risk. As a kid, he made pretend investments and was content to chart the slow growth of his fantasy account. When a couple of uncles got wind of this, they encouraged him to invest small amounts of their money, and before long—Ken was only twenty by this time—half of his large, extended family were following his advice. Ken dropped out of Penn State and started Adler Associates with thirty clients, all of them relatives. He treated their money as if it were his own. His successes were moderate, his failures were few and far between. Adler Associates was, by the time he hired me, larger than he had ever wanted it to be, and Ken was always nervous, slightly gloomy.

Some of our investors were impatient, but most were content with their wealth increasing slowly and steadily. Nevertheless, in anticipation of the initial public offering of Tawk, underwritten by Paine Webber and SG Cowen, Ken wanted me on the road to gather firsthand information about the company. There was a Tawk outlet in New York, near Battery Park. It seemed well run and full of customers, and had a pleasant welcome-to-the-future atmosphere, but in fact the New York store was the very best of the four hundred Tawks, and had been opened so close to Wall Street in the hopes that brokers and bankers would travel no farther than that one anomalous outlet, walking distance from their offices and afterwork watering holes. It took me two weeks on the road, on the rails, and in the sky to visit forty Tawks and not one of them approached the attractiveness of the New York branch. Some Tawk outlets were in major cities, but most were in the Elkhart, Indianas, of the world, where commercial rents were reasonable. The Tawks were almost always dirty, some smelling of corn chips, others smelling of disinfectant, or what a teenager might use to cover up the smell of pot. Many Tawks featured brands of cell phones that few people wanted or had even heard of, and they were staffed by people working on commission, infusing the atmosphere with an air of anxiety and illegitimacy. My strong recommendation was to stay away from the IPO, no matter what the stock opened at, or how many others stampeded into it—tech IPOs were just about fail-safe at the time.

Ken thanked me for my work and my insight and proceeded to take a position in Tawk anyhow, not a huge one, but about $12 million spread evenly through the portfolios of his investors. By the end of the first day of trading Tawk had gone from $25 a share to $37 a share; at the end of the first month Tawk was listed on the NASDAQ, sixty outlets were closed and the stock cratered at $8. But it was a measure of Adler's decency that he didn't forget I had tried to steer him away from Tawk and he didn't want to punish me for being right. Instead, he hired someone else to take over my duties writing those long long long letters to our investors, gave me a larger office, and a raise, and now road work investigations of companies was my full-time job.

After my Tawk road trip I was sick for a while—respiratory illness from all the regional jets, I suppose—and I wasn't able to get upstate to look at the land until the end of April. I arrived at the train station in Leyden, New York, but Thaddeus was not there. Grace had come to pick me up, dressed in a brown leather jacket and tight corduroy pants, her hair closely cropped, lightly flecked with gray. She was standing rather far from me, but she didn't move when she saw me. She waited for me to come to her.

———

Strange now to think of it, it all went by so quickly, but Grace and I met more than twenty years ago, when I was living on Jane Street,

in an outlier building, a big, 1960s-style monstrosity, in an en-
clave of town houses and low-rise apartment buildings.

The plan had been for Thaddeus to come to New York with
the bit of money he had saved working for his parents and to live
with me while he looked for a job. I took the day off and spent it
cleaning the clean apartment, making up the bed in my second
bedroom, and buying a dozen purple irises, and then throwing them away out of embarrassment. I resisted the impulse
to wait outside for him, as the day hobbled along. The plane
from Chicago was due to land in New York at 2:00 P.M., but it
was 4:30 by the time Thaddeus was at my door, and he was not
alone. Without bothering to alert me, he had brought Grace.
I'd heard he was seeing someone named Grace, but Thaddeus
was always seeing someone, and it had never occurred to me,
not even for a moment, that he would be bringing her along.
And it wouldn't have occurred to him to alert me. He would
have assumed delight, or at least easy acceptance on my part.
We were all of us still in the more-the-merrier time of life.

"Welcome to my humble abode," I said, with a buffoon's bow.

She was five foot ten inches, with broad shoulders, with one
of those brutally beautiful Irish faces, long, narrow, with suspicious green eyes and heavy dark brown brows. She wore bright
red lipstick, which I guessed she had reapplied while in the elevator, but other than the lipstick she was not going out of her
way to be feminine. All of Thaddeus's previous girlfriends had
exuded estrogen. Maybe Grace having a bit of boy in her was
part of the allure, the perfect choice for the guy who needs
the social approbation of conventional coupling, while helping himself to some of the pleasures of same-sex sex. As Jiminy
Cricket almost sang, Let your unconscious be your guide! Grace
was watchful, poised between gaiety and stubbornness. Here

was someone who did not assume she would be welcome—
anywhere. What she had in the world was hard-won, including
the man at her side. Her voice was pure and deep, but her
pronunciations were bewildering. She sometimes gave words a
weird British inflection—*rilly* for *really,* and a few others—an
Audrey Hepburn–ish tone that climbed like ivy over her true
speaking voice, and was meant to camouflage the enunciation
of a girl born in Wisconsin, raised in Chicago, a girl without
a high school diploma. (The GED was in the mail.) She was
twenty-one years old and the flight from O'Hare to LaGuardia
was her first time on an airplane.

"We made it," she announced. They dropped their suitcases to the floor, clunky maroon monstrosities upon which
they had x'd masking tape, as if someone might actually steal
them.

"I see that," I said.

"Uh-oh, Thaddeus didn't tell you I was coming, did he."

"Of course not!" I said, as if Thaddeus's spontaneity, as ex-
asperating as it might be, was also endearing, something she
and I might appreciate together. "Come," I said, touching her
shoulder. "I'll show you to your room."

It was a room that could just about accommodate a bed, a
chair, a chest of drawers, a small bookshelf. I could see their
disappointment.

They were tired from traveling, but nevertheless, Thaddeus
wanted to walk around the neighborhood. I was relieved; I was
worried they might close the door and fall into bed together.

"The White Horse Tavern's near here, right?" he asked. He
explained it to Grace. "All these great writers used to go there.
Delmore Schwartz and Dylan Thomas. I've always wanted to
drink a beer there."

Before we left, Thaddeus insisted Grace show me the drawing she had brought for me as a house present. She lifted her suitcase, threw it onto the bed, and found what she was looking for at the bottom, a manila envelope, which she handed to me.

It was a pencil drawing of Franz Kafka. I was familiar with this image, modeled on the photograph on the back of my copy of *The Castle*. Grace's drawing was more or less an exact replica—I would soon learn that exact replica was her métier. Here was Kafka with his Ashkenazi bonnet of dark hair, the protuberant fairy tale ears, the deep-set eyes radiating inquisitiveness and dread.

"Isn't it amazing?" Thaddeus said.

"That's Frankie K all right," I said, on the off chance that a bit of jokiness might bring him to his senses.

No possibility of that, however. "She can draw anything. Anything! It's almost scary. And will you look at her?"

"Thaddeus, come on, take it easy," Grace said. To me: "I'm glad you like it." She made a quick half smile. It was like one of those obligatory handshakes the winner of a tennis match makes, barely touching the sweaty hand of the vanquished opponent.

CHAPTER 5

Enter Jennings

Meeting me at the train on the day of my pre-purchase due diligence, Grace was with Hat Stratton's son, Jennings Stratton, who now lived in—and owned—the caretaker's house with his wife, Muriel, and their two children. Jennings made himself essential around Orkney, but he had his own business to run—removing asbestos from homes, churches, schools, government buildings. Half his life was spent in a Hazmat suit. Years ago, Jennings had been the county's Casanova, and even now, with silvery hair and a paunch, he retained the manner of a handsome man, with a quick, confident smile, a swaggering gait, and a way of looking at you that implied you two shared a funny, risqué secret—namely, your attraction to him. He was a hard-charging alpha male, tuned in to four channels: See, Want, Take, Defend. If he'd been born to a different family, he'd be raking in a fortune on Wall Street. As it was, all he had ever been able to accumulate was women, and now they were safely locked away in the memory bank.

When I got into Grace's car, Jennings was sprawled out in the backseat, swigging on a bottle of Dr Pepper. His hair was in a ponytail and smelled of coconut-scented conditioner. He wore a white shirt, the sleeves carefully rolled, and a pair of sharply creased gray trousers. I had nursed my share of suspicions about Jennings and Grace. I had seen him look at her with a little glint of ownership in his eyes. He'd built her a studio in an old shed, though there were plenty of places for her to work inside the big house. He had posed for her. He had driven her down to New York to buy paints and canvases.

"Where's that husband of yours?" I said, as soon as I fastened my seat belt.

She smiled. She knew exactly what I meant by that question. Thaddeus was in Hollywood. He was pitching a movie idea and wouldn't be back for a couple of days—he could get a cheaper ticket if he stayed over on a Saturday, and these days he was paying for those flights to L.A. out of his own pocket.

"Any sense of how it went?" I asked. We hadn't left the train station's parking lot. People were tossing their suitcases into backseats and trunks, hugging their hellos.

Jennings slid farther down in the backseat, quite obviously not wanting to be seen. Maybe there was actually someone he wanted to hide from, or it could have been muscle memory from years on the prowl.

"Thaddeus tells his stories and it always goes well," Grace said. "But nothing ever seems to come of it." She put the car into gear while glancing at Jennings in the rearview mirror. "Do you have any idea how much sugar is in one bottle of that stuff?"

"A lot!" he said.

"Right. A disgusting amount. You should at least drink the Diet, which has zero calories."

"Those fake sweeteners are just chemicals, Grace. Rat poison. Way better off keeping things natural."

"This from Mr. Asbestos?"

"Hey, if you want to pay me twenty-five dollars an hour to drink Diet Dr Pepper, I will." Their repartee was easy and intimate. I looked down, feeling the shame that ought to have been theirs. We were passing a farm. A woman on a tractor was dumping bales of hay out of the front loader onto a stubbly field where six tan and white cows patiently waited, their tails flicking, presumably with no idea why they were being fattened.

Grace poked me on the shoulder. "We have to make a quick stop. Sorry about that."

"Two minutes," Jennings said.

It was annoying that they hadn't run their errand before picking me up, but I didn't want to be a jerk about it. I think I sighed. And Jennings, preternaturally attuned to slights, looked sharply in my direction before sliding out of the backseat and slamming the door behind him.

"Wow," Grace said. "He's so noisy!" She had her eyes on him as he walked toward Leyden Home and Garden, with its sidewalk display of paint cans, rolls of window screen, a backyard grill, and an old gumball machine with a card taped to it that read Ask at Register. When he was finally out of view, she took a deep breath and slowly let it out. I don't know what I was supposed to make of it.

"So, Kip," she said. "Why the sudden interest in seeing the land?"

At some other time, the abruptness of the question would probably have caught me off guard, but the combination of having Jennings with her and then stopping at the hardware store had already put me on alert. I figured three possible motivations for her question, which were, in descending order of awfulness: she was aware that I had simply created an excuse to come upstate and spend time with Thaddeus, or she was worried that despite my reassurances I did in fact have some vague plan to one day build something on that land, or it had dawned on her that bringing Jennings to the train station might have been an error and now she was nervously making conversation.

"I'm paying a lot of money for that land, Grace. Of course I want to see it."

"You never saw it? All the many times you've come to visit?"

"Well, if I saw it, I wasn't paying proper attention."

"Anyhow, it's a small investment. For you."

"I'm not nearly as rich as you think I am, Grace. And it's not a small investment."

"I'm sorry. Sorry sorry. I'm in a shit mood. There's nothing like running out of money to make a gal hate the rich."

"But I just told you: I'm not rich."

"You are to us, Kip." She put her hand to her forehead, and was silent. "We're lost. I don't know what to do next. I can't stand waiting for the ax to fall."

"Things could change. Maybe some rich collector will discover you. Maybe some rich producer will finance a movie for our favorite boy."

"Right. And what are we supposed to do in the meanwhile?"

It was a moment to push back, if only slightly. "We could each and every one of us follow Henry James's three rules for living," I said. "Be kind, be kind, and be kind."

"And you think that will be enough?"

"I think it's a lot."

"Well, as Thaddeus says, isn't it pretty to think so?"

As Thaddeus says? Did she not know the line belonged to Hemingway? Had Thaddeus taken credit for it? My god! The ideal marriage. Let no man intrude upon this perfect union.

Jennings emerged from the hardware store with a small red and blue box of dust masks.

"They jumped the prices," Jennings said, getting into the car and closing the door with a maximum amount of noise. It wasn't meant to be angry, it was just how he closed a door. "But Oscar gave me the old price."

"Oscar's a good guy," said Grace.

"Hometown boys stick together," Jennings said. "Right, Kip?"

"I wouldn't know," I said.

Abruptly, Grace pulled out of her parking spot and wedged her way into the flow of traffic, which was moving slowly. By the time we were close to Leyden's center, we were barely inching forward. Finally, we arrived at the source of the traffic jam. Three middle-aged men stood in the middle of the road soliciting donations for the Windsor County Volunteer Emergency Services. They were a matched set, burly, with long hair, flannel shirts, suspenders, blue jeans, and black rubber boots.

Jennings powered down his window and called out, "Hey, Itchy, what's the what?"

Itchy pretended to adjust his glasses when in fact he was giving Jennings the finger.

Grace scooped out quarters and dimes from the car's ashtray.

"That's not going to do it, Grace," Jennings said, reaching into his own pocket, pulling out a couple of bills, and handing them to her. "Shit gets noticed."

And recorded, too, it seemed. A woman in a print dress and ski jacket stood to one side, and as a car in front of us passed the three guys with their buckets without dropping in a dime, the woman bent at the knee and photographed the back of the Infiniti with her Polaroid. When the photo emerged, she shook it dry and dropped it into an open guitar case at her feet.

"Who's she?" I asked. "Madame Defarge, keeping track of people who don't give so they can be dealt with later?"

"It's always the ones in fancy cars who don't give," said Jennings.

We made our way to Riverview Road, with its wrought-iron gates and gingerbread gatehouses, the stone walls, the Corinthian columns, the security cameras perched like buzzards in the trees. Orkney had no gate, no gatehouse, and only a few flowers, the hardy ones that had made it through layers of leaf litter to show their shower-cap faces to the sun. The driveway had fallen onto hard times, and Grace's car shuddered as if we were driving across an immense washboard. Suddenly, she braked and pointed to an area off to the right. "Your acres would be right there, Kip. If you want, you can walk around, check them out, then come to the house in a while and I'll see what I can do about lunch."

Startled, dismissed, I got out of her car and stood there with the wind whipping at the cuffs of my trousers, and watched Grace and Jennings drive toward a sharp turn in the driveway and disappear from my sight. So here they were, my mute, innocent acres, the trees' crowns moving with the wind, their roots sunk deep into the earth.

I knew a few things about trees, learned in my youth during weekend trips with my grandfather to his musty little cabin near a trout-rich Michigan lake, near the town of Farwell.

Grandfather's name was Leslie Woods. He lived in the pricey Detroit suburb of Grosse Pointe Farms, in a Tudor mansion overlooking Lake St. Clair with more than enough nature to satisfy what seemed to me his rather glancing appreciation of the great outdoors. If it was solitude he was seeking in that musty shack in the middle of nowhere, he surely could have gotten his fill of alone-time at home, with his wife long deceased and his only son, my father, permanently out of favor for marrying my mother, who he considered a gold-digging social climber. Grandfather showed no interest in either of my two older sisters, but at last my mother did something right in his eyes by giving birth to a boy. From the very beginning of my life, Grandfather paid attention to me. You would have thought my parents would have told the old tyrant to take his model trains and autographed footballs and shove them up his ass, but they submitted to his selective largesse, my mother grudgingly, my father abjectly. I adored my father but he was not strong. Raised affluently, he now lived with a wife and three children in a two-story house of about twelve hundred square feet, 88 Hydrangea Court, three little bedrooms, one bath, zero privacy. I would have traded an arm for my own private bathroom, and I would have rather been struck blind than to ever again see my sister tormentingly holding her nose upon entering the washroom after I had used it—which she would do even if I'd only taken a leak or combed my hair.

After bouncing around a few retail jobs, my dad was fortunate enough to reconnect with Joe Schultz, an old army buddy with textile factory contacts in Hong Kong. Together they opened Hilary Custom Shirts, called after my father's given name. Dad and Joe worked out of the old Michigan Central Station, carefully measuring the necks, arms, chests, and torsos of their customers and sending the measurements off to Hong Kong to be made. They would pick up the shirts in their blue and white boxes at the Wayne County Airport and hand them to the men, not exactly saying that either my father or Schultz had handcrafted the shirts, but not averse to giving the impression that they had. Even after fifteen years of exile from his father's affections, ever hopeful Hilary Woods still believed that one day he'd be welcome again in Grosse Pointe Farms, and he saw Grandfather's interest in me as an early promising sign that the old man was slowly undergoing a change of heart. Alas, Dad was dead wrong. My grandfather favored me out of boredom and loneliness and, really, as a way of reminding my father of all he had thrown away by marrying my mother. Beyond that, the old man's supposed fortune, made brokering cement and stone, was wholly dependent on the auto industry, and when the auto industry faltered, and the town took a nosedive, Grandfather's coffers were soon empty. After he died, the government seized his property to offset five years of unpaid taxes.

But we had no idea he was living so close to the edge of financial ruin. To my family on Hydrangea Court, he was like a king and I was encouraged to be close to the old man, which meant attending hockey games, boxing matches—he owned a tenth of a middleweight named Billy Diaz—and spending an occasional weekend at that cabin, where there was no phone, no TV, no radio, no music, and the lightbulbs were so dim that reading was impossible after dark. Much of the first day was spent making the place habitable—sweeping out the droppings, the spiderwebs, the leaves and acorns, the occasional weightless corpse of a bird that had found its way in but could not find its way out, and which lay like a mournful shadow on my hand. The cabin was filled with booze, locked away in his absence. Usually, he grabbed a bottle and wandered into his bedroom, and that would be the last I'd see of him for four or five hours. He had come there for the silence and the silence reigned. There was only wind, birdsong, the occasional plane passing overhead. While Grandfather rested (or drank himself to sleep) I took walks in the woods, careful not to get lost. There were few books in the cabin, but there were wildlife guides, bird books, and *The Collins Guide to Trees,* by Norma and George Collins. Their illustrations never quite matched the trees in those Michigan woods but nevertheless I learned how to recognize shape, bark, and leaf, and I still remembered my lessons.

And so I wandered through my soon-to-be-acquired acres and spoke their names aloud, as you would incantate the names of saints—locust, oak, spruce, hemlock, Douglas fir, maple, ash, wild cherry.

CHAPTER 6

Cozy and Threatening

I stood now before a white oak, quercus alba, its grayish bark like the skin of an elephant, with a bumpy carpet of acorns scattered beneath it.

"See this tree over here?" a voice behind me asked. Startled, I turned to see Jennings. "That's your honey locust. My father planted it." He patted the tree's reddish bark, like a trainer stroking a prized horse. "This one's young, one of the last Dad put in the ground."

Jennings stood close to me now, cozy and threatening at once. "People treat them like they was weeds, but Dad thought they were a good tree. Not a great tree. But a good one. Fast growing, good for fence posts, and they drop these pods the deer really like. It's a delicacy for deer. Gracey won't let hunters in so you're going to see a lot of whitetails around here, whole herds of them hanging around like a bunch of bums." He smiled his clean, confident smile.

He was carrying something that looked dug out of the earth. It was about two feet wide, one foot high, made of wood. When I looked more closely I saw it was an old radio, a Philco, with two black plastic knobs, one for volume, the other for moving the square orange and black dial, which was beneath its plastic cover. Next to the dial was another square, the same size, this one covered in fabric, or what was left of the fabric, where the speaker was housed.

"Does it work?" I asked.

"Don't know. We shall see." He looked at it fondly. "Every time I go poking around these woods I think of Dad. He used to take me with him, I can still hear him say 'Son, we are going prospecting just like the forty-niners of old.' First time out we found a spoon worth three hundred dollars. Solid silver. Paul Revere, I think he made it himself. I was so excited. I was always asking When we going prospecting? But Dad was usually too tired. Man, they worked that guy, they just wore him out like a pair of shoes. But we'd go out some Sundays. We found coins. Once we found some old stock certificates, really beautiful, with all this scrollwork. I thought it was the Declaration of Independence or the Constitution. Dad got a good laugh on that."

Jennings put the old radio down for a moment and flexed his fingers, over and over, as if he were milking a cow. He had long fingers, perfectly proportioned. You could look at those hands and think, Yes, I get it, I can see how this man was once beautiful. He may have sensed what I was thinking because he smiled at me, not in a friendly way.

"This is a beautiful spot," he said.

"Yes, it really is."

"I don't understand how you city people find out about this place. I don't know jack about the city, but you guys swoop up here and land in the most beautiful place."

"Well, back in the day, Thaddeus used to work at a place

called B. Altman, and he met Gene Woodard, who worked there, too, and Woodard invited Thaddeus and Grace up for the weekend."

"Them," said Jennings with an unpleasant laugh. "They're long gone. Some guy from television's got that place now and all he's got is Mexicans working the place for two bucks an hour."

"The Woodards are gone? What happened? Did their money run out?"

"Money," he said. "I find it really weird. I mean money is crazy, isn't it? A bunch of paper, or maybe just numbers on a screen somewhere—and you get a piece of God's own earth. Blows my mind. I know, this ain't the stuff you're supposed to think about except for kids, right? But if being a grown-up means you believe that some numbers on a screen gives you permission to say to the whole world that you own this"—he waved his arm at the treetops, the sky—"then I don't know what to tell you. I'll take being weird over believing something like that."

Jennings walked slowly and I followed him. We traipsed through weeds and vines, past towering hemlock. The wind was up and the clouds moved swiftly; the daylight came and went, as if a hand were moving across the sun.

"This will be your north border," Jennings said. "I mean once it's all paid for." He said *paid* as if there were something unclean about it. We came to the remains of a stone wall like a set of aged teeth that followed the undulations of the land. I was abreast of him now and my feet got tangled in a swirl of vines. I made the mistake of trying to power through, impatiently yanking my foot forward, but the vines were as stubborn as steel and I fell forward. Jennings grabbed me beneath both arms and held me suspended for a moment before setting me straight on my feet.

"You right?" he asked.

"Thanks," I said.

My armpits ached from where he had grabbed me. I felt foolish and weak—not only for having lost my footing but from the pain of being caught. Hard hands. His touch was still on me, as if I were clay. The cawing of crows. The zizzing sound of car wheels on the distant blacktop. The tattered sound of music disappearing with the car. The desiccated crunch of winter's carpet of casualties beneath our feet as we walked.

"So pretty soon this land belongs to you," he said. "But you should know—it won't really be yours. No one owns land."

"Except legally," I said.

"Money money money money money money money," he said, his voice getting quieter and softer, his head shaking back and forth.

"I didn't make the world, Jennings. I just live here, okay?"

"So, is this like an investment for you?"

"No."

He smiled, as if he were used to hearing a bunch of lies from people just like me. I resisted the impulse to amplify my no, and to tell him I was buying the land to help a friend out of a jam.

"We can keep an eye on things for you, if you want," Jennings said.

"We?"

"Me. My kids. Last thing you want is to come here and see someone's put a deer stand up in one of your trees and left a bunch of beer cans and candy wrappers as a thank you note. Thing is, if folks know we're looking after you, that way they'll know. All the folks in the big houses don't realize it, but the hometown boys know everything that happens around here and if a place is empty or there's some land no one's taking care of, we know, we all know. We see it all. You know." He lifted a finger, thick and battered. "Like red-tailed hawks, right? Riding the thermals. It's our world, it's how we prosper." He laughed. "Not that anyone's doing much prospering, but you understand."

"You really think these trees need guarding?" I said. I felt queasy. We were stopped now, but it was as if he were closing in on me. Whatever egalitarian impulses I'd had as a young man had atrophied within the confines of my cossetted New York life and, shamefully, at this point I had very little contact with workers who weren't obliged to be polite to me. Cabdrivers, doormen, sales clerks, prostitutes, painters, plasterers, plumbers, electricians, bartenders, tennis teachers, personal trainers, waiters, concierges, bellmen, housekeepers, receptionists, tour guides—with them I was open and easy, friendly and kind, curious about their lives and no need to call me Mr. Woods, Kip's my name. Good old Kip, friendly Kip, secure in the knowledge that my position was impregnable for no other reason than sooner or later I would be writing the check or handing over the credit card or peeling off one or two bills from the knot of twenties and fifties I always had in my front pocket. All that bonhomie was shaped by the fact that I was the boss, the client, or the customer. When was the last time I'd spoken to someone who lived paycheck to paycheck and our material inequality was irrelevant? In high school, and maybe never since. But here with Jennings I was nothing more than some stranger from the city walking around these soggy, brambly acres in the wrong shoes.

But wait, I thought. He *does* want to be paid. I relaxed, the way you do when you realize that you get off the train at the next stop.

"So yeah," I said. "You and your kids? If you want to look after the place when I buy it? That would be great."

"Okay then," he said.

"How much do I pay you for this?"

"Not much. We can work it out."

"No, let's settle on a price. It's cleaner that way."

He smiled. "Okay. Cleanliness. It's next to godliness. How about five hundred dollars?"

"Five hundred?"

"A year," he said.

I was taken aback by the modesty of his proposal, but I could not resist the impulse to close. "All right," I said, offering my hand to seal the deal. His hand was like stone.

CHAPTER 7

Stoned

We finally had a date for the closing on the property, at the end of June, on a Wednesday afternoon. It was not a good time for me to be away from Adler, but I'd already had to cancel the closing twice. I took Amtrak up, so the 110 minutes riding north could be used productively, writing a long memo to Ken summarizing what I'd so far learned about Sears.

One of the traders at Adler was buying a lot of Sears stock and wanted to load up on more. Sears's earnings were at that point well north of the disaster they became, but Ken nevertheless did not believe the board's estimates of where profits and stock prices were heading—it was his guess that things were a lot worse than the board was letting on. I was sent out to visit Sears stores in malls and on Main Streets across the country, starting in Honolulu and ending in Bangor, Maine. I took notes, recorded testimony from employees, and photographed the countless clues I found to suggest mounting infirmity— plastic buckets beneath leaks in the ceiling, stained carpets such as you would find in a fleabag hotel, a cracked window repaired with masking tape, Kenmore washing machines three years out of date but still on display, a Kenmore refrigerator ostensibly for sale but plugged in via a tangled network of extension cords and being used to cool sandwiches and sodas by the store's cost-conscious (i.e., underpaid) employees.

I went over my notes as the train moved north. Most of the passengers chose to sit on the side that offered a continuous view of the Hudson, but I preferred the other side, where you could see human life unfolding. Little river towns, many not yet touched by real estate speculators. Junked cars, Irish saloons, cluttered yards, chained dogs. Normal life. I felt like a ghost longing to be corporeal. A little town slid by, replaced by a marshy pond choked with cattails. It was a lovely day out there, sunlight diamonds sparkled on the water, the sky so still that it looked like pottery. I drifted away from my work.

In the *New York Times*, I read a piece about the guy who was the architect of Clinton's proposal regarding gays in the military. Everyone from Morris to ACT UP to the guy skating backward down Hudson Street in a wedding dress thought Don't Ask, Don't Tell was demeaning, while the homophobes thought Bill Clinton was giving people a license to commit sodomy. I was one of the few who thought Don't Ask, Don't Tell was a decent idea—I liked the respect for privacy in Clinton's executive order. Yes, it was sort of mealymouthed, but not all of us are temperamentally suited to uncloseting ourselves. From Stonewall on, I looked upon gay activists with admiration of the most distant sort—the way people thought of the Vietnamese monks who set themselves on fire to protest the war. And once AIDS became a reality, not being seen as a homosexual was even more important to me. I didn't want anyone—not in my family, or in business, or at breakfast at the Regency—wondering what microbes might be swimming around in my bloodstream, or if I was practicing safe sex. Oh! Even the two-word phrase *safe sex* was a kind of verbal saltpeter—not to mention a total and excruciating invasion of privacy. My privacy was paramount, though it made me unheroic. Not everyone can be a hero; if everyone was heroic, then heroism would be nothing but doing what was expected and we would have no actual heroes. You understand?

Just as I turned back to my report, something struck one of the windows in my car with astonishing blunt force, like a gunshot. The noise was terrifying. It was startling in itself, but it was also connected to lurking terrors that were already in me—it was as if the noise pulled back a tent flap to reveal frightened faces huddled within.

Two seats behind my row, the window had been smashed and a silent scream of cracks engulfed it. A moment later another window was hit, this time with more of a thud than a crack, and then another was hit, and the window made an almost human sound, an ooof, like someone who has been punched in the stomach. The noise filled the car like smoke. No one knew what to do. We were ambushed from both sides of the track. And from above. Stones rained down on the top of the train and the clang of it entered the car and we were pinned beneath it as if we were being buried alive by sound. I'd once read about a man who heard voices and he said they bombarded him like a fusillade of stones—but here the stones were like voices, wrathful, the cries of a world gone mad.

People scrambled out of their seats and stood in the aisle, looking for someone who might bring a sense of order, someone to look up to, someone who could tell us what to do—a conductor or some other Amtrak employee. Someone I couldn't see was shouting, "Goddamnit! How many more times does this have to happen?"

CHAPTER 8

Closing Time

When the lawyer pulled open the top drawer of his Pickwickian desk, the old wood screeched a bit, startling me so much that I half stood up, and knocked my chair back into the three-stack of glassed-in bookcases. We were closing on my purchase of the land in Thaddeus and Grace's lawyer's cluttered, low-ceilinged office. My hands were still clammy from the autonomic chaos unleashed by the attack on the train, the adrenaline no longer surging but its side effects present—a fluky heartbeat and inappropriate vigilance.

Fortune Harris reminded me of one of the members of the Ale and Quail Club in *The Palm Beach Story,* rotund and brimming with absentminded good humor, his cheerfulness resting upon his assumption that everyone thought well of him, and life today would be pleasantly similar to life yesterday. Also present for the closing was an officer from the Leyden Savings Bank, where T&G's mortgage was held. This fellow, Arthur Holdridge, was decidedly not Ale and Quail material. Skeletal and colorless, he exuded a sour complacency, quiet and judgmental. Holdridge had a secretary with him, an elderly woman with large ears who seemed entirely terrified as we passed the contracts around for inspection and signature, her dark glittering eyes darting back and forth as if lives hung in the balance. The banker and the lawyer both were surprised I hadn't brought my own lawyer with me, but I knew how to read a simple real estate contract and frankly it didn't occur to me to come to the closing with a lawyer in tow. The lawyers I knew charged at least five hundred an hour, usually a lot more than that, assuming I could have lured one of them away from New York, where deals floated in the air like dandelion spores. I had a cashier's check in my jacket for the entire amount and some of my own checks to cover the incidentals.

While Fortune and Holdridge muttered on, I told Thaddeus and Grace about the rain of stones that had hit the train. Thaddeus downplayed it. He thought it was somehow his mission in life to make certain that those around him didn't overreact. "Yeah, that. I know. It's so annoying. They tend to stone the trains coming from the city, but the ones going in the other direction they tend to leave alone."

"Who is they?" I asked.

"Well, there's the question," Thaddeus said. "That's always been the question. Who in the hell is they?"

"The first time my train got hit I completely freaked out," Grace said. "I just couldn't understand why anyone would do something so . . . stupidly violent."

"But who's doing it?" I asked.

"There are a lot of hometown guys who think their lives were a lot better before people like us started moving up here. It's a kind of radical nostalgia for the past. Very Pierre Bourdieu."

"We don't know who's doing it," Grace said. "We're not sure. It could be quite a few people I can think of. Or it could also be a couple of stoned teenagers. Literally."

"It's more than two people," Thaddeus said. "It's all up and down the line. But mainly around here—once the train gets to Windsor County, that's when it usually gets bombarded. Terrorism, right? Hezbollah on the Hudson?" He laughed and pointed at me.

When had he developed the habit of pointing after he made a joke like some cornball comedian whose life depends on getting a laugh? Everything about him seemed torqued an extra turn of the wrench. Pierre Bourdieu? Why would he want to draw attention to himself in this way? I felt some dismay, the way you do when you turn on a Fred Astaire movie on TV and find out it's been colorized, and the glamour, depth, and crisp chiaroscuro swapped out for a pastel palette that looks like a bowl full of Necco wafers. Here's something else about us torchbearers. We are possessive of the one we love and we are determined to maintain our hold on the idea of them. Our idea of them is really all we have. When you think about someone more or less constantly, you begin to believe—though you would never say so, not even to yourself—that they belong to you. You are like a jailer forever pacing past the cell, looking in on the prisoner to make sure he's where he belongs, and is doing what is allowed him. Thaddeus's life was disordered but there was always something about him that was steady and predictable and I counted on him to be essentially unchanging. But to make a joke and to indulge in a bit of physical business to goose it along? That was a new one. To drop the name of a French theorist? It was beneath him.

We continued to talk as the lawyers instructed us where to sign the documents, where to initial riders, etcetera.

"So what's happening here?" I asked. "Have I bought land in some sort of hot zone?"

"It all started with a fucking cement plant," Thaddeus said.

"Some people wanted to stop it from being built, because it was going to go right on the river, and they wanted to protect the view, the water, the feel of the place, the fish, the swans, whatever. And other people wanted it to be built because of jobs. And guess what?" He feigned a look of wonder. "The opinions broke down more or less on class divide. The leisure class doesn't want the plant; the working class does. Shocking, right?"

"And in the meanwhile, we alienated both sides," Grace said. "It's so frustrating. We do our best—and we always have, from the day we moved out here. We treat everyone with respect."

"We're basically saints," Thaddeus said. "It's strange they don't recognize us as saints."

"I'm serious," Grace said. "We don't treat anyone as if they were 'less than.' Our nannies were part of our family. They had the run of the place, and we paid like a real job and if one of them got sick, it was me who brought them soup and drove them to the doctor. When people came to take care of the fields, or to deal with the woods, we served them lunch in the house, not like some who just bring out a bunch of cruddy sandwiches and throw them out on the ground like they're feeding the animals."

Holdridge wasn't going to let that pass without comment. "Really?" he said. He was quickly paging through the contracts, to make certain the signatures and initials were where they belonged. "Throwing sandwiches on the ground? I've never heard of such a thing. The people of means have always treated our workers with all due respect."

"Maybe this is a moot point," Thaddeus said. He rotated his shoulders, stretched his neck. "We ain't hiring anyone, baby. Not anymore."

CHAPTER 9

George Washington Inn

The contracts were signed, the check was in Thaddeus's possession, and we stepped out into a day that had turned sultry. We walked across the main street to the George Washington Inn, a kind of miniature White House, with Doric columns, copper roof, and fussy plantings. Over the past two hundred years, notables from General Lafayette to Soupy Sales had spent the night in one of the inn's spartan rooms. We made our way through the lobby to a sitting room with pale green furniture and a salmon and white Aubusson carpet, and into the tavern, snug and windowless, and smelling of beer and Pledge.

Thaddeus and Grace had been buoyant when we'd left the signing, but now the rush of money was behind them, and the full force of what they had done and why they had to do it seemed to hit them all at once. Sawing off a piece of their land was like a lifesaving amputation—great to be alive, but, you know, where's my leg?

Thaddeus took the cashier's check for $130,000 out of his pocket, gazed at it for a moment, and said, "Aren't you a handsome devil. And you've come home to Daddy."

"I didn't realize this was a Daddy thing," Grace said, taking a seat at the square wooden table. Thaddeus put the check in the side pocket of his suit, turning in his chair and peering into the darkness of the empty tavern, looking for someone to serve us. When he turned toward me, his expression was stricken and his eyes were full of tears.

"I feel awful," he said. "Orkney's land has never been broken up before. You're supposed to keep those properties intact. It's what you're supposed to do." His voice was steady, but now his eyes were overflowing and tears coursed down his cheeks. He seemed not fully aware of them.

"Thaddeus," Grace said, reaching for him. "It's all stolen land anyhow, right? Like from the Indians?"

"She's right," I said, "And fuck keeping the properties intact. In business people are always buying and selling, back and forth. It's just how it is."

He nodded, somewhat brusquely, the way you do when you are acknowledging the fact that someone has spoken but have not really listened to them.

"We said we weren't going to cry," Grace softly said.

"Right," said Thaddeus. "It's just not . . . Well, you know."

And I did. I knew. Thaddeus understood that selling the land was a desperate move and when you are desperate things don't normally get better. We love those stories about dramatic turnarounds—adult fairy tales of people rising like a phoenix from the ashes of failure, of the alcoholic actor who suddenly turns in the performance of a lifetime, the Kentucky Derby won by the horse nobody wanted ridden by a disgraced jockey paroled for that one afternoon, run-down cafés in little towns serving you the best dinner you've ever eaten, missing children returning years later—but they're black swans occurring just an inch north of never. And Thaddeus knew it. From that first call he made to me at six in the morning, I could hear it in his voice. He was being swallowed by the sea and would in all likelihood disappear without a trace. He feared going back to where he had started—the unloved son of two gloomy booksellers, the unknown writer whose ambitions far outstripped his talent. The only thing that he was holding on to was Orkney—and now that little island of deliverance was ten acres smaller.

"You know you can buy those acres back from me whenever it's feasible," I said.

He blotted his tears with the heels of his hands. "I'm going to," he said. "That's the plan right there. Just as soon as the old gravy train rolls around again." He mimed digging up and madly clutching a handful of earth. "As God is my witness, I'll never be hungry again."

"Knock it off, T," Grace said. "Kip is saving our asses. Let's just be grateful and leave the jokes out of it."

Thaddeus reached across the tavern table and clasped my shoulder. "I know, I know," he said. "I love you, man, you know that. Right? Right?" The last time he had touched me in such a sustained manner was in my old loft on Park Avenue South, at the end of his wedding party. Then, he embraced me, and half lifted me off the floor. I ought to have more thoroughly enjoyed that embrace, but I'd had quite a lot to drink, and had endured watching Thaddeus get married, his legs trembling, his voice cracking, and who knew what else was going on beneath his rented morning coat. As Thaddeus gave me that long goodbye embrace, and breathed several hours' worth of cucumber sandwiches and cocktails into my face, my main thought was: this is the thanks I get for giving you and your girlfriend a place to be married in, and paying for the food, the drinks, and two waiters? My opinion was that a boozy hug and a couple of mumbled platitudes did not do it. In my opinion what should be forthcoming was a kiss, a goddamned kiss on the lips, a kiss so hard and so meant that I'd feel it like an umbrella opening in the pit of my stomach.

CHAPTER 10

Another Man's Child

"Oh, there she is," Thaddeus said, half rising from his chair.

One of the inn's waitresses made her way toward us. I ordered a Diet Coke, Grace a Corona, and Thaddeus a martini.

"You make it, okay, Sue?" he said to the waitress. "You've got the touch." She nodded, neither friendly nor unfriendly, just doing her job. She had narrow shoulders, thin brown hair, something of the ascetic in her expression. When she was away from our table, Thaddeus said, "I've been trying to get Sue Briggs to like me for two years. I think I've got her to the point of not actively hating me. That might be the best I can do."

"I'm sure you can do better than that," Grace said. "If you really give it your all."

"People up here seem rather angry," I said. "What's up with that?"

"If you're nice to people they'll be nice to you," Thaddeus said.

"You think so?" Grace said with a married laugh, mirthless and knowing. Then, to me: "Are you staying over?"

"Alas, no," I said.

"We're having people for dinner," she said. "As usual." She gestured, indicating the empty tavern. "This place should have the human traffic we get."

"It's called hospitality," Thaddeus said.

"Is it? I thought it was called auditioning."

I actually agreed with her. From the moment they moved to Orkney, Thaddeus had courted the approval of the other riverfront-estate families. "I feel really really dark and Jewish and out of my element around these people," he had said to me, early on. By *these people,* he meant the Family Tree crowd, the self-centered, self-satisfied Episcopalians whose mansions were scattered twenty-five miles to the north and south of Orkney, and whose long deceased relatives had raked in sufficient assets to keep several generations' noses above the waterline. It had been Thaddeus's project to ingratiate himself to his skeptical neighbors, and some of them were, in the beginning of his ownership of Orkney, reluctant to drink his wines and eat his roasts and celebrate even lesser holidays like Labor Day on his verdant lawns. But Thaddeus persisted and they got used to him, even as one by one the old estates were sold to the winners in a new economy—an actor, the owner of a cable TV network, the founder of a company that trained and dispatched security personnel to airports all over the world. Now, Thaddeus was playing host to a whole new cast of characters.

Our drinks arrived. Thaddeus did one of those *I salute the divine within you* bows to Sue as she placed his martini before him. The mix was off on my Diet Coke. Grace took a long swallow out of the bottle of Corona and then announced she was leaving.

"How am I supposed to get back home?" Thaddeus asked.

"Kip can take you."

"Kip? Kip took the train up here. Remember? You don't remember?"

Ah, he had her there. He seemed to take some dark delight in the possibility she had forgotten my Amtrak adventure. There it was: marriage. The pettiness, the ever metastasizing need to show the other up, to win, like two lunatics in a contest over who can collect, accumulate, and protect the larger ball of aluminum foil.

"Well, either leave with me," Grace said, "or find another way home. But Emma is alone in the house and that kitchen is filled with uh-uhs."

"'Uh-uhs' are forbidden foods," Thaddeus said to me. "Grace is trying to make Emma lose weight."

"What I'm trying to do is save her life," Grace said. She was standing now. Like Thaddeus, she had dressed formally for the closing, in a dark blue skirt and matching jacket, with a white blouse and a strand of pinkish pearls. "Being overweight ruins your life and shortens your life."

"She's a kid. There's too much emphasis, and too much pressure. And you're always policing her."

"I wouldn't have to if we were both on the case."

"She's not a case," Thaddeus said.

Grace sighed, shook her head. "Words," she said, and that was that. She leaned over me and kissed the top of my head. "Thank you, Christopher Woods," she said, using my government name. "I hope everyone in the world has at least one friend as good as you."

Thaddeus followed her with his eyes as she made her way out of the tavern. "I wish she'd lose her looks," he said.

"Yes, she's a handsome woman, no doubt about that."

"I still lust after her. Pounding heart, dry mouth, the works."

"You're a lucky man."

He nodded, but with a look of sorrow.

"You okay?" I asked.

"Sure. How about you, Kip?"

"I worry about you," I said.

"I'm okay, considering. Unemployment is a nightmare, so there's that."

"How's the marriage holding up?"

"The marriage?"

"Yes. You are married, aren't you? I hope I didn't get that wrong."

"The marriage is okay. Like life, up and down. I don't understand people who get divorced. Maybe they were never so much in love in the first place? I don't believe it when people say—what is it they say? We grew apart. What the fuck does that even mean? Our lives are short, we don't actually have time to grow apart. Divorce is a panic move. Quitting on the person you loved is like rejecting God because your prayers weren't answered."

"And Grace?" I said. "Is this how she feels?" I was appalled that I had asked such a thing but to take it back would make it worse.

But Thaddeus didn't seem to have heard it. He seemed for a moment lost in thought. He tapped his finger against his lower lip, and then, suddenly, seemed to revive. "Remember when we saw *Notorious* during the Film Society's Hitchcock festival?" he asked.

Yes, I did. I was living in a grungy group house a couple of miles off campus and because there was always something going on and nothing was in place and it was never really quiet, it was a house people liked to congregate in. After the movie Thaddeus and six or seven others came back there and we talked about the movie and smoked pot and drank tequila, and around midnight Thaddeus was in a stupor, falling asleep, waking, dozing off again. I managed to steer him into my bed. Otherwise he would have slept on the sofa in the common room, with its unending human and feline traffic. Falling leaf silent, I got into bed with him. "This okay?" I whispered. But he was unconscious as soon as his head hit the pillow, whereas I was up until daybreak listening to him breathe. Wondering if I would have a second chance. I was half insane from the temptation to touch him, to caress his skin or feel his hair or even kiss him. I understood it would be a wrong thing to do. Beneath me, really, but not so far beneath me that I could stop from thinking about it. This is where the Jews have it all over us so-called Christians. The Jews say all that matters is what you do and don't do, and your thoughts are your own private business.

"Yes, *Notorious,* great movie," I said. Perhaps he'd only been feigning sleep. "Who wrote it?"

"Ben Hecht. My parents had a copy of his autobiography at Four Freedoms."

"Right," I said. "Ben Hecht. Great two-fisted name."

"So do you remember like at about the halfway point, when Claude Rains comes into his mother's big Nazi bedroom and she's there in her fussy Nazi nightgown and he says, 'Mother, I think I married an American agent.'"

"Yes," I said. "Amazing moment. We almost feel sorry for him. Like his mother is going to completely humiliate him."

"Well, do you want to hear my version?"

"Something you're working on? An update?"

"Unfortunately not. Real life."

"Go ahead."

"It's about Emma," he said.

"What? Is she okay?"

"Well, it's like this, old bean," he said, taking a swipe at a British accent. "I think I may be raising another man's child."

The Spurned Artist

Why would Thaddeus say such a thing? On the train going back to the city, gazing out at the lingering light of early summer, a light so golden and soft it almost seemed tangible, I wondered if what Thaddeus was stating was a verified fact or a theory. Was his suspicion the side effect of marital malaise, the dulling of desire? Was their marriage in trouble? I had often asked myself that, wanting it to be true, which is not very nice, I know, but people like me, the unchosen ones, we're not always very nice, though some of us may appear so. At any rate, it was a ridiculous question, a child's question. Of course their marriage was in trouble. All marriages are in trouble.

But what treachery, what deceit on her part! Not confined to the infidelity, but the toxic spillover—letting Thaddeus believe Emma was biologically his. Could Grace have been capable of this, a lie that would have to be sustained and protected day after day, year after year?

I dealt with some pretty tough and nasty characters in my job, men terrified they might have to give up one of their beach houses, or fuck someone their own age, or make less money than their cousin, but I don't know that I've ever encountered indignation that equals that of the spurned artist. Even the spurned lover has only been rejected by one, maybe two people. The spurned artist has been rejected by the world. Grace came to look at each of her hundreds of unsold paintings and drawings as love letters that came back with Return to Sender stamped on the unopened envelope. And as her own art became a source of pain and humiliation, she turned sour regarding the art of others. What the galleries showed was repulsive to her—she saw more art that she approved of in antiques stores than in galleries. She had expended so much of her effort on learning how to draw and paint with perfect verisimilitude that anything abstract, expressionistic, conceptual, or minimalist was an affront to her sensibilities. She went on making art for as long as she could, until finally her energy ran out and she could no longer protect herself from feeling rejected. For all her outward toughness, she didn't have the self-confidence to promote her own work. She was turned down by three or possibly four galleries in New York, and the experience was so painful, and shaming, that she chose the strategy of waiting for the world to beat a path to her door. And every year that this failed to occur was further proof to Grace of the art world's idiocy, until her anger turned to shame.

Please take everything I say about her with a grain of salt, which Pliny counsels will protect you from certain mild poisons. And bear in mind that not only did Grace lie nightly (both definitions) with the man I loved, she abused the privilege.

Here is what I believe. Without a career to strive for, Grace needed some other kind of adventure in her life. She needed drama, consequence, suspense, something to obsess about, something to hope for, something to dread, something to give her life shape and meaning—and what easier way to achieve all that than to have an affair? Infidelity is an avenue to adventure available to all, rich and poor, immigrant and native-born, the pious and the unbelievers, anyone who feels crushed by the dailiness of settled life, anyone who needs a window in a life that suddenly seems all walls.

So, yes, I did believe that Grace was not only capable of betraying Thaddeus, but in all probability had done so. I was prepared to be wrong about this, wrong on all counts, but my guess was that the most likely candidate for Emma's biological father was Jennings Stratton.

Strange now to think of it, but when Thaddeus first talked to me about Grace back in 1976, my feelings were generous. He told me about her over the telephone. Long-distance phone conversations were an expensive rarity for most people our age, but from my desk at EF Hutton, I could make discreet calls without fretting about cost, though I did worry someone at a nearby desk would overhear my conversation and know I wasn't doing business. Thaddeus, too, was at work, sitting on a three-legged stool near the cash register at his parents' store, while they were at lunch.

This new girl, Grace! Her artistic genius, her fierceness, her almost feral determination to survive, her pot-dealing older brother, her unhappy, well-marinated mother. And then Thaddeus waxed on about her tenderness, her honesty, her absolute and total inability to lie or even shade the truth. I knew I was listening to someone who was completely under the spell of new love. It was as unmistakable as the slurred speech of someone who has called you after slugging down half a bottle of vodka, and embarrassing as seeing a friend, having volunteered to be hypnotized at a party, quack like a duck or bark like a dog or twirl like a ballerina. But it was Thaddeus, and he was dear, and he needed to be loved, and I was happy for him, and happy for myself, as well: to picture him as fully ensnared, fully engaged, fully committed, would hasten to end my mooning obsession with him. I would be free to stop worrying what he was up to, if he was all right, if he was thinking about me, if he was laughing or making love or driving drunk, and I would be free to find love of my own, free to face forward and get on with the great adventure of making a life for myself, a better life, a real life. "I love her so much, man, so much," he said, not even trying to make it interesting and adult and unique. But the unadorned ardency moved me, it truly did, and for a moment a better me rose from the ashes of ego.

Alas, those rare moments of satori are not self-sustaining. They fade quickly unless you work at it, daily work, hourly. They need prayer, sacrifice, you have to devote your life to keeping them alive. That initial response to Thaddeus telling me about Grace, the feeling of peace and happiness that it gave me? It could only point me in the direction I must go, but it could not and did not take me there. Before long, I was again pacing up and down that hall of mirrors, the corridor called self-interest. I can tell you what you already know: ego is the sworn enemy of happiness.

CHAPTER 12

Bruce

On that train going back to New York, satori may have already been out of reach, but at least happiness lingered. At first I was too busy with Sears to realize it, but then it struck me as the train lurched out of Yonkers and began its final run to New York City. I was happy. My internal landscape had been altered. At last, at long last, I had something new to worry about, new information, new *possibilities*.

The man sitting next to me looked in my direction, nodded his head, and smiled.

"Was I chortling just now?" I asked.

"You were," he said. "Please, don't let me stop you."

He had gotten on the train the first stop south of Leyden. The car was by no means full, but as chance would have it, he chose to sit next to me. He was about my age, a kind of standard-issue, old-style American man, with neatly combed brown hair, the beginnings of a double chin, sloped shoulders, small hands, well-polished shoes. I could smell his spearmint chewing gum. He was reading an old hardcover edition of *The*

Seven Storey Mountain, by Thomas Merton. He had marked his place with a tasseled bookmark.

"Well," I said. "I'm in a good mood."

"You don't recognize me, do you?" he said.

My heart sank—I did not recognize him, not even faintly. It wasn't one of those names on the tip of the tongue situations. His face meant no more to me than that of anyone else on the train, and I replied with something I must have seen in a movie. "I'm afraid you have me at a disadvantage," I said, in a voice that was a blend of Ray Milland and Frank Langella.

"It's Bruce," he said. "Bruce Grogan."

As soon as he said his name, I did, in fact, remember him. He used to live near me in Ann Arbor and he didn't look all that different than he had in college. He used to affect the look of a college student circa 1930, in sweater vests and pleated pants, his hair carefully parted on the left side. We hadn't been close friends, but every now and then he'd come to my apartment, and we'd get high together and listen to Glenn Gould over earphones, making little aahs and mmms of potted appreciation. I was dating a girl named Daphne Holt, who sometimes spent the night with me, and whenever she did, Bruce dropped by the next morning—he might have been keeping track of her. He was a philosophy major and tried to work his education into his approach to Daphne, saying once to her, "Hey, Daph, you've got hair like Hannah Arendt's," as if that might win her over. On the other hand, who knew what Daphne liked. She was, after all, with me.

"Bruce, my god. What the fuck? What a great surprise." I gestured to the book. "Still philosophical, I see."

He turned the Merton over in his hand, looked down on it. "Ah, the Trappists, don't start me on the Trappists."

Don't worry, I won't, I thought. "So what's happening, Bruce? You look great. Are you living up there or are you in the city?" I reached over, patted his shoulder vigorously; seeing someone from college had increased my good mood. The jolly cup runneth over! "What the fuck, man? This is such a treat!"

"I'm going to Yankee Stadium. The Tigers are in town. I'll probably be the only one in the whole place rooting for them. Anyhow, I live upstate, sort of. It's temporary. Finishing up my studies at St. Philip's and waiting to be assigned."

"So fucking great to see you. Assigned to what?"

He smiled, a little bashful, a little pleased. "I'm a priest," he said. "Well, not quite. Ordination in September."

"Wow. You're a priest on your way to a baseball game and I'm a gay guy on his way home," I said, much to my own immense surprise—and horror. I thought it was the funniest thought that had ever passed through my mind, but it was not meant to be said aloud and actually heard by another person, and like many neuronal bursts of ersatz inspiration, it lost a great deal in translation. "Of course, I'm kidding," I said. "And sorry for all the foul language."

"Couldn't care less about cussing," said Bruce. "We learn to let all the petty stuff go by." I wondered if my being gay was also petty stuff in his view, or if he'd even heard me, or if I'd actually said it out loud. "And what about you?" he continued. "Still doing that master of the universe stuff on Wall Street?" He shook his finger at me in mock admonishment. "I hope you know there is only one true master of the universe."

"And he's doing such a bang-up job," I said. "How did you know I was working in finance?"

"Oh, Thaddeus mentioned it to me."

My brief flight of unencumbered joy was over and now I

was in the weeds for good—Bruce and Thaddeus were in conversation? Did that mean I had just blithely blurted a secret about myself that would be revealed, or at least alluded to, the next time they spoke? Was this protected conversation? Was what passed between you and a priest sacred and secret, even though Bruce was not quite a priest and I wasn't Catholic?

"So you and Thaddeus hang out?" As far as I could tell, my voice was steady.

"Oh, a little. We met at a party at his . . . What does he call that place?"

"Orkney. The name wasn't his doing. It came that way."

"Right. Orkney. One of the deacons was invited to a lawn party there, and he took a bunch of us along with him. All I knew was it was a party at someone's big old estate and the owner was very easygoing. I was worried about being a gate-crasher. But then I heard we were going to a home owned by Thaddeus Kaufman and I thought, Holy Moly, it's got to be one and the same. I had heard about his movie career, but I had no idea he was living so close. It wasn't like we were best friends in school, but I always thought he was a good guy. Everybody did, right? So friendly."

Bruce was distracted for a moment as we moved into the outer reaches of the city. Several public-housing towers were going up. Idled for the evening, candy-striped cement trucks were parked in a semi-circle and immense cranes like dinosaurs were etched against the darkening sky.

"Anyhow," he continued, "it was about a forty-minute drive. We were all sort of jammed into this little Renault. I called it God's Clown Car. There were seven of us, seven is the number of spiritual perfection, though we were getting pretty sweaty and crabby by the time we got to Orkney. Before we knew it, a huge thunderstorm came in—it was out of nowhere—and we were wondering if there was even going to be a party, since it was supposed to be a lawn party, one of those August things. And if it was going to be moved indoors, having the one person who was invited bring six others was going to pose quite a dilemma. But we persevered. There were about twenty other cars, maybe forty. We couldn't park that close to the house and the seven of us ran with our hands over our heads. We must have been quite a sight, seven seminarians running around the circular driveway and up the stairs and onto the porch—it's not something you see every day. And it was Thaddeus himself who opened the door for us. Even in the rain with all those dripping seminarians around me, he recognized me—like that!" Bruce snapped his fingers. "He threw his arms around me, dragged me into the foyer of his mansion like I'd just returned home from the Third Crusade."

"Ah," I said, a little squeamishly. How could I not take this description of Thaddeus's ebullient hello to Bruce as a critique of my own?

"Thaddeus walked me through the place. I assume you've seen it."

"Many, many times," I said.

"Well, then you know. Lordy, what a spread. I asked him, What's the occasion, what's this party about? And he says, This crazy old house needs people in it. And there were people everywhere, all ages, all colors. Someone was making a fire in one of the fireplaces and folks were draping their wet socks and things on the fire screen to dry them out. And this guy, this singer . . ." Bruce screwed his eyes shut and tapped his forehead. "I can't remember his name. Had his moment in the late sixties? Well, there you have it, the fleeting nature of worldly accomplishments. Anyhow, he was there with his guitar in one room, and a lot of people were listening to him. And Thaddeus's little girl was playing along with him on her guitar."

"Emma," I said.

"Pardon me?"

"His daughter's name. Emma." There must have been some unintended grit in my tone, an unwashed leaf or two in the salad.

Bruce gave me a quizzical look. "Anyhow, it was quite a shindig. I met the beautiful wife. Grace. That's not a name I can forget, obviously. And his son . . . David? And Thaddeus introduced us. . . ." Now it was Bruce's turn to chortle—my chortling days seemed suddenly far behind me. "He introduced us to everyone as the Seven Samurai."

"He loves that movie," I said.

"Oh, is that it? Everything he tells me about Hollywood and the people out there . . ." Bruce shook his head. "Worse than the Vatican, in terms of infighting."

"I was just with Thaddeus," I said. "And Grace. I bought some land off of them."

"Now isn't that something? I remember how close you and Thaddeus used to be, so it doesn't surprise me, not in the least. So what about you? You look healthy, youthful. Are you in a committed relationship? Hey, do you ever hear from Daphne Holt?"

"No. So, uh, when was this party?"

"Last summer. And we've met for lunch a few times since then."

"Is that a fact?" Unrequited love is a petri dish for jealousy, and after years of envy that extended from his sex life with

Grace to the brave little chickadees that landed on his shoulders when he came out to pour sunflower seeds into their feeders, the image of Thaddeus and Bruce chatting away over beers and BLTs in some Windsor County café was galling to me.

"Yes, yes, I only wish we'd made more time. But we're both very busy—Thaddeus, as you know, is always writing. And my studies can be somewhat of an endurance test. But he is always eager to meet and I love talking to him. He has a way of listening that makes you think most people don't listen at all. He's so present. He's always asking me about what it's like to make the choice I've made. At first, he was so intrigued by it."

"I'm not surprised you're going to be a priest," I said. "In college, the way your mind could engage with these very abstract philosophical ideas."

"But it's not the mind that brings you in, at least not for me. The mind sees all the inconsistencies, the impossibilities, the absurdity, really. The mind's mission is to make mincemeat out of faith. It's the heart that brings you in. And the hunger. And that was the main thing that seems to interest Thaddeus. What gives our life meaning? And how can we tolerate life without meaning? Is it money, prizes, notches on your belt? These things that are so transient and that cause us so much anxiety? He's starting to wonder if life without God—some kind of God, maybe not mine, maybe not the God of the Holy Mother Church, but God nevertheless—if we are without it, what possible meaning can there be to life?"

Oh please, give me a fucking break, I thought, just as you would shield your eyes if someone emerged from the darkness to shine a flashlight in your face.

"But we know this to be true," Bruce said. "Without God, our lives are intolerable. Without meaning, how do we live?

Thaddeus sometimes wanders into churches. Just to sit there. And it's always one of ours."

"Well, yours are the ones that are always open. The other ones are usually locked."

"Yes! Exactly!" Bruce said, as if I might be on the path to agreeing with him about a great many things. "I don't think he'd mind me saying this to you. He has considered conversion. Taking instruction. Making the choice."

Really? My Ashkenazi dreamboat raised on Trotsky? How dare he! What was he really looking for? A new hiding place, this one reeking of paraffin?

The train entered one of the tunnels leading to Penn Station and our car went dark. I closed my eyes and felt the tears pulsating behind my lids. I cleared my throat, shifted my weight in the darkness.

"Well, we made it without anyone casting stones," invisible Bruce said. "Thank God."

Yeah, sure, I thought.

"Are you okay?" Bruce asked quietly.

In my bitterness, my loneliness, my furious nostalgia for the happiness I had felt only half an hour ago, I fled all possibilities of God and sought my refuge in the familiar embrace of Mammon, which is to say I wondered what a priest pulled in. I had read somewhere the average salary was about 40K per. If I was given a year-end bonus of forty thousand dollars, I would start looking for another job. In my business, a 40K bonus was a fucking pink slip. And Bruce wasn't even making that, in all likelihood. He was a seminarian. Living in a dorm. Listening to the snores of other celibates. Happy with a sandwich, a glass of beer. On his way to becoming a kid diddler, as Kenny Adler would say. Pope blower. Mackerel snapper. I never asked Adler why he hated priests so much. But he did. He asked, How can any of them be trusted, ever again? Call one if you're in trouble and you just might end up thinking that the curate was worse than the disease. (Rim shot!)

We pulled into the station and the lights in our car stuttered back to life. Bruce stood and retrieved his bag—black leather, shaped like a doctor's satchel—set it on the arm of his seat, opened it. I saw a flash of purple satin, and a Detroit Tigers baseball cap. He placed his book in the bag, deliberately, as if it was something of a ritual, and redid the clasps. I shoved my work into my briefcase and wordlessly followed behind Bruce. We stood in the aisle while two people helped a woman in a wheelchair off the train and then we filed out with the rest of the passengers. The light in the tunnel was gauzy and gray, it must have been one hundred degrees, and the air smelled of diesel. Up one flight of stairs to the Penn Station mezzanine and then up another to the main hall, with its throngs of people, smells of scorched tomato paste and doughnuts, urgent gibberish coming through the public address system.

Bruce stopped and we shook hands. It was time to say goodbye, go our separate ways. There seemed to be something that needed to be said, but I didn't know what it was.

"So long, Bruce," I said. "Maybe we'll meet again soon."

"I hope so, Kip—do people still call you Kip?"

"Yes. Everyone. I was Kip in the crib."

"I don't think I ever knew your given name."

"Christopher, actually."

Bruce smiled broadly, shaking his head.

"That's as far as it goes," I added.

There was a small disturbance to our right. A collective

murmur, a small parting in the sea of humanity. I generally think something awful is happening when there is a sudden shift in the intricate urban routine—if traffic has stopped there's been a horrible wreck, if there's a bad smell in the corridor one of the locked doors will lead to a decomposing body. But in this case, the excitement was benign. Several balloons, red, orange, and silver Mylar, were heading in our direction, and as they drew closer I saw they were being held by a phalanx of men who I could immediately identify as seminarians—with their well-scrubbed faces and assembly-line haircuts, dark slacks, and white shirts. Mixed in were a couple of actual priests. "He's here!" shouted one of them, older than the others, jolly and red-faced, his white hair springing out on either side of his Yankees cap.

"I knew it, I knew it," Bruce cried.

"We were stuck in traffic," one of the seminarians said.

"We prayed that your train would be late," said another. "Hey! Happy birthday!!"

"We have to get to the subway to the stadium," the white-haired priest said. "Ready? On three?" He counted out loud and the group let go of their balloons and let them float away and they all fell silent, and craned their necks and followed the balloons' uncertain ascent. The bright silver Mylar balloons, decorated with sparkly stars, nuzzled against the station's low ceiling while the others meandered.

"Mine's winning!" one of the guys called out.

I was slowly backing away, as you would creep out of a child's bedroom after the last lullaby. "So long, Bruce, happy birthday. Go Tigers." He was absorbed with his friends, the birthday, the balloons. Back five steps and then turn. Walk away toward the Seventh Avenue exit. Luck was on my side! I was in a taxi within a minute and on my way home. The driver had rosary beads wrapped around the stem of his rearview mirror. That's what piety will bring you—sixty hours a week fighting traffic in Midtown Manhattan.

I closed my eyes. I had nothing to do that night. Of course that wasn't precisely true. I had a lot of work. Nothing I cared to do was more like it. Nothing. I thought about Bruce and his Bible buddies rattling toward the Bronx on the D train for that night's game, and felt . . . I couldn't identify what it was that was making me miserable as the taxi brought me downtown. I felt such emptiness and rejection, even though I didn't know these people and I didn't want to go to a baseball game in Yankee Stadium, or anywhere else. If Bruce had turned toward me and said, I don't suppose you could be tempted into joining us. . . . It actually would have been the polite thing for him to do. We had been traveling together, side by side. We'd shared confidences. And suddenly it was as if I didn't exist. It was actually quite rude. All this concentration on eternity, while the here and now slips through the cracks. Yes, I thought, he should have invited me. I would have said, No thanks. I would have said, Oh, I'm jammed for tonight. Enjoy! And that would have been that.

Priests have horrible manners, I thought.

CHAPTER 13

Motown

Adler Associates was small. We weren't moving markets or making news. We had sixty or seventy investors, each of whom had between $8 and $15 million with us, though Ken let a few friends and cousins in for a smaller commitment. We had the endowments of three colleges and the pension fund of the advertising company where Ken's father had worked. AA took an annual fee of 0.075 percent out of your account if you had over $5 million and 1.2 percent if you had less. All in all, Adler collected about $9 million in fees every year, enough for Ken to pay himself a large salary and to keep the rest of us fairly happy. Though the heavyweights at places like Merrill Lynch or Lehman Brothers would have considered it paltry, I was astonished by my compensation.

Ken wanted me to form personal relationships with some of our clients—the cultured ones, the ones whose names were listed as donors by their local symphonies or museums of folk art, the PEN supporters, and in one case an affluent surgeon who was part of an effort to buy *The Atlantic Monthly*. Lunches, dinners, sailing parties, confirmations, weddings—it was a version of the monetized friendliness I'd been encouraged to show my grandfather. What I was there to do was make the investors feel they had entrusted their money to people who were not only savvy but elegant, and who, in the person of me, took a special interest in their financial well-being. I suppose it's baked into the capitalist soufflé that every transaction is to one degree or another an exaggeration, a hustle, or a lie. All we had to do at Adler was outperform the overall market, even by 1 percent, and give our clients the sense that, for reasons that may have been difficult to explain, we saw them as individuals, quirky and fascinating, decent and lovable, and that our own sense of well-being hinged on our ability to protect and grow their capital. This mercantile chumminess made more sense when the majority of AA's clients were either closely or distantly related to Ken, but over the years our roster of customers had grown and helping to maintain the illusion that we had some overarching, emotionally charged commitment to our investors became part of my job.

One of the people with whom I had formed a business friendship was named Parker Brown. He had been disastrously married to one of Ken's cousins but stayed with us after the divorce. Poor Parker had succumbed to cocaine and lost his medical license, but he still owned several McDonald's franchises in Detroit, which, selling chopped-up cows, were cash cows themselves. The scandal surrounding the lost medical license and the toxic aftermath of the messy divorce left Parker isolated and more or less friendless. He needed a lot more hand-holding than most of our clients, but I was willing to give it to him, partly out of duty, but mainly because I could combine a trip to see him with a visit to my parents and sisters.

I would spend the night in my childhood house. My sisters' shared bedroom was now where my mother had graded papers while she still taught seventh grade and where now she spent time on her computer and read—I noticed her library reflected a growing concern with health issues. I sensed something was unspooling within her. Her hands trembled and sometimes when she spoke her lower lip trembled as well. My old bedroom still contained my childhood bed, but I had to share the space with stacks of Hilary Custom Shirts' signature blue and white boxes, now that Dad ran what remained of his business from home. When he met with his few customers, it was at a nearby Marriott, generally on the first Tuesday of the month.

Sometimes my sisters, Lois and Loretta, would come to the house when I was there. Lois, solid and hardworking, had followed Mom's career path and worked at a day school in Lansing. She was married to a Nigerian named Daveed Okafor, who taught geology at Michigan State, and they had two kids, whose pictures were all around my parents' house, mixed in with photographs of Loretta's child, Joy, who was born with a defective heart and had not been expected to live beyond her first birthday. Thanks to Daveed's brother, a pediatric surgeon at the Cleveland Clinic, Joy lived but Loretta's marriage had not survived. The last time we were all of us together, I noticed the united front between Loretta and Lois had gaps in it—their once steady stream of smirks and eyerolls had become a parched trickle, and the avid nods one would make while the other spoke had been supplanted by quizzical looks and interruptions. Now unmarried Loretta, slimmer than I'd ever known her, wearing futuristic earrings, her hair boyishly bobbed, was saying things that implied she and I, the unmarried siblings, shared an understanding of the world that the others, deluded by togetherness, could not perceive.

"Kip and I have a singles lifestyle," she would say. "It's way more of an adventure." Then, resting her chin in her hand and opening her eyes, signaling her receptivity to the wildest story I could tell, she would ask me, "So? Who have you been dating?" She had that alcoholic way of inserting people into a drama that seemed primarily to be taking place in her own mind. She'd point to you when she wanted you to say something and wave you off the moment she'd had enough. I maintained I was seeing several people but no one too seriously. She had always been suspicious of me. *Hey there, Batman, how's Robin?* was her regular greeting when we were young.

On this late April visit, however, I didn't reach my parents' house until it was nearly 10 P.M., too late for my sisters to make an appearance, and I was leaving the next morning for New York. My father let me in, his expression worried, as if I'd been out with the family car and had broken my curfew. He looked tired, dressed in pajama bottoms and a Red Wings sweatshirt. The sweatshirt gave me pause. Recoiling from his own father's mania for sports, Dad didn't follow any sport— Grandfather had owned shares in two welterweight boxers and had held season tickets to Pistons and Lions games, and, when the Red Wings won the Stanley Cup in '55, Mr. Super Fan had catapulted from his second-row seat and bounded onto the ice, where he slipped, fell, and was knocked unconscious.

"Mom's not feeling great," Dad said, "but she hopes to see you in the morning." He took my suitcase from me. It was a pricey little one-suiter from Mark Cross, with my initials embossed near the handle, and he looked at it admiringly. More and more, he seemed to catalog the outward signs of his son's success, commenting on my suits and shoes and, of course, my shirts, even mentioning the details of my personal grooming. "Where do you get your hair cut?" he'd asked me the year before. "It always looks so good." Now, as I followed him from the little entranceway of our Hydrangea Court house and into that familiar kitchen, where he had already set things up for a late night talk—a bottle of good vodka and a bowl of high-fiber pretzels—I debated with myself whether or not to mention I had recently purchased ten wooded acres in upstate New York. I wasn't sure whether this information would interest him and make him happy for me, or if any further evidence of my affluence would make him feel diminished. I did not want to bum the old guy out, I truly did not, yet there was a temptation to do so, like how you protect an inflamed tooth from anything that might set it off, but every once in a while you suck some cold air over it, just to make sure it hurts as much as you feared.

"So you in town for Parker Brown?" Dad asked as we sat at the kitchen table. He lifted the bottle and asked by raising his brows if I wanted a drink.

"How do you remember these things?" I asked. "Do you know Parker?"

"No, no. Mr. Parker Brown and Hilary Woods are in very different circles. And he's years and years younger than me."

"He doesn't look it," I said.

"Is that a fact?" Dad asked, his expression brighter for a moment.

"Dad, you're filling my glass to the very top. I'll be out of my mind."

"Ah, minds aren't all what they're cracked up to be. Try one of these pretzels. They're whole wheat with just a little bit of sea salt." He scratched his arm through the fabric of his sweatshirt and then pushed the sleeve up and pulled off a big star-spangled Band-Aid, beneath which was a bluish splotch.

"What you have there, Dad?" I asked.

"Blood test. I've got squirmy veins and they have to keep poking before they get a hit." He lifted his glass. "Poke poke poke," he said, by way of a toast.

"Why the blood test?"

"Because that's what you do after you round the clubhouse turn, as my dear late father used to say."

"He certainly did."

"Speaking of your grandfather . . . ," he said, his tone cagey.

"As we so often do."

"Well, wouldn't he just keel over if he were to see my son becoming so successful. You're going to end up more success-ful, at least in terms of m-o-n-e-y, than that old buzzard ever was, even at the pinnacle."

"What does it matter?"

"Ah, modesty. The luxury of success. Problem with me, I was always worried that people would think too little of me. I never had a thought of downplaying it."

"I don't feel successful, to tell you the truth."

"Really. Well, if you don't feel as if you've been successful, then I may as well shoot myself." He took a gulp of vodka and shook his head as if a bell had clanged within it. The drinks were absurd. I'd be hard-pressed to drink a full glass of water, much less a full glass of his vodka. "Mom says I owe you an apology," he said.

I prepared myself for whatever was about to be said.

"She says I never should have encouraged you to cozy up to the old man. She says I shouldn't have encouraged such a thing."

Encouraged? I wanted to poke-poke at that word. My courtship of Grandfather was not encouraged—it was required. Dad would brief me on what constituted acceptable behavior in my grandfather's house, urging me to feign being a Tigers fan, and a Lions fan, and to pretend to look forward to those dreary, humid weekends in the cabin. I was a spy and Dad was my handler. In 1970, my hair was long, and one Saturday, waiting for Grandfather's car to arrive, I braided it, inspired by Iron Eyes Cody, the crying Indian in the anti-littering ads on TV. When I emerged from my room in braids, Dad said, "Are you out of your fucking mind?," and frog-marched me back to the bathroom. "This is not a game."

"I made a very bad mistake," my father said, taking another sip of his vodka before putting the glass onto the table and moving it farther away, out of easy reach. "All those weekends with that jerk. What I"—he hit the heel of his hand against the side of his head. "I was too wrapped up with my own parental issues to understand how it felt to you to spend that time with a man who had so disrespected your mother."

"Mom?"

"Yes, that was the main thing, wasn't it? When your mother and I got together, that jerk said"—here Dad's voice became an ignorant growl—"'She's ten miles beneath you, boy. Her father is a house painter. She is trash. And if you don't do exactly what I say, you're finished around here. Finished!'" He stopped for a moment, massaged his throat. "This is how he spoke about the woman I loved. A woman who, by the way, anyone without poison in their blood would recognize as one of the finest people who has ever lived. I see now that what was happening . . ." He squinted and turned his head, as if a vision was materializing in the dreary light of the fluorescent tube that softly hummed above the kitchen sink. "I was put smack-dab in the middle of my earliest childhood traumas, which all involved protecting my mother from his tyranny, his moods."

Was Dad in therapy? Parental issues. The recapitulation of childhood traumas. Since starting at Adler, I had gone through four shrinks; when I traveled I kept my appointments via phone. I believed in psychotherapy and I needed it, but nevertheless there was something unsettling in picturing Dad with a box of tissues at his elbow. Even at their most disappointing, we prefer our parents to remain fixed poles, unchanging and predictable, not works in progress.

"These feelings," Dad was saying, "controlled me more than I could control them. I wanted to be a good father to you, Kip. In light of what my father did to me, I wanted that more than anything."

"But you were. You were a terrific father. You were the best father I ever had!" The joke stabbed into the back of the emotion, which was my intention, but Dad took it differently and his eyes filled with tears.

"There's a lot of regret, Kip."

I knew this was where we were headed. I could sense it, the way you can smell the nearness of rain. We were about to revisit the conversation in which he blurted out how repulsive it was to measure the necks and limp wrists of the various fairies who came to him for customized shirts. As much as it had wounded me then, I had also taken a kind of comfort in the outburst, figuring that my father—who loved me, who was gentle and kind—would not make odious remarks about the men he measured if he suspected for a moment I might take them personally. Yet even then, rendered half stupid by my need to believe in my father's love, a smaller yet persuasive part of myself suspected that Dad sensed in me a vulnerability to a so-called lifestyle that was abhorrent, disgusting, and disqualifying, a subculture of the contemptible who he imagined were making up for their inability to multiply in the normal way by luring unsuspecting suckers into their doomed community.

"I remember you were extremely accommodating when it came to my weirdness about what I could eat and what made me sick," I said. "You knew this pizza place where they put hardly any tomato sauce on it, just brushed it on like a pink wash in a watercolor."

"Oh yes," he said. "Taste of Capri. I knew the owner quite well. Poor guy just passed. Not really all that poor, actually. He took the franchise route and made important money. There were seven Tastes of Capri in Michigan alone. Good old Andy Manzardo. I can't tell you how good it makes me feel that you remember those pizzas."

"Well, all right then."

"He never married," my father said. "Everyone used to pester Andy about it. I guess that was pretty stupid. What did we know, right? It was a long time ago."

"I don't mind tomato sauce anymore," I said. "I actually like it, done right."

"The thing about marriage is, it's not for everyone," my father said. "And that's okay. It's a big world and there's room for everyone."

He looked relieved, unburdened. This is what he'd wanted to say. He was as close to speaking the truth as he dared to venture. Not to actually speak the truth, but to scale a little promontory from which the dim outlines of the truth could be seen. That great gated city in the mists.

"I made a lot of shirts for that man. My clients are the cream of the crop, men who don't hesitate to pay three or four times the store price for the right shirt. The funny thing is when I am seeing customers I make sure to wear a custom shirt, but other than that I buy most of my shirts right out of Macy's." He squinted at me, took in what I was wearing, and nodded approvingly. "Very nice, by the way."

"Probably Bergdorf Goodman."

"Ooof," he said, rubbing his thumb and two fingers together.

"Or maybe Macy's."

"Somehow I doubt it. My son is a rich man, a very wealthy man indeed." He saw I was about to object, but he stopped me with a raised hand. "Which comes as no surprise. I always knew you were going to be special. And a smart cookie, too, make no mistake about it. Smarter than your old man, that's for sure. I don't see you getting tied down to any one person. Hey!" He slammed both his hands onto the table and the sudden noise almost made me yelp. He was closing the door to the room in which his innermost unhappiness lurked, but I had gotten a glimpse of it. "You know what I'm going to do? I'm going to make you three shirts."

"You don't have to—"

"No, no, I want to. It's an honor. And you know what? It's good business. The people you mix with, the hoi polloi? They see you in a Hilary Custom Shirt and they say, Hey, where'd you get that shirt? And some of them could end up right here, getting measured for shirts of their own. Right?" He struggled out of his chair. To my great regret, the head of his penis came through the pajama flap, like the head of an anxious actor parting the curtain to see if the house was full. "Wait right there," he said.

"Where are you going?"

"Upstairs. I'll bring down the sample books, do the mea-surements, and we're off to the races."

"Dad, it's really so late. . . ."

"I'm striking when the iron's hot. I'll be right back. Help yourself to anything in the fridge. There's yogurt, real New York yogurt. I'm going to check on your mother, and then I'll be right back with everything we need to get you the best shirt money can buy. Which will be free. I'm still the father, right?"

"What does that have to do with paying?"

"Just . . . just let me do this my own way."

I heaved the exasperated sigh of an adolescent but did nothing more to stop him. The house now was fully carpeted, wall to wall on every square foot of it. It was a continuous pale green, all off the same roll. When I lived here with Lois and Loretta, the floors reverberated beneath our hormonal hoof-beats, room to room, up and down the staircase, but now, when it seemed to me my parents needed it least, footsteps were soundless.

I checked my phone to see who had been trying to reach me. A call from the Manhattan Theatre Club, probably to re-mind me to renew my subscription. Three calls from my office. A call from the airline, something they'd instituted the year before, a kind of faux concierge service, checking in with fre-quent first-class passengers to make sure everything had been to our liking. A call from Thaddeus. Another call from Thad-deus. I checked my watch. It was too late to call him back, no matter how much I wanted to.

Fifteen minutes passed and I decided what had happened—I was sure of it—was he had stretched out next to Mom and ac-cidentally fallen asleep. I waited a few more minutes just to be sure. Finished my drink. Took my notebook out of my jacket's inside pocket and tore out a piece of paper and wrote him a note. *See you in the morning. Great talking with you. Much love. By the way, hoi polloi doesn't mean fancy people. It actually means just the opposite.* I slipped the note under the sugar bowl and sat there for an extra moment or two, just enough time to come to my senses. I grabbed the note and ripped it in half, and in half again. I didn't even want to put it in the garbage, though nothing I had ever touched deserved more to be put into the garbage. I shoved it in my pocket, turned off the kitchen light, and climbed the silent stairs to my boyhood bed, thinking to myself: In a sense, all of us continue to sleep in our childhood beds.

CHAPTER 14

Stoned Again

*I returned Thaddeus's call from the Detroit airport right before board-*ing but he didn't answer, and I called him when I landed at LaGuardia, and a third time around eleven in the morning, from my office.

"I'm so glad you're back," he said. "But I'm frantic right now. I'm supposed to go to Florida in the morning. Grace is having a show there—a solo show, isn't that fantastic?—and tomorrow's the closing party. I missed the opening and I can't miss this. David was supposed to come down from Skidmore to look after the place and, frankly, look after Emma, who's having some difficulties and we don't want to leave her on her own. But the little jerk just canceled on me. Completely spurious reasons."

"I'll stay with her," I said. "I'll hop on a train and be there at the end of the day."

"Oh man, that would be amazing."

"Emma? Come on, it's a pleasure. Great news about Grace, by the way. Really."

I boarded the three o'clock Amtrak, out of Pennsylvania Station. Though it was Friday, the train was half empty.

We rolled north, through the catastrophe of the Bronx, the looming catastrophe of the nuclear power station farther up the Hudson. Several insurers had refused to write policy for it until a credible evacuation plan could be presented, some way for the hundreds of thousands of jeopardized people to escape the radioactivity should there be a meltdown or any other serious malfunction, and so far no such plan existed. I fell asleep. One moment my brain was full of chatter, hyperbole, justifications, and theories of human behavior, a few of them road tested, others shaky to say the least, and the next moment I just went dark, a plunge so precipitous it was like a dress rehearsal for sudden death.

A stone the size of an orange struck the very window upon which my head rested. The Amtrak windowpane was thick enough to absorb the blow; a starburst of cracks appeared. I looked around at the other passengers, feeling somehow sheepish that my window had been the one to be hit, but no one was looking my way. Had no one heard? Were they all so accustomed to these attacks that a mere solitary stone failed to register or registered as something so trivial that it didn't warrant interrupting their reading, their conversation, their telephone calls, their laptops, their idle contemplation of the passing landscape? I was underslept, dislocated, full of anticipation to see Thaddeus, my mind a palette onto which color from too many tubes of paint has been squeezed, making the whole thing a blurry mess. The conductor dozed at the back of our car, with his arms folded over his chest and his cap balanced on his knee. My heart was racing and I stood in the aisle like a child who cannot fathom the willful blindness, the sheer hypocrisy of the adults in the room. "What the fuck?" I shouted. "Didn't anyone see what just happened?"

The person sitting in the seat across from mine was an exquisitely groomed woman in her forties, with pearl earrings and an ecru silk suit that matched her hair. Her left arm was in a sling and she had been working on her laptop using one hand. "It's actually getting better," she said, in a voice that was calibrated to calm you down. "They're slowly but surely giving up."

"But who?" I asked. "Has anyone figured that out?"

She made a dismissive sound, and waved her hand, as if to indicate a world beneath her contempt. The train sped around a curve and, stumbling, I allowed the momentum of it to return me to my seat, where I sat next to the cracked Plexiglas, feeling both ridiculous and self-righteous. Forty minutes later we arrived at the Leyden station. I pulled my bag down from the luggage rack and made my way to the exit. The ecru woman was continuing north, but she looked up from her work as I waited in the aisle for the doors to open. She smiled at me, winked, and gave me the good old thumbs-up. We were somehow on the same side, in it together.

CHAPTER 15

Faux Pair

"There's my au pair!" Thaddeus called, as soon as he saw me in the train's open doorway, getting ready to step down onto the platform at Leyden. The wind came off the river strong enough to make you think you could lean your weight against it, as if it were a wall. Thaddeus was dressed for milder weather in a thin, zippered jacket, hatless, gloveless, ever the optimist. As he reached up to take my bag from me, his jacket hiked up. All he had beneath it was a T-shirt and that rose, too, revealing a patch of stomach, with tight little black curls of hair on it, like drops of rain. I felt desire as a kind of wretchedness.

"Kip, what can I say here? One day you're going to get fed up with saving my life and I don't know what I'll do after that."

I told him about the stone and the window and the woman in ecru and what she said about the attacks coming less frequently.

"Well, that's good to know," Thaddeus said, as he patted his pockets, looking for his car keys. "Did you see your family while you were in Detroit?"

"I slept at my parents' house. But I was late and my mother was already in bed. Her health isn't that good right now."

We were halfway up the steep staircase that led from the train platform to the little station, but Thaddeus stopped right there. "Oh no," he said. "What's going on?" He looked at me with his startling receptivity. Even if it was an act—what was the difference? Most people wouldn't bother making you feel so listened to, wouldn't make you feel that your words had such weight that they could hang on to every one of them. "What's wrong with her?"

"I don't know. Maybe nothing. She doesn't really trust doctors. Western medicine and all. She's worried, though. She thinks it might be Parkinson's. Self-diagnosis is dangerous, and now that my parents have a modem, the world is her osteopath."

"I'm really sorry, Kip. Should you have even come here? Maybe you need to be back in Detroit."

A couple in their thirties passed us on the stairs and waved hello to Thaddeus; he waved back at them without taking his eyes off me.

"I'm happy to be here," I said. "There's nothing I can do in Detroit, except go insane with boredom and irritation. She doesn't listen to reason and my father is being . . . He's turning into an old man, that's what's happening." I started up the steps again and Thaddeus followed.

"Your parents are beautiful people," he said.

"Didn't you only meet them once?"

"Twice actually. Ann Arbor. And New York. Actually three times, twice in New York. But I'd think they were beautiful people because you're their son, they raised you, and you are the kindest person I've ever known. That doesn't happen all on its own. They gave you a lot."

We made our way to the parking lot. Through all the financial upheavals Thaddeus had managed to hold on to his BMW, but it had surely seen better days. The casing on one of the taillights was missing, the side-view mirror on the passenger side was held in place with electrical tape, and the leather seats were cracked like my window on the train. We Michigan boys were taught to believe in the iconography of vehicles, that they tell as much about you as your clothes or your haircut. We believed that those who drove Buicks were Republicans, those who drove VW bugs were hippies, a Chevrolet was for a worker bee buzzing his life away in the billing department at AT&T, a Peugeot was for an assistant professor who wanted to look cool but couldn't swing getting a car that was actually good, a Honda was every bit as sexy as a spinach salad, and the Volvo owner believed in safety first and read *Consumer Reports,* and probably wore two rubbers when he screwed. I knew it was nonsense, but I was relieved Thaddeus had held on to the Beemer.

It took four tries before the engine caught, the fan belt shrieking.

"It does that," he said with a grin. "But if I give up this car, I give up the ghost."

"Totally agree," I said. "This is a quality ride."

"Reading anything good?" he asked.

"Not really. Kind of bogged down. What about you?"

"*Winesburg, Ohio,*" he said. "I think I might be nostalgic for the Midwest."

I wondered for a moment if he was telling the truth. Those Sherwood Anderson stories were what he had read aloud to me at my hospital bedside when I was in St. Vincent's with a lung infection. He and Grace were living on Twenty-Third Street at the time; he was writing advertising copy for B. Altman. I can't remember how I learned I was sick. Maybe I called him. But he was there hours after I was admitted, and he looked much more frightened than was warranted by a lung infection. Half the people in that hospital were dying. Most of the staff wore surgical masks for their entire shift. I was feverish, coughing, but I knew I was going to get better and I wondered how I could reassure Thaddeus that this was far from a worst-case scenario. His chair was close to my bed and his knees touched the skimpy yellow blanket. He read beautifully, softly tapping his foot against the linoleum to keep an even pace. In "Hands" there's a line that goes, "I am a lover and have not found my thing to love," and when Thaddeus had read it, there was a catch in his throat and his foot was still for a moment or two.

"You brought that book to me in the hospital," I said.

"I did?" he asked. He shook his head and smiled. "Well, how do you like that?"

It was a short drive to Orkney, beneath gray skies. I felt the familiar nausea of suppressed desire. The clouds had massed in two distinct regions, separated by a narrow ridge of blue that bisected the sky like the part in an old-fashioned haircut. I usually found Leyden and environs rather glamorous, but the place did not show well until spring was fully present. The trees were partially bare, broken limbs dangling. A dairy farmer had turned his herd of Jerseys out onto a dark brown pasture and the cows were just milling around, swaying their Illinois-shaped heads back and forth, waiting for someone to feed them.

"Exciting about Grace," Thaddeus said.

"Definitely. How did all this come about?"

"Oh, a friend of her brother's. They were both in the weed business together. And now they're both retired. Liam's avocado farm is this guy's art gallery."

"Different strokes."

"Hyperrealism is hot. At least in Coral Gables. She's sold quite a few of them and she's really happy."

"Long overdue," I said, feeling a tug of worry. I was as close as I was to Thaddeus—to the lot of them—in large part because he was on the skids, Orkney was on the abyss, and I was their primary source of funds. And even though it often worried and galled me that I was more *needed* than wanted, money secured my little lair at the edge of their lives.

"The rest she'll leave down there so we don't have to worry about shipping them back here," Thaddeus said. He tapped his fingers against the steering wheel, and cleared his throat. "Jennings drove all that work down to Florida. He rented a padded truck. An art truck. He had to go down to Canal Street to pick it up. They spent three days packing it just so, with a wooden box he made for each piece. He's so good at that kind of thing."

"So . . . is Jennings still down there, too?"

"No." He glanced at me. "You don't really like him one little bit, do you?"

"I don't know him. Anyhow, we're too old for liking and not liking."

"I'm not a complete fool," he said.

"There are worse things in the world," I said.

"This has been her dream ever since I've known her."

We were on Riverview Road now, gliding past the wrought-iron gates at the foot of each driveway. We were closing in on Orkney. A guy in a T-shirt and a multicolored Peruvian wool cap was replacing stones in a border wall that separated the winding macadam from the maples that lined the road. A woman with a small child sat on the ground near him, her dark blue skirt spread out around her like a blanket. Her eyes lifted and met my gaze.

Thaddeus took the sharp right turn into Orkney's entrance, and onto his half mile of driveway. The driveway branched off, with an auxiliary blacktop leading to the yellow house, where Jennings and his family lived. An orange and white panel truck bearing the name Windsor Asbestos Solutions was parked in front of his house. And there, suddenly, was the man himself, so stately and hypermasculine, working with his son, Henry, on replacing some spindles on the side of the front porch.

The main house floated into view, a mash-up of architectural styles—Gothic here, Victorian there, four chimneys, a messy scatter of windows over which there were occasional stone outcroppings, everything a sudden inspiration, or perhaps an afterthought, an architectural cacophony that would have rendered Orkney virtually worthless had it not been for its location. Its pristine view of the Hudson meant Orkney was known as eclectic, just as bizarre behavior in a rich person is called eccentric.

"There it is," Thaddeus said. "My folly."

"It's just a house, man, just a pile of stones."

He looked at Orkney with an expression that suggested he was seeing it with new eyes, but finally he shook his head and smiled indulgently at me, as if I'd said a poem was no good if it didn't rhyme. Then something caught his attention. An old dark blue Subaru hatchback was parked at the side of the house.

"Goddamnit," Thaddeus said. "David is here."

"Which is a good thing, right?"

"I wouldn't have dragged you up here if he hadn't already said he couldn't come home this weekend."

He looked far more upset than the situation warranted.

"Well, I'm more than happy to be here," I said. "And it will be nice to see David."

"Good. Tell him his parents are fine, upstanding people and he should let go of this fantasy of joining the CIA and stop using this house as his laundromat. Those three things. Okay?"

"The upstanding part might be a bit of a reach."

"Oh, you've pulled off bigger scams than that."

I heard what I first thought was heavy furniture being dragged over bare floors inside the house, but it was Grace's gray and mauve Weimaraners, their paws on the glass of the French windows, barking wildly at us, turning now and again to bark at each other.

CHAPTER 16

In Dreams Begin Responsibilities

There was a chill inside the house. It wasn't so cold that you'd see the vapor of your own breath, but you were certainly not in a rush to take off your jacket. The dogs circled us, gliding gracefully as if on skates. "Ignore them," Thaddeus said.

It was a house divided, with the Weimaraners patrolling the downstairs and a half dozen cats roaming above. With David away at college, it fell to Thaddeus to care for and protect his cats. The five-foot-high accordion gates at the bottom of the staircases were scratched to hell by the dogs' futile attempts to scale them.

These gates were only one aspect of the overall feeling of slippage that had overtaken Orkney. There is something vagrant and a little wild in the atmosphere of an unheated house, and this sense of dishevelment—a kind of shabbiness that seemed to have a moral dimension as well as a material one—extended to the worn-through upholstery, the pale blue paint scaling off the ceiling, the presence of low wattage bulbs in the formerly blazing lamps, and most notably in the two shopping bags filled to bursting and waiting to be schlepped to the supermarket, where a nickel would be rewarded for each empty can or bottle.

Thaddeus waved wildly at the dogs and made noises to keep them at bay after opening the gate to the main staircase. First I went in and he came after, quickly pulling the gate closed behind us. "I know," he said, as we climbed to the second floor, "it's insane. But those cats are David's inner life. And the dogs are Grace's. Pure hatred on both sides and all the work is left to Daddy. We're a house divided! Come on, I've put you in David's room."

"He won't mind?"

"I made the room cozy for you and he doesn't get to upend everything at the last minute."

That sharp juniper bush feline scent greeted us as soon as we were on the second floor landing, and one of the cats, a pale gray Persian with long whiskers and eyes as devoid of warmth as sequins on a dress, came bounding toward us, only to skid to a stop—evidently, it had been expecting someone else. I was relieved to see an electric heater in the room assigned to me—one of my favorite rooms in the house, full of odd angles, the windows offering a view of the river beyond the steep slope of the lawn.

Thaddeus left me to unpack my bag and to rest for a few moments while he put together our dinner. Another of David's cats came in, this one a seal point Siamese. It looked at me and made a cat sound, and I crouched down and put my hand out.

But before I could induce the cat to come closer, David came hurrying in. "Oh, there you are," he said to the cat.

The cat, upon seeing David, ran under the bed, and was silent.

"You can stay there for all I care," David said to the cat. He folded his arms over his chest. He was dressed in a Thaddeusian outfit of jeans and a T-shirt.

Unlike Thaddeus, whose face, when I met him, had been soft, still childlike, David's adult face was starting to emerge. His cheeks were sunken, and his expression, at rest, was suspicious, as if his path through life always took him through rooms where people had been talking about him. He had Thaddeus's dark eyes and hair, and skin that was at once pale and ruddy, like someone who has taken a long cold journey on foot and stood now at last in front of a roaring fire. Both Thaddeus and Grace had low voices—roughly in the deeper registers of a clarinet—and David's was similar, though without the warmth of his father's, or the rich trill of his mother's.

I asked him the cat's name—Jeane Kirkpatrick—and invited him to stay and wait for the creature to emerge. David flung himself on the bed and landed with enough force to cause its slender wooden legs to tremble, but not enough to stir Jeane Kirkpatrick. Sprawled out, his hands behind his head, his T-shirt rising a bit to show the ragged path of dark hair traversing his navel, David looked too much like his father for my comfort and I turned away from him, walked to the window to take in the view. The river throbbed bright silver in the sunlight.

"I've taken your room," I said to him. "I'm sorry. Your father insisted."

"I don't care. I'm not staying overnight anyhow."

"He wanted me to have a river view. Will you look at that river?" I said. "No wonder so many artists have painted it."

"Fucking artists," David said. "The scum of the earth."

"Really," I said, turning, smiling. "Scum of the earth? That's a new one on me."

"The most despicable people in my school go around calling themselves artists. These people have got their heads so far up their own asses it's a wonder they can breathe."

There was no reason for David to be saying these things to good old Uncle Kip except to gauge my reaction, but then I realized he was serious. His lips were pressed tightly together and his eyes were blazing with that most intransigent sort of conviction, the kind that comes from personal injury. I should have seen it coming, the collateral damage of it—both his parents had dreamt of being Artists, with that telltale capital *A*, and the failure of it, the heartbreak, the bitterness, and the suspicion that a great party was taking place to which they had pointedly not been invited seeped poison into their daily lives.

"Your mother's a good artist, David," I said. "You know that, I hope."

"You think so?" He stretched himself in a way that he might have learned from observing his cats. I wondered for a moment if he was flirting with me—not out of desire but to test his power. "I always thought you thought her stuff sucked. From the expression on your face when she talked about her stupid paintings."

"I actually own some of her work," I said.

"Owning it isn't the same as putting it up on your wall," he said.

He had me there.

"She's ridiculous," David said, "my whole family is. My dad's parents, stupid Communists, hating their own country? My mom's mother comes here and does nothing but drink and we don't even know where Mom's father is." He slapped himself on the chest. "Thanks, Mom and Dad, thanks for the legacy."

He rolled out of the bed and peered under it in search of the cat. He extended his arm and somehow caught the thing. It yowled in protest as he dragged it across the floor, and only quieted down when David cradled it in his arms and stroked the top of its head with his chin. "Out of their gourds. Both of them. They gave away that whole house to the Stratton clan, a house I could have lived in myself if I wanted to. Not that I ever would, but maybe I would. I don't know. And it's not like we're rich. Not anymore. My father saw to that. He threw away his career and now all he does is worry about money. It's pretty weird, don't you think, when your own parents act like they're on drugs or something. Like the real world isn't enough, those two have to live in make-believe."

"What about the idea that art is more real than anything else?" I offered, and he looked at me as if we were old pals and he knew I was kidding.

"Are you into cats?" he asked me.

"A gay man has to be careful about pets," I said. "Cliché avoidance and all that."

"I always thought you might be gay," David said.

"Really? That's interesting. What made you think that?"

"I don't know. That you take good care of yourself? That you're funny? Maybe just the way you're looking at me right now."

"David. What the fuck? I'm not looking at you weird."

"I didn't say it was weird. If you must know, I like it."

"I guess for your generation it's a lot different," I said. "People can be whatever they are."

He put the cat on the floor and looked at me with a frankness I found completely unnerving. He sensed my unease and smiled. He moved in my direction. Stopped. Gave me a moment to wonder what he was up to. And moved still closer.

"Would it be okay if I hugged you?" he asked.

"Sure," I said, thinking that if I answered casually it might not flip our relationship into the realm of transgression. I could be just an honorary uncle giving my honorary nephew an honorary hug. What was the emotional value of a hug anyhow? Golfers hugged their caddies, Formula One drivers hugged their sponsors from Valvoline, celebrants at Episcopalian mass hugged whoever happened to be seated next to them. And kisses? Social life since 1980 had been raining kisses, one cheek, two cheeks, sometimes on the lips. By now, a handshake was an affront.

And so I embraced him. Here was a knock-off of the original object of desire that I had spent years searching for in rent boys, in porn reels, in passersby. Yet I was careful not to presume any desire greater than a desire for comfort on David's part. I even did that thing that people do to drain the emotion from an embrace—I pat-pat-patted him on the back. But he would not allow me to put a veneer of nonchalance or innocence on the embrace. He held me tighter and moved his hips and then reached up to put his hands on either side of my pale and astonished face so that he might kiss me.

But none of this happened. There was not a confession, I did not make that remark about gay men and cats. There was not a touch, and there was certainly not a kiss. It did not take place and it never will, would, or could. Please discount and dispose of everything I have said after *Are you into cats?*

What really happened was this. The cat ran back under

the bed. I asked David how school was. He said it was fine. I asked him if he'd decided what to major in, and he said he was studying international relations. And then we heard Thaddeus calling up, telling us dinner was ready.

Did Dante ever mention this, Your Honor? Here is what unrequited love feels like: no matter how many times you strain to swallow, your mouth is always full.

CHAPTER 17

Dinner

Emma was waiting at the kitchen table, with her hands folded and her head down, like a defendant waiting to be called to the stand. Thaddeus was at the stove, shaking a long-handled skillet; sizzling vegetables and tofu released their calm, virtuous aroma.

"Hey there, Emma," I said. "I'm starving. How about you?"

Thaddeus turned, looked at me with slight alarm.

But of course: I had wandered into forbidden territory. Emma's weight! Emma was a little heavy, and I might not have noted it had Thaddeus not told me that it was a subject of not only disagreement between him and Grace, but a flash point, a subject they shouted about, stalking out of rooms, giving each other cold shoulders and permafrost stares. This from Thaddeus's point of view, but even if he was shading the story to put himself in the best possible light, the cherry-picked facts as he presented them suggested an ongoing battle between a child and her mother over food, one that was not only ill advised but could conceivably lead to a lifetime of eating disorders.

From the age of four on, Emma was weighed every single

Sunday morning. The results were fixed to the door of the refrigerator by a magnet in the shape of a ballerina. At meal-time, her portions were radically smaller than David's, and often her meal was something completely different from what everyone else was having. Even if she had a little school friend at the table, and the dinner was, say, a roasted chicken, Emma was served steamed vegetables and a small piece of fish. If dessert was served, Emma was given an apple, and sometimes the apple was diced to conceal the fact that it was really half an apple, the other half tithed to the Church of Slender Children.

All of this was done under the highly dubious banner of Tough Love. Grace believed—and this wasn't a belief she kept to herself—that she was saving Emma's life, staving off diabetes, heart attacks, and cancer. She was saving her from being socially ostracized. She was saving her from lovelessness. She was saving her from developing what Grace called a Fat Personality, which I suppose meant some form of compensatory jolliness. She was saving her from unemployment and/ or lower wages, too, according to the statistics she lobbed at Thaddeus. And as Grace's mission to slim her daughter down to the dimensions of a fetching little upper-middle-class girl continued to fail, her frustration intensified, and the frustration resulted in a kind of paranoia, the kind that afflicts tyrants who begin to suspect there are traitors and secret deals afoot. It was like the Red Scare at Orkney—Grace suspected subversion everywhere.

And so after that remark about starving, I could hardly believe something so idiotic had come out of my mouth and I tried to bury my embarrassment in an avalanche of chatter, seating myself next to Emma and asking her all the inane questions you nervously ask a fifteen-year-old girl. How's school? Looking forward to summer? What are you listening to, what are you reading?

"So," I asked her, "do you have any ideas about what you'd like to do when you grow up? Or is grow up a stupid concept?"

"I'd like to be a marriage counselor," she said.

"Really?"

"I think so. I think I'd be good at it."

Thaddeus cackled merrily and Emma looked anxiously at me. "Dad told me to say that," she pleaded.

"How'd you know I was even going to ask the question?" I asked him.

"Childless people always ask that," Thaddeus said. He gave the sauté pan a final shake and turned off the gas, and the blue chrysanthemum was sucked back into the cast iron burner grate. The dogs immediately stood up and began pacing, their claws clattering nervously on the wooden floor.

"Those dogs totally suck," said David.

"Can one of the cats sleep in my room tonight?" Emma asked her brother.

"No."

"Please."

"Which one?"

"Dullest likes me," she said.

"His name's not Dullest," David said, wearily. "I told you. It's Dulles."

"Sorry," Emma said.

"John Foster Dulles?" David persisted, as if the confusion was a personal affront to him.

"You guys know how long I've known Kip?" Thaddeus asked, seating himself next to me. "Longer than either of you have been on the planet." He threw his arm over my shoulder, practically unseating me. "Right, Kip? Isn't that right?"

"Yes," I said, resisting the impulse to squirm away. I felt overwhelmed, weirdly diminished. Somewhere along the way, Thaddeus had learned to turn his outgoing nature into a form of aggression, weaponizing the sweetness. Do we all of us become steadily shittier as we grow older? Thaddeus's jokiness, his affectionate nature, his unending project to make you comfortable, now they all had an element of smoke screen to them. He wasn't so much amusing as distracting. No matter how I enjoyed the infrequent occasions in which Thaddeus and I made physical contact, there was something manic and evasive in his touching me now that put me on guard. It didn't seem like touch so much as a satire of touch, an imaginary bridge over a very real boundary.

CHAPTER 18

Aria

Maybe he was wound up more tightly than usual, anticipating Coral Gables, his reunion with Grace, but as we ate dinner Thaddeus dominated the conversation, not bothering with his food, pouring himself glass after glass of last year's beaujolais nouveau. When it was empty, I thought aha, he will either have to stop drinking or take the time to get another bottle, and maybe someone else can get in a word or two. But he had planned it out in advance, and all that was necessary was for him to reach down and grab the second bottle by the neck, like a gambler with a losing hand pulling a pistol out of his ankle holster. David, frowning, moved his food around his plate without eating it, while Emma, for the duration of Thaddeus's aria, remained hunched over her dinner, obediently chewing each mouthful fifteen times. At one point, a spectacularly pregnant woman in her twenties waddled in and took a pitcher of ice water out of the refrigerator. She was tall, bare-legged, and wore a plaid robe. Her pale, frizzy hair was beaded with moisture. I learned later her name was Ruthie Horn and she was giving birth in one of the back bedrooms, which Thaddeus had offered to her after the midwife refused to do it where Ruthie and her husband lived because their A-frame in the woods was too far from the hospital, should complications arise. She huffed and puffed Lamaze-style, scarcely acknowledging our presence. David shook his head in disapproval.

Also tucked away in one of Orkney's rooms was the gear, and occasionally the sleeping body, of a photographer named Lee Garnett, whom Thaddeus had met years before on a movie set, and who was traipsing around wooded areas throughout Windsor County, setting up and collecting motion-sensitive cameras, in order to capture the secret life of bears, deer, fox, weasels, bobcats, raccoons, herons, swans, ducks, turtles, snakes, and teenage lovers.

"You guys remember me telling you about my new agent, right?" Thaddeus asked, reaching over and patting my forearm, petitioning my forbearance. "I liked her from the start. My guess was either she's too young to have even been in the business when I had that trouble or she thinks it's such a huge ridiculous unjustifiable overreaction. And her name, she has a great name. Victoria Stern. A total don't-fuck-with-me name."

"You said she wore that weird hat," Emma said.

"A pillbox hat, yes."

"With a feather in it, right?" Emma said, possibly without the knowledge that those would be the last words she would be able to interject for quite some time.

"Yes, with a feather. Like a middle-class matron strolling around Vienna. She wears it everywhere, at lunch, at her desk. It's like Tom Wolfe and his white suit, only worse. Anyhow, she was going to set up some meetings for me with producers and studio execs, and I sent her some pitches, including that one I told you kids about, about the early part of your mom's and my relationship, moving to New York when the city was going crazy."

A movie about him and Grace? The idea struck me as absurd, but I counseled myself to maintain a neutral expression. And you never know. Long ago, I'd been at a party on Crosby Street after a show of Nam June Paik's video installations at some unheated, cement-walled gallery on Houston Street. I tried to get Thaddeus and Grace to come with me, but they had no interest in avant-garde anything. They were against everything new and strange. And when they weren't working their office jobs, they were either fucking or making dinner or she was doing a portrait of a pineapple and he was banging away at his fiction. I remember how furious I was. They were so insulated, they were missing everything. At any rate, at the party I found myself in conversation with this Englishman with a comb-over and a long scarlet scarf. He asked me what I was working on and when I told him I was working at a brokerage house, he didn't seem surprised or disturbed. "Lucky you," he said. This was Tim Rice. I had no idea. He smelled of pâté and expensive aftershave. I asked him what he was working on and he said he was preparing a musical about Evita Peron, and the idea was so preposterous to me, so doomed, I just assumed he was being satirical. I wanted to laugh in Tim Rice's overtly ironic face. Lesson learned: shut the fuck up about other people's projects.

And yet. A movie about Thaddeus and Grace? Who did Thaddeus think he was? These kinds of projects might get financed if Ingmar Bergman or Francis Ford Coppola wanted to make them, but nil were the chances of someone paying the persona non grata getting sloshed at the table in Orkney's kitchen so much as a dime to write something like that. They wouldn't have paid him to do it even before that mimosa was tossed.

But then it got worse. Here he was trying to find a way out of the briar patch of ignominy into which he had stupidly thrown himself, and once again talking about writing a modernized version of *Lady Chatterley's Lover,* an awful idea he had been trying to flog since the early days of his career. He had even gone to London on the delusionary hunch he might interest Stanley Kubrick in directing such a movie. While working on-set doing a rewrite for a Jeff Bridges movie, Thaddeus became convinced Bridges would make a perfect Oliver Mellors and he persisted in discussing the matter with Bridges to the point where Bridges felt compelled to take his meals in his trailer while the rest of the cast and crew enjoyed lovely alfresco lunches in the little Italian seaside village where the movie was being shot.

The Lady Chatterley idea was not only misbegotten but, knowing what I knew about Grace and Jennings, or at least suspecting what I suspected, I could only believe that Thaddeus's pursuit of this project suggested suppressed knowledge of the fact that he himself was something of a Lord Chatterley. While the Outer Thaddeus exhausted himself trying to dig his way back into the movie business, an Inner Thaddeus was also hard at work, patiently tunneling toward the surface to deliver some very bad news.

Just then, Lee Garnett walked in, wearing camouflage pants and a sleeveless T-shirt, with the Rolleiflex on a strap, bouncing on his chest like an external heart. He was tall, though his spine was as curved as a scythe, and his hair was gray, worn in a ponytail. He opened the refrigerator and pulled out another pitcher of water. This one had little yellowish shreds of lemon peel floating in it.

"What do you have there, Lee?" Thaddeus asked, as Lee tried to leave the kitchen as unobtrusively as he had entered it.

"Oh, it's just my ginger infusion."

"Sounds amazing," Thaddeus said. "You know how to live, Lee."

"Trying to learn how to die," he said, and was gone.

"The idea Victoria thought was going to work best," Thaddeus said, "was my OPEC thriller. She thought it could be another *Hostages.*"

He glanced at his wineglass and his eyes showed a flicker of surprise; he had refilled it to the brim and now he carefully sipped it down to a respectable level.

"So I go out there, which means I have to miss the opening party for your mother's show. And pay for my own flight. The Wilshire is out of the question, Four Seasons, ditto, even the creepy Chateau Marmont. I checked into this really barebones hotel, the Martin on Sunset, the kind of place hookers take their clients, but only if they plan to slit their throats."

One of the party boats that sailed the Hudson was drifting by, music blaring from its speakers. This one must have been carrying an older crowd because it was Jerry Lee Lewis singing "High School Confidential." Most of the people with houses on the river raged about the profusion of sunset cruises for people without the means or skill to go onto the water on their own, denounced the assault on the river's ancient peace. Thaddeus never seemed to mind those tubby pleasure boats owned by companies with names like Cap'n Hudson's Floatin' Groove, Booze & Blues Cruise, or Zowie River Tours. The more the merrier remained his motto. The music faded as the boat motored south.

Thaddeus did not pause as he poured. He barely paused

as he drank. A bottle and a half of the beaujolais was gone, of which I had had one glass. I had never seen him drink like this. He was never one to refuse a drink—or a toke or a sniff—but there had always been an air of moderation in his recreation, a sense that part of him was going to be kept in reserve in case someone might need a ride home or someone else was hungry and omelets were in order or if he wanted to keep himself together enough to make love to his wife at the end of the evening. But tonight he drank with a kind of fury, like someone trying to break a padlock with a hammer. He continually rearranged himself in his chair. His face softened, his handsomeness eroded by waves of alcohol.

"Hey, Dad, tell the truth," David said. "Are you going to lose this house?"

Maybe Thaddeus hadn't heard the question. More likely, it was not one he cared to answer, and still even more likely than that, it was not a question he knew the answer to.

"My first pitch meeting is at Disney, where I've worked three times. Bubkes. Fine, I'm tough, I can take a punch. Next stop, I have a meeting at this newly minted, very well financed production company called Anastasia Pictures."

He paused to reach for the bottle. He kept his eyes on the glass this time to guard against overfilling. Movements very deliberate, his stab at precision.

"So, yeah, on to Anastasia. Which is right in the middle of Beverly Hills, on Canon Drive, in a little office building, with no place to park, except a garage a block away, so there goes another twenty bucks. And the whole thing was an ambush."

His voice suddenly broke; his eyes filled with tears.

"I walk in. Nice offices, you can tell some serious coin was spent. Beautifully framed movie posters, *The Bad and the*

Beautiful, Sullivan's Travels. The smell of espresso in the air. The receptionist a dead ringer for Nicole Kidman. And the main guy, Hap Wasserman, massive guy, a linebacker, Hap meets me in the reception area, he's like a bouncer with a manicure. He's giving me that awful two-handed sandwich handshake. And he's flattering the hell out of me. Another so-called huge *Hostages* fan. Meanwhile, leading me into his lair, this huge office that was decorated like he had spent a weekend in Santa Fe and just grabbed whatever wasn't nailed down. Hap orders coffee and while we're waiting he tells me all about how great Anastasia's business is doing, and all the great people they have deals with, and I'm getting that sinking feeling, the one you get when someone is telling you all about a party they had and—oops—they forgot to invite you."

Thaddeus suddenly stopped, cleared his throat, breathed deeply, raked a clawed hand through his hair.

"I asked you a question, Dad," David said. "Are we going to lose the house?"

"Why is that so important to you, David?" Thaddeus said.

"You always do that," David said. "You never answer directly. Answering a question with a question is the height of sophistry."

"Is it? Well, it's nice to be at the height of something."

"Dad, I am asking you a direct question, yes or no."

"Be here now, as Ram Dass tells us, David. Be here now."

"Thanks for the downward mobility," David said, his voice splintering.

Most of the color drained from Thaddeus's face, except for those two rough blushes that were always there, and which now seemed to burn hellishly. His lips, whose resting point was normally a slight, bemused smile, twisted into a villainous sneer.

"Do you even know what happened to me in that office?" he said. A bullying finger jab. Another.

"Come on, Dad, you don't have to be so upset," Emma said, her eyes fixed on her empty plate. "It's not a big deal."

He will destroy you. It was what Morris said one night. Where were we? Cafe des Artistes? No . . . it was at his place, his and Robbie's. Robbie! I would never have a Robbie in my life.

"Your father was set up," Thaddeus said, after a couple of deep breaths. "A total ambush, a hit job. I think that's something you could care about, both of you."

I glanced at the kids. They were poker-faced.

"As if I haven't had enough," Thaddeus said.

Ah, there it was! *As if I haven't had enough.* The Magna Carta of self-pity. Another poor sap in the Job market.

"No, apparently none of that constitutes enough," Thaddeus said. "Someone picturesque brings the coffees. It's probably the most delicious coffee I've ever had. But I feel something coming. It's like you're in the woods and you start feeling maybe there's a bear out there. Hap picks up his phone—it's an old-fashioned phone, like out of *The Maltese Falcon,* because everything has to be special, right? We're ready to begin, he says. Hangs up, smiles, looks at his watch. And who in the whole miserable world walks in? Like two seconds later? Like he's been waiting on the other side of the door, waiting for this moment? Craig Epstein!"

I glanced again at David and Emma, not sure the name Craig Epstein would mean anything to them. Craig's was the face into which years ago Thaddeus had thrown a mimosa. The scene of this career suicide was Arlene Epstein's house in Los Angeles, at a birthday brunch for Craig himself, on the occasion of his twenty-seventh year to heaven. With the exception of Craig, no one was more surprised than Thaddeus when he threw his drink in the birthday boy's face. Thaddeus was later to claim Craig had threatened to sock him in the face, but I never found that entirely believable. Factor 1: Thaddeus had been quarreling with Grace. Factor 2: Thaddeus had been wondering if his talents might be being wasted in the movie business. Factor 3: Craig was attending the party thrown in his honor wearing pajamas, a sloppy presumption of adorableness and worldwide acceptance that Thaddeus could not abide. Factor 4: Craig was wandering around his mother's house eating peanut butter out of the jar. When I had mentioned to Thaddeus that the peanut butter might have been the real triggering factor—four-year-old Thaddeus, after all, had been scorned and scarred for spooning peanut butter into his mouth the morning his parents staggered back into the apartment after leaving the corpse of their baby daughter at the University of Chicago Hospital—he gaped at me as if I had suddenly developed an interest in phrenology.

"My mind is racing around like a trapped rat," Thaddeus was saying. "Was I being set up? Of course I was. But by whom? Was my agent in on it? Or did Hap, recognizing my name, do this as a favor to Craig? Craig is there, making himself comfortable. The years have been extremely kind to him. He's slim, he's fucking radiant, with beautiful curly hair. Smiling. This is just totally making his day. His year. Who knows how long he's been waiting for this? Well, go on, Hap says. Vicky tells us you've got a terrific international thriller in mind. We here at Anastasia love international thrillers. Isn't that right, Craig? Sure, Craig says. Done right? They're money. And all I can think is the last time this guy saw me he was wiping orange juice and champagne off his face and I was being marched to the front door. I could hear him crying, My eyes, my eyes, like

I'd thrown Drano at him and not a goddamned mimosa. So now he wants to hear my pitch? Like hell he does.

"Me? I'm dumbstruck. Hap clears his throat. Craig cocks his head, raises his eyebrows. And I think, Wow, they're actually going to make me go through my pitch. I'm going to be like one of those guys in a Western doing a little jig while they shoot bullets at his feet. Meanwhile, the seconds are ticking by and it's like my body has figured out what to do before anything is clear in my mind. I just stand up and say, You know what? I've thought better of it. And I walk right out of that office. Right out of the building. Back to my car, back to my motel, back to the rental-car return, back to the airport. I pay more money to have my flight changed. And for a while I was actually quite happy. I stood up for myself. I didn't allow the humiliation to continue. But now . . ." He took another deep breath, trying to steady himself. His eyes were suddenly filled with tears. "It's back to the drawing board," he said. "Right now, ladies and gentlemen, and children of all ages, I got nothing."

You did this to yourself, I thought, but the bilious twist of impatience was subsumed by pity as tears began to stream down his face.

Pity! I tried to smother it, thinking, as I had been told so often, that there was something base about it, that there was no more dehumanizing thing you could feel for another person. But I wondered: How did pity come to be so despised? Who came up with the idea that if you truly respected someone you could not pity them? It must have been a banker or a killer or a thief.

As Thaddeus reached for his glass, I reached for him but was seated too far away to touch his arm. His hands were shaking and as he brought the wine to his lips it rose from the glass and seemed almost to leap onto him, creating a wet spot on his shirt between the top two buttons, and also a bit of transparency. I could see the hair hibernating in his chest's concave. Unbidden, a memory came—a wet T-shirt contest in a gruesome little bar on Chambers Street, where I'd been dragged one day after work by my EF Hutton boss and his brother, a pair of demonic dunces in seersucker suits, slicked-back hair, who howled like cowards at a prizefight as the four women were drenched by a bartender wielding one of those old-style seltzer bottles. Breasts! They went mad at the sight of them as if they were babies starving for milk. Hey, heterosexuals, seriously: Get a fucking grip! And yet, seated at Thaddeus's table, I stared. It was not his skin that arrested my attention. I saw a cross, the outline of a crucifix as stunning as any other intimacy.

"Goddamn," he said, brushing at his shirt as if it had gotten dusty. Now he plucked at the shirt and pulled the fabric up, shaking it dry, or trying to. With his free hand he made a resting place for his forehead and his tears continued to fall, hitting his empty plate with a barely audible plink, like time passing in another room.

Emma did what I would have liked to have done. She got up from her chair and went to Thaddeus's side and patted his shoulder. Of course it was much better, coming from her. Yet even Emma's kindness seemed not to register on him. He seemed unaware of her, or of any of us.

"You didn't answer me," David said, unmoved. "Are we going to lose the house now?"

CHAPTER 19

The Curtain Call

"I went too far," Thaddeus said, *as soon as the kids were out of the* room—David to the upper floor to feed his cats and gather his things before driving back to Saratoga, and Emma to the yellow house, to help Henry Stratton repaint the old Taurus Jennings and Muriel had given him for his sixteenth birthday. "I never saw my father cry. Or my mother. Maybe there's something disgusting about too much emotion from a parent. Like seeing them naked."

"I think it's okay. Anyhow, it's not like you planned it."

"And I'm drunk."

"Well, yes, there's that."

"Not as drunk as I'd like to be."

"I know the feeling."

"Kip . . . man."

"What?"

"Nothing. Just . . ." He made a face and shook his head.

"Do you mind if I ask you a question?" I said.

"Of course not."

"Why are you wearing that crucifix?"

He placed his hand over it, as if he had forgotten he was wearing it, or was surprised it could be seen through his shirt.

"I'm not really sure," he said. "It feels . . . I don't know. Lucky? Not that it's brought me any great luck."

"It's kind of strange," I said.

"I always wanted to be Catholic. I need a rule book and someone to tell me what the hell to do. And an old friend gave it to me. Hey—you remember Bruce Grogan, don't you? From Ann Arbor? Remember when you said the philosophy department at Michigan was really a front for the church? Maybe you were right because Bruce became a priest. He's a total priest! He was up here for a while and we hung out. He'd bring a bunch of the other guys, too. I loved giving them the run of the place. One minute they'd be tossing a Frisbee around, the next minute they'd be debating Deuteronomy. He's in Houston now. He's second banana in this big church in Spring Branch."

He went on to relate some of Bruce's impressions of Houston, but I was finding it difficult to pay attention. I was hearing his voice the way you can hear the muffled murmur of people talking poolside while you are underwater. Why oh why oh why had I so blithely told Bruce anything personal about myself? I must have been out of my mind. That they were still in contact with Bruce a thousand miles away filled me with dread.

It had been years since I had felt such fear of exposure. In my thirties, I had a couple of dinners with an ascendant woman writer who normally lived in Alaska but who was in New York on a one-year appointment to teach writing at Columbia. We had a nice time and when I brought her to a Christmas party Kenny Adler was hosting in his apartment, she was a tremendous hit—funny, friendly, and she taught everyone how to make a lethal cocktail she called the Fairbanks. Based on a couple of remarks and her body language, I suspected she might want something more overt and romantic in our relationship, and my uneasiness was confirmed when I asked her out for the third or fourth time and she said, "Come on, let's get real here. Okay? Can we do that? Kip." It was the way she pronounced my name—as if it were a scarlet letter only she could see. But it was not the first time that I had dealt with friendly dating's expiration date and her apparent pique didn't bother me for more than a few minutes. A year later, however, she published a story about a closeted gay man with jug ears and an unfortunate face who worked on Wall Street, dated women right and left, and called himself Cap. It was titled "The Insider," with its suggestion of unethical professional behavior, and its insipid assonance with "inside her," that erotic Maginot Line that Cap could never cross. It came out in *The Paris Review,* not exactly required reading for everyone I knew, but hardly an obscure journal, and for weeks and weeks I was sick with anticipation that someone in my family, someone with whom I worked, or Thaddeus would read it and know for sure that Cap was Kip. People had seen me with her after all; the whole pitiful purpose of her was people seeing us together. And even though no one ever mentioned the story to me, I never did fully recover from the dread.

Thaddeus and I walked out onto the front porch with the dogs, who immediately took off into the dark, with manic sidelong glances to each other as they ran, their tails whirling around like helicopter blades. The bamboo chairs with their deep seats and canvas covered cushions were gone—had they been sold?—and we stood, leaning on the railing, listening to the dogs whine and yip as they plunged into the spirea.

"Now, may I ask *you* a question?" he said. "Mine's a bit personal."

Are you gay? Do you want to kiss me? I tried to anticipate, I tried to prepare.

"Go right ahead," I said. "Ask away." And why not? Perhaps it was time. My secret life had by now probably turned into Miss Havisham's wedding banquet. Touch it and stand back. Yes, we could talk about the elephant in the room. Maybe elephant wasn't how to say it. What? The candelabra in the room? The red red rose in the room? The little lilac love seat? The leather jacket? What the fuck was in that room? If there was a room at all.

"Are you happy?" he asked.

"Happy?"

"Yeah. I know. Who is? Who cares? But still. We're here for . . ." He snapped his fingers. "What else can we hope for?"

"Didn't you once say happiness is for children?"

"I don't think my children are particularly happy," he said. "And I think that's . . ." He looked out into the darkness. "I'm dragging everybody down." He shook his head, rather violently. "But you, what about you? Are you happy?"

"I don't know. I don't really think about it."

"I do. And I think about you. I think about you and your life," he said. "You have this . . . job. And money, and you have this very full calendar, and travel, and all the things that people want. But I worry about you. I can't even say why. But I do."

My heart was racing, pounding so loudly I wondered if it could be heard in the stillness of this Windsor County night. I know a heart beating like a drum has been said before but it happens, it's true. It's an old song and I was singing it. It was my turn.

He was standing three feet away from me. Thirty-six inches. I was unraveling. Passion—untapped, untried, untested, and above all unsullied by compromise or even reality—surged through me with such force that I gripped the railing of the porch to keep my balance.

"Maybe I worry because you're alone," he said. "I know you don't have to be. Anyone would feel lucky to be with you. You check all the boxes. Kind, cultured, great job, great apartment. You're really a total prize. What are you waiting for? Is it the job? Is that it? Does it just take too much of you? You work so hard. Maybe you should take time off? Come up here. It's nice up here. Or you know what? You know what we should do? Hike the Appalachian Trail. We wouldn't even have to do the whole thing. That would be a bit much. But just to be two creatures in the great outdoors. I think that would be amazing."

The dogs were barking in the distance, and we listened to them.

"It's either a mouse or a vole," Thaddeus said. "They feel about them the way people do about money."

"To each his own," I said.

He took a deep breath and exhaled with a sigh of pleasure. "The night air is sobering me up," he said. "Don't ever let me drink like that. And shut me the fuck up if I ever start boo-hooing about the goddamned movies again. The movie business is supposed to break your heart. That's what it's there for."

"I can't control what you do," I said with a small laugh.

"I do follow your lead, you know that, don't you? You tell me about music or a film, I always check it out. And when I don't listen to you—you always thought Orkney was a bad idea— then I sort of end up wishing that I had."

"I didn't want you to leave New York."

"Yeah, I know. I felt the same way. I always thought we looked out for each other and it was a little scary, the distance. I blame Woodward and Bernstein. That whole follow-the-money thing? I followed the money and went right off the side of a cliff."

"I don't know what to tell you, Thaddeus," I said.

"Oh, you've already done so much. Too much. It should be my turn." He rubbed his hands together. "What can we do for old Kip?"

I knew he was being playful but the question provoked me. My face burned and I was grateful for the darkness.

"I'd love to do that Appalachian Trail thing sometime," I said.

Had he even heard me? He was looking off into the distance—maybe he was listening for the dogs.

"You always had the money thing figured out, Kip. You never let it get the best of you. Most people . . . Well, forget most people. Me. I let money get the best of me. Not that I was anything so special to begin with. But money just made everything worse. I was sort of stupid when I had it and now not having it doesn't seem to be bringing out the best in me. Any advice? You know, tips. Whatever."

He put his arm over my shoulders. Nothing remotely romantic, total 100 percent palsy-walsy.

"Just tell me what to buy," he whispered.

My future had been holding two cards and after teasing me with the possibility of laying down one of them it played the other one instead.

My stock had crashed, the train had left the station, the blood test results were not too good, my house had been broken into, and vandals had shit in every drawer. I felt sick.

"It's chilly out here, isn't it?" I said. "We should go in."

"I'm waiting for the dogs to come back."

"Call them."

"They don't listen to me. It's better if I don't try."

But even as he was saying that, the dogs were approaching. The jangle of their collars, their deep chesty breaths, their paws in the scrub, and now the lawn, and now the paving stones—and an instant later they were on the porch, greeting Thaddeus, slinking their heaving massive torsos against his knees. They looked like seals swimming in circles.

"Well," I said, "they came back."

"They're like what Bruce told me about Jesus—they may not come when you call them, but they're right on time."

CHAPTER 20

Emma

Before dropping off for the night, I fiddled with the shades so they fit the windows as tightly as possible, but it was to no avail, and a few hours later the rising sun sent out its first probing rays, somehow able to get through not only the window shades but my eyelids as well. Ugh, those rosy fingers—rarely a welcome sight. However, this day, rather than my usual lustful mourning him, I woke wanting to strangle Thaddeus. A barrier had been breached and I understood that from this day on I would always have a degree of unease—I was not made for any activity that was even slightly criminal. I did not give tips; I did not do whatever. Maybe my extreme caution about my personal life had mutated into a generalized timidity. I had no stomach for the outlaw life. I could still turn my own stomach and make my hands shake by recalling the time I was caught shoplifting a first edition of a Djuna Barnes novel from Odyssey Books, oh and the nights of despair that followed, not to mention never daring to enter that store again, or any of the nearby used bookshops down on Fourth Avenue, relegating me to a lifetime of buying the first editions I like to collect via mail order or from overpriced antiquarians on the Upper East Side, used to selling their wares to interior decorators rather than real collectors.

And now here I was, with the weekend before me during which I'd be Emma's guardian and in charge of this house—this monster of brick and lumber, this trophy Thaddeus had given himself to celebrate his success and which now he was willing to ruin my life to hold on to.

David's bedroom was in decent repair—the paint was fresh, the plaster showed not a peel or a pucker, and the carpet carried not a whiff of mildew. There were scratching posts and the cat toys, but the cats themselves hadn't joined me. They wandered the second floor of the house in the safety they presumed was theirs, though all that protected them were accordion gates at the tops and bottoms of the stairways. I went to the window and looked out just in time to see Thaddeus tossing his travel case into the backseat of his car. Mist rolled across the fields like an ocean of gauze. Thaddeus wiped the moisture from the windshield, using just his hand. He gave the house a farewell glance, and moments later he was on his way to Albany for the early morning flight to Miami.

Back in bed I relieved my sexual tension and was fortunate to fall back to sleep. A weakling wasp ticked between the shade and the window, which I incorporated into a dream of standing in Orkney's foyer next to a noisy grandfather clock, looking for someone and wondering if I'd come on the wrong day. The next sounds, however, were not so easily sublimated—Emma was screaming, Oh god, god, please no. No, no, no!, her voice pleading and frightened. I scrambled out of the bed; my legs failed me for a moment, but I righted myself.

Emma was on her knees, her arms around the neck of

one of Grace's Weimaraners. It was either Marcel or Marceau. Grace said she had named them so to keep them from barking, but the dog barked, as well as whined and growled, as it tried to wriggle free from Emma. One of David's cats, a huge black and silver tabby, was pressed into a corner, tail flicking, back hunched up like a Halloween cutout.

Emma was in pajamas decorated with delicate little pink carnations like an English teacup. Her face was feverish, her hair plastered to her sweaty brow. I tried to help her hold the dog at bay, but I screwed up. When I grabbed the dog's collar, Emma let go, probably thinking that now an adult was in charge and she was relieved of her responsibility. The dog, however, did not owe me the deference it showed Emma and it quickly turned its head, snarling and showing its shocking teeth, and I let go of the collar for a moment, plenty of time for the dog to realize it was free to go on its murderous errand. Emma, screaming, tried to catch it by the tail, but the dog was past her, its head down, its entire body close to the floor, like one of those swimmers who move like a torpedo just above the tiles on the pool's bottom.

From bad to good is a long journey, but going from bad to worse is generally a quick commute. Moments later, the second dog was with us and now the interchangeable Marcel and Marceau charged around the once forbidden, cat-rich territory of Orkney's second story. The black and silver tabby lit out for a tall, freestanding bookshelf about forty feet down the hallway. It was stable enough to withstand the impact of the cat scrambling to the top of it, but it couldn't remain standing when the dogs leapt upon it. The entire bookcase tipped over, sending down a pounding sharp-edged rain of Sendak, Seuss, and Silverstein. The wall opposite the case prevented it from falling onto the dogs but they were nevertheless in a panic, and now the question of their own survival supplanted their desire to tear the cat to shreds. Marcel's and Marceau's claws clicked wildly against the bare floors and their legs whirled around cartoonlike as they scrambled to the top of one stairway, where the accordion gate was partly open. Thaddeus! It must have been him. What an idiot! He'd left it open. His mind already filled with visions of Grace. And now: you see? In the meantime, Marcel and Marceau were recovered from the shock of falling books and seemed to be planning a reengagement.

While the dogs were still far enough away for her to risk it, Emma grabbed the terrorized cat, which looked electrified, its fur bristling, its claws extended, and ran back to her bedroom. I followed her in and she slammed the door shut. Her bed was bare, save for one pale blue fitted sheet, the walls displayed a couple of Bob Marley posters, and it smelled faintly of cat. Her windows offered a view of the back lawns sweeping down to the river. I remembered Thaddeus's saying *A kid raised with a beautiful view will always think the world is a good place.*

As for the cats, I didn't know if they'd taken refuge in Emma's room, or if she kept them there when David was away. One of them—another Siamese, taupe and mahogany— amused itself by batting around a candy wrapper. Emma glanced guiltily at me to see if I had noticed it. I think I was able to keep it from her. I felt so awful for the poor kid, but I wasn't able to sustain that feeling for long because moments later Marcel and Marceau were hurtling themselves against the door. They were not exactly well versed on the art of persuasion. Somehow the cats maintained an air of indifference.

"I hate those dogs," Emma said, retrieving the candy wrapper and stuffing it in her pocket. "They love Mom but they're not even friendly. They're the worst." She kicked furiously at the door with the side of her foot—even I knew better than to do that. The dogs revved up again, as if Emma had started a motorcycle, and now, at last, the cats began nervously milling around, inspecting the perimeter of Emma's room and looking for avenues of escape.

"We're going to be okay," I said. "We can figure this out."

She looked at me skeptically. I was in my undershorts and a T-shirt. "They're too strong," she said, sadly, in that tone people use when they regretfully disabuse you of your illusions.

"We'll very carefully open the door and go out to the hallway and take those two crazy dogs downstairs and make sure those gates are properly closed. Okay?"

"They want the cats, Kip," she said. "They won't follow us."

"We'll force them," I said.

"They're too strong."

"Okay, how about this? We lure them. I noticed one of the cats was playing with a candy wrapper. Do you have anything to use as a treat?"

She was silent. How could a girl whose diet was so closely monitored, who snacked on carrots and celery sticks, drank eight glasses of water daily to slake hunger and flush the system, and who was pushed to do calisthenics with her mother at her side, admit to having a treat in her room?

"I don't think so," Emma finally answered.

"That's okay."

We stood there for a moment. The cats were silent and the dogs were persistent, whimpering and whining.

"Maybe I have something," Emma said.

"That would be great. They'll follow us right down the steps, I'll bet anything."

"I'll look around," she said. "I don't know."

I tried to imagine where she had hidden food in this room. The closet? Her little black and gold dresser, with its bowed drawers and filigree? She would have had to have done better than that—surely Grace tossed the room from time to time, probably with the ruthlessness of a federal agent. But of course. Grace was in Florida. "Want me to go out there first?" I asked.

"Okay," Emma said.

"The dogs won't bite me or anything, will they?"

"They don't really bite."

"They don't *really* bite?"

Emma laughed, a dear little burble, half nervous and half grateful. I carefully let myself out of her room. The dogs tried to charge past me but I stopped them with my legs and closed the door very loudly behind me, on the off chance the noise would startle them. I stood there with my back to the door, and the dogs looked at each other and then at me and then at each other again. I wondered what Emma was unearthing in her room and some of the terror and claustrophobia of being young and harboring secrets from your family came rushing back to me.

Marcel and Marceau kept watch as I stood there. They seemed to be inching toward me.

"How you doing in there, Emma?" I said through the door.

"I think I found something," she said. I heard the scrape of furniture. "I'm sliding something." A moment later, a slice of American cheese in its plastic wrapper slid under the door. I quickly picked it up, peeled off the plastic, and held up the bright Crayola yellow square for the dogs to behold. When I tore the cheese in half and flung it down the hallway they went clicking and clacking after it. I quickly let myself back in to Emma's room, where she stood holding a second slice of cheese.

"They'll definitely follow us down now," I said.

By the time we had closed the door behind us, the dogs had already found and eaten the cheese and were back waiting for more. Emma tore the second slice in half and we each dangled a piece before the dogs as we walked quickly to the staircase. Grace had taught them enough manners to prevent their jumping up and grabbing the treats from our hands; they followed us down the steps, toward the half-open accordion gate at the foot of the stairs, a wooden accordion paused mid-polka.

"It's working," I said to Emma, sotto voce.

She took my hand as we made it to the bottom of the stairway. We tossed the cheese onto the inlaid floor of the foyer and Marcel and Marceau went bounding after it, at which point we secured the accordion gate.

"Mission accomplished," I said.

Emma took my hand again. She lifted it toward her face and bent slightly to plant a kiss on my knuckles. At first I thought she was just goofing around, then I thought she was celebrating our getting those dogs away from the cats. But the kiss was her thank-you for my giving her privacy while she tucked into her storehouse of hidden food. The inexplicable tingle of art, the sweet oblivion of sex, the fleeting elations of money, travel, wine, all of life's pleasures, I cherished them all, but this, this moment, this little grateful kiss, this recognition that I for a moment at least had helped a child feel safe, this was the happiest I had ever been. If it pleases the Court, my life would have ended on a high note if I had died then and there.

CHAPTER 21

Deal

Emma and I secured the other staircases, put Marcel and Marceau outside, and settled into our late breakfast, one that clearly delighted Emma—scrambled eggs, apricot jam, and buttered toast. She asked for coffee and I gave her coffee. She asked for more toast and I toasted more toast. She wondered if she could have the blueberry preserves and I said I hadn't seen them and she said there was a jar in the fridge behind the wheat germ, and I got her the preserves.

"What do you have planned for today?" I asked her.

"Just hanging out, I guess. Maybe go over to Henry's house. Maybe I'll bring my guitar over. We like to jam together."

"I didn't know you were musical," I said.

She shrugged. "I know like seven chords. Mainly I sing."

"You do? No one tells me anything. I love music. I always wished I was musical. So what do you like to sing?"

"Songs. All kinds. Do you want to hear?"

"Definitely," I said with an enthusiasm I didn't feel. I was leaping into a pool without first checking if there was water in it. Everything was going so well between us and the last thing I wanted was to sit there with a suffering smile on my face while she butchered some pop song that I would probably hate even if it was sung well.

"Wait here," she said. "I'm going to get my guitar." She practically ran out of the kitchen, and when she returned with her guitar she was flushed from the exertion of running up and down the stairs.

Suddenly shy, she did not make eye contact with me, but busied herself with tuning her guitar.

"Dad says it's proof that there is a God," she said.

"What is, Emma?"

"Music. And not just because it's beautiful. It's not like other beautiful things like flowers and mountains and stuff. He says you can make scientific reasons for those kinds of things but there's no scientific reason for music. He says it's there to remind us that there is something holy in us. That's what he says."

"And is that what you think?"

"I don't know. I guess I agree with Dad."

Finally satisfied with the tuning, Emma played a G, an E minor, a C, and a D, and her expression, a moment ago so soft and uncertain, became confident and serene.

"If I should stay, I would only be in your way," she sang, the tempo slow, her voice brocaded with longing and nostalgia and kindness entwined, like soldiers helping each other off a battlefield. She continued to sing and then paused, perhaps to gather herself, or for the effect. Slowly, her eyes closed and she sang, very softly, *"And I will always love you,"* each word fainter and fainter, down to an incandescent whisper trailing off even further until all that remained was your own memory of the song.

Was this the most beautiful singing I had ever heard? Suddenly, it seemed so and I felt my throat closing like a drawstring purse. "Oh no," I muttered, and leaned forward and covered my eyes. But it was too late. I had been ambushed by the fragility of her voice, and if I had had to answer for myself and explain why suddenly tears were coursing down my face I don't know that I could have said. I still can't explain it. It's the mystery of music.

But that mystery was supplanted by the sudden appearance of Jennings Stratton, who had walked in without knocking or even calling out, and now, with Marcel and Marceau at his side, he was in the kitchen, dressed in green and pink Bermuda shorts—impossible to imagine he had bought them or even found them himself. His legs were muscular and dark, rather trim and well turned, especially on a man who had otherwise succumbed to fleshiness. By any normal measure of allure and sexiness, Thaddeus had it all over Jennings. But, of course, Cupid is a drunken archer. I knew this, yet I could not look at Jennings, with his sweat socks pulled high, and his Allman Brothers T-shirt taut over his belly, without thinking that Grace's unhappiness must have mutated into a kind of madness for her to choose this man over her husband, even for a night.

Meanwhile, Jennings exuded ease and self-confidence. Apparently, early sexual success is indelible. Like someone who has lost his fortune but still expects the deference afforded to the rich, Jennings seemed to assume everyone wanted him. His luminous sea green eyes rested on me for a moment and he showed his teeth in a smile as hokey as a cocktail lounge pianist running the keys from low to high.

"Hey, Emma-Bemma," he said, "you should get your behind

over to the house. Henry is going to take the canoe over to Lark River and we got an extra pair of oars. You should go."

"Can I?" Emma asked me.

With the two of them in the same room, I was all the more sure that Jennings was Emma's father, and though she asked me for permission, I could feel her leaving me as soon as he was present. Of course she knew him so much better than she knew me. They had shared these acres from the beginning of her life. They breathed the same air, the sun hit them at the same angle. I wondered if he had ever heard her sing—but of course he had. What to me had been a revelation was for him an everyday matter. He was there, he had always been there, patching the screens in her bedroom windows, carrying her on his back through snowdrifts so she could catch the shuttle bus to her twee private school, appearing midafternoon sweating and shirtless with an old milk can filled to the tarnished brim with dark purple wild berries.

I didn't know if this Lark River was dangerous. I didn't know if she was a strong swimmer. I didn't know anything about Henry. Maybe he was a risk taker, a show-off. I did know this: he was beautiful, with large eyes, more violet than blue, blond hair more silver than yellow, full lips, pale skin, a dreamer's slow-motion walk. Before I could gather my forces, Emma had grabbed the last piece of toast and was out of the kitchen and on her way.

"Be careful!" I cried out behind her.

"Nothing to worry about," Jennings said, taking Emma's seat at the table. "She knows what she's doing. She's a terrific girl. We take her on our drills and she's way ahead of the pack most times. Even in the rain."

"What kind of drills?"

"Up the mountain."

"I don't get it."

"If we ever had to get out of here. You know?" He started to cough, deep, dry, painful sounding, as if he was tearing away at something that needed to be dislodged.

Asbestos, I thought.

"Can I get you something?" I asked. "Water? Anything?"

He shook his head no, but the hacking continued. It seemed to feed on itself like a kind of hysteria. His face reddened, his eyes watered. Both of his hands were raised now and he made a pushing motion, as if to keep something at bay.

At last, the coughing stopped. I handed him a glass of water and sat down again. "Christ, Jennings. What's going on?"

"It's okay."

"You should drink some water."

"I don't need water. But thanks," Jennings said. He composed himself. The coughing had subsided and he stroked his chest, as if to subdue a distressed child. "Muriel's got me on the wormwood. She makes it into tea. It's pretty good." He shrugged. "She thinks I've got a cancer."

"Oh no," I said. "Jennings. Man. What does the doctor say?"

"So many of the things you need to beat it grow right here on the property. I think it's going to be okay. And remember that radio I showed you, the old Philco? Well, me and Henry got it working and the first thing that comes on is this guy Reverend Cobb out of a church way far away, in Florida, and he's talking about healing through prayer. And then next thing I know the radio goes dead and we haven't gotten it to work since. Isn't that so cool?"

"There are good doctors up here, right?"

"Everything happens for a reason," he said.

"You think?"

"I know."

"Do you have a doctor?"

"You know a lot of people say Emma looks a lot like me."

"Really? Like who? Who says that?"

His smile was at once radiant and horrifying.

"Well, she's really something, Emma. Hey, I've been think-ing: What about building you a house? You've got those acres just sitting there. I could help you with that. I know the people who do the best work around here. Hometown boys, always the way to go. I could supervise and do some of the work myself. Save you a lot of money."

"I'm not planning on building," I said.

He took a small, polite sip of the water I'd handed him and placed the glass carefully on the table before standing up.

"Well, it's something to think about. It's a beautiful spot, shame to waste it. Back in the old days, we all had this fantasy that we were going to live here, Grace and Thaddeus in the big house, Dad and me and the family in the yellow, and we were all going to work in the gardens and the fruit trees and fish and the kids would grow up together and we were all going to be one big happy family. Right?"

"Right. Well, like you said. Fantasy."

"Yeah. Fantasy. There's our plan and there's God's plan, not the same thing, that's one thing we can all agree on. And don't worry about Emma. Okay? I'd be the last person to ever let something happen to that girl. I love her like she was my own."

He left me with that.

I sat at the table for a few moments, more or less staring at Emma's plate, so bereft of food you'd think it had yet to be used. A wasp, black as oil and droning deeply, staggered drunkenly across the table, perhaps on its way to the sugar bowl. It crossed my mind that I ought to kill it before it gathered the strength to fly up and sting me. The wasp scuttled onto Emma's plate, and watching it make its feeble way across the plate—I saw it! I saw it as if it were happening right before me: the canoe turning over in the Lark River. And I heard her cries as she struggled to stay afloat, trapped in a mesh of weeds and lily pods.

I didn't know where Lark River was. I would have to go to the yellow house and get Jennings to tell me. Hatred hissed through me like a sudden rain. I stood at the windows for an hour watching for her. The dogs slept at my feet. Upstairs, the cats scampered. I heard their footsteps through the ceiling. At last, I saw Emma and Henry walking up the driveway. They looked happy, but soaked through, with weeds in their hair.

CHAPTER 22

The Paris Commune

Thaddeus was in the city more and more often. He'd signed with a new agent, a young guy named Milos who promised career resurrection and set up lunches, drinks, dinners, and meetings at which Thaddeus could trot out his wares and run through his well-practiced routines of charm and enthusiasm to producers and studio executives Milos's age, which was about thirty. Thaddeus was meeting with people who were not even in the movie business when he became a pariah, yet nevertheless he sensed in their demeanor—the wry smiles, the carefully folded hands, the way they sat deep in their chairs, creating the maximum amount of space between them and him, as if his breath was offensive or his behavior a matter of nervous conjecture—that his ragged reputation had been passed down to a new generation of gatekeepers.

When I could, I'd meet Thaddeus after one of these disastrous meetings, willing to absorb his feelings of rejection and desperation before sending him back to Orkney. I suppose it could be argued that this was a classic wallflower move on my part, but it's also what friends are for. Sometimes we met for a quick drink, but if there was time we had dinner, always with an eye on the clock—now that his pied-à-terre on Horatio Street was someone else's pied-à-terre on Horatio Street, he needed to be on that last train out of Penn Station.

It was awful to hear about the meetings he "took" and to hear the stories he proposed. I could not bear to see him treated so disrespectfully, so dismissively. Yet even though I loved him, I had my own way of seeing things, my own standards, my own purchase on reality, and I wondered if Thaddeus might very well lack the skills he would need to write himself back into contention. In the eerie, unnerving silence of failure, the question posed itself, perhaps not to Thaddeus but, alas, to me: Had the time arrived when that lifelong dream needed to be set aside? Aren't they called *youthful* dreams for a reason? Don't nearly all of us abandon them? Aren't they the first things jettisoned, thrown over the railing and into the sea the moment the ship of self starts to take on water?

It was a warm evening, the daylight had faded but still remnants of it were scattered here and there. After work, I'd gone with Ken Adler to a gallery on Fifty-Seventh Street; he was on the verge of buying an Albert Pinkham Ryder painting, and he wanted my opinion about it. I was hasty in my judgments. Ken wasn't clear about his intentions—did he love this broody, crepuscular canvas or was it an investment? And I was distracted because earlier that afternoon I'd agreed to meet Thaddeus downtown for dinner at a restaurant called the Paris Commune. He was already at our table and halfway through a bottle of white wine when I arrived. He was in jeans and an expensive shirt and sport jacket. He'd taken off his tie and stuffed it in his breast pocket like a pocket square. His legs were crossed and his chin rested in his upturned palm. Even in a funk his dark eyes were keen, and his hair glistened like the healthy fur of an animal in cold moonlight.

"This place is lovely," he said, "and the wine is delicious, but how dare they call it the Paris Commune? For a place where an actual worker can't afford to have a meal?"

I smiled neutrally. He had a point, of course, but the question remained—did he have a right to make it?

We ordered our customary dinners—Thaddeus ordered some kind of chicken, thinking it was somehow slimming, and me the shrimp provençale because I liked seafood but never cooked it at home. While we ate he told me about meeting at the Carlyle for drinks with a producer named Curt something or other, a middle-aged man who'd made millions in Florida real estate and who now wanted to try his hand at movies—Warner Bros. would of course indulge his folly until his pockets were empty. "I thought I'd pitch him *Mass Deception,* but that's sort of scorched earth for me since that disaster in L.A. And I have a new idea right now I'm tremendously excited about." He may have caught something in my expression because he laughed. "Yeah, tremendously excited—you heard me. And yes, I'm still limber enough to blow a bit of blue sky up my own ass. Anyhow, I won't bore either of us with recounting the story; suffice to say, he loved it and needed a little time to think about it—in other words, Pasadena, baby, sayonara, see you in hell." He ended with an extravagant wave, like an acrobat acknowledging the audience after a perfect landing.

Our waiter, mistaking Thaddeus's gesture for a summons,

appeared at our table. He refilled our glasses, relit the votive candle.

"Are you still working on these?" the waiter asked, indicating my shrimp provençale and Thaddeus's poulet aux olives.

We told him we were and he poured the last of our Chablis into our glasses and left. Thaddeus said, "'Working on these.' As if we were working, and not just sitting on our asses, paying more for this bottle of wine than he'll take home at the end of the night."

"Well, if we weren't here, he might take home even less."

"I'll give you that," he said. "By the way, don't even look at the check. Dinner is on me."

"Whatever for?"

"Because it's my turn. Because you're true blue. Because you're my best friend and I love you."

"Ditto."

He carefully picked the linen napkin off his lap and folded it slowly but haphazardly, longing for order but having little talent for achieving it. He did his best to smooth it into a presentable shape and tucked it under the rim of his dinner plate, after which he placed his knife and fork on top of it.

"Now it's perfect," I said, hoping to lighten the mood.

Our bill was on the table and Thaddeus slipped his Visa into the folder and handed it to the waiter. A few moments later, the waiter came back to say the card had been declined, the news delivered casually, with no embarrassing deference or concern. More of an oops than an oh-no.

Nevertheless, Thaddeus was crestfallen. "I'm sorry. I thought that one was still okay." He stood up and pulled some money out of his pocket, but it was clearly not going to be enough.

I had a cold feeling that all of this had been premeditated, but I pushed the thought away. Which I would do again. If love is a sinking ship, you do want to go down with it.

"Sit," I said. "Let me take care of it. I'll expense it, if that makes it better."

I gave the waiter my card. The bill was nearly $200 and I was relieved that Thaddeus wasn't paying.

"Tell me a stock to buy," Thaddeus said, as soon as the waiter was out of earshot. "I can't stand this much longer."

"Any valuable information I have is called privileged information and I'm not allowed to use it. That's called insider trading."

"I have a feeling it happens all the time."

"Some people probably get away with it, but it would be a tremendous risk. And that's why they overpay—keep us happy and discourage us from taking big risks."

"There must be ways to do it," Thaddeus said. "You wouldn't be buying the stock yourself."

"Wow, what a great idea. No SEC investigator could ever figure that one out."

"I'll bet it happens all the time. I'll bet that for every one person who gets caught there are a thousand who get away with it. And what difference does it make? No one gets hurt. It's the quintessential victimless crime."

"It's not victimless."

"But it's all fixed, top to bottom. Isn't it? That's certainly the impression I have. All those people who made a fortune on AOL? Don't you think some of them were given a few very helpful hints about what was going on with that company? A brother, a neighbor, a best friend? You know as well as I do, every time they bust some guy on Wall Street there's at least a thousand other people doing the same thing or worse."

"Do you read the newspapers?" I asked. "People go to jail."

"Okay. So every once in a while there's a sacrificial lamb."

"I don't want to be that lamb, Thaddeus. This is crazy. We shouldn't even be having this conversation."

He put up his hands, signaling surrender.

"I'm sorry. If anything bad ever happened to you, I'd never forgive myself. I really thought . . . I don't know. Probably not thinking that clearly. The money thing is really getting worse."

"But Grace."

"Grace is happy. She's getting attention. But the money . . ." He shook his head. "Anyhow, I sell one script." He raised one finger. "It gets made." A second finger raised. "It does okay." He held up three fingers. "Then I need never worry again. I will never be put in this position again. It'll be fixed. I will be all set."

"Good. You're the man to do it."

"But in the meanwhile, I don't know what to do."

He was looking at me searchingly, and fury scorched a path across my thoughts.

"You could live like a regular person."

"You don't live like some regular person! You live in a beautiful apartment on a fantastic block in probably the most expensive city in the solar system."

"I have a job. One that I intend to keep. What about you?"

"I do not at this moment have a job. Why would you ask me that? I am *officially* unemployed. But that doesn't mean I'm not working. I work like a fucking dog. And things are starting to shift. For sure."

"What about in the meantime?"

"In the meantime I am trying to get a job. I am writing outlines. Pitches. Spec scripts. None of which I would be able to do if I was bagging groceries somewhere."

"You could teach."

"Where? I'd do it if someone called me. That would be great. Columbia, NYU, I'm not choosy. I'll do it. The money will basically suck, but I will do it."

"Sell the house, Thaddeus. Sell the house. You'd have money."

"What? If I sold Orkney?"

"Yes. That's what I'm saying."

"First of all, I can't. It would destabilize everything. I'd lose Grace."

"No you wouldn't."

"I don't even own the place anymore, Kip. I've mortgaged it up the wazoo. If I sold it now, I'd probably walk away with enough money to buy a one-bedroom apartment in New York."

"Then live somewhere else," I snapped.

He looked at me, his eyes full of injury.

"Where would I live?" he finally said. "Kalamazoo, Oklahoma City? I need to be where I can take meetings. I can't give up. I don't have any other way. And I need that house to entertain in. People in the business, you know? They see me in that house and they know I'm viable, I'm a player. It's my marker on the board. Without it, I'm a nonentity. I'm supposed to invite some producer up for the weekend to sleep in a mobile home? Can't be done. I'm sorry. I really am. I love you, Kip. And you've been so generous. I wish . . . I don't know what I wish. But I'm sorry. I know I'm putting you in a weird position. Please, please forgive me."

"Okay."

He breathed out his relief. There was sweat on his brow and his philtrum glistened with moisture.

"Thank you," he whispered. "I have to go. Train to catch. And I think it's time to relieve you of the sight of me."

"Johnson and Johnson," I said. "Buy it in the next few days. The stock's been dormant but we think it's undervalued, and I heard"—I looked around the restaurant, to make sure none of our fellow communards might be listening in—"I heard Bayer might be interested in a takeover. You won't make a fortune but J and J is going to move—and when it does, sell it. Don't wait for a double. Take twenty percent."

E. M. Forster wrote that given the choice of betraying a friend or betraying his country, he hoped he'd have the guts to betray his country. Understandably, he left out the part about betraying yourself.

CHAPTER 23

Grace Ascendant

A few weeks after her great success, Grace called me in my office late on a Thursday afternoon to ask if she could spend the night at my apartment. She'd come to the city to show slides of her work to Justin Kent, a newly minted gallery owner with a space on Broome Street, and Grace thought the meeting had gone well. Kent had liked her work enough to invite her to a dinner he was having that night for a painter named Lou Trachtenberg. Perhaps he had realized that his guest list of forty people included only five women. Trachtenberg's work involved smashing glass and pouring it artfully onto paint-spattered tarps, and though Grace's narrow taste in art didn't include smashing glass or paint-spattered tarps, she was excited to attend the dinner. After so many years feeling herself a non-being in the art world, any kind of inclusion encouraged Grace—who could blame her?

The dinner was in Kent's SoHo loft; and Grace had been seated in the semi-Siberia between a morose South American man with a tiny mustache and painted fingernails, and Kent's mother, an ENT who practiced in Amagansett. But the placement did not dampen Grace's spirits. Nothing could.

Good food, great booze, and she arrived at my place around eleven glowing, like a girl coming home from her first real date.

It was a warm early summer night. Parts of the city were already quieter than usual as people of means had left town to get a head start on the weekend, allowing me to open my windows and run a couple of portable fans rather than the air conditioning. I showed Grace to the second bedroom, which I had prepared for her, with Stargazer lilies and a bottle of cold Evian water, as well as one of my T-shirts, which she could wear as a nightgown. I wanted everything to be as swell as I could make it because my intention was to speak frankly with Grace about Jennings, and to bear down on her should she decide to be evasive. I have a single person's understanding of marriage, which is that most are dressed in camouflage. Each marriage has its own Constitution, its own code of conduct, its own language, always with something distinct, and recondite, obscure, complicated, and private—when a marriage dissolves, it's as if a little nation ceases to exist. Perhaps in some fit of passion or remorse Grace had already confessed to Thaddeus, or in some moment of rage, or some mood of wanting to know the worst, Thaddeus had pressured her to reveal her relationship to Jennings and Jennings's relationship to Emma. It was all guesswork, like hearing your parents murmuring behind the bedroom wall and not being able to understand what they are saying.

She admired my apartment, in some detail, while reminiscing about my old loft on Park Avenue South, where she and Thaddeus had tied the so-called knot one frantically snowy January afternoon. We reminisced about that day, the guests, the food, the Ethical Culture minister who had arrived on cross-country skis. Grace talked and talked in a way that seemed chemically induced. Her footsteps were heavy. She picked up the various little objects that caught her eye—the scrimshaw church, the framed pastel postcard of the GM plant in Flint, circa 1955, a dozen or so pricey knickknacks, until she settled on the green glass art deco diver. She continued to talk, asking what I thought a studio apartment in the Village would cost, even chiding me for not hanging any of the pieces I'd bought from her over the years. Had this voluble person been sullenly lurking within Grace all the while, furious over not being heard? I also wondered if she was talking to keep me from talking, if she had somehow deduced that I was going to come after her, and her defense was to build a wall between us made of words. She described Justin Kent's expression while he looked at the slides of her new work (delight, amazement, etc.). She homophobed about his appearance. ("So handsome, and in perfect shape. I don't know why we can't get guys like that on our side of the street.") She indulged in personal mythology (journey from rank basement apartment to dinner in perfect SoHo loft, parallel journey of artist who no one took seriously to artist on the cusp of renown). She asked for ice water. She wondered if I had something sweet to eat on hand—she'd been, she admitted, too nervous at the dinner to do more than pick at her food. She fiddled with her wedding ring, twisting it around and around. She did something odd with her eyes at the end of nearly every sentence, opening them wider than they were meant to go, a kind of ocular exclamation mark. And when she was running down a bit, she suddenly said, "The guest room has its own bath, right? I think I should shower. I feel like a tea bag that's been left on the bottom of the cup. If you wait up for me, I wouldn't say no to a nightcap."

I waited in my favorite leather chair for her to return, which she did, her dark hair wet and swept back. She was barefoot and immodestly cloaked in the pale green T-shirt, which extended barely to her knees. She seated herself in one of the Mandle-brod chairs I'd recently acquired.

"I need to chill out. I am so excited. I am just so completely jazzed, I can hardly stand it."

"Yes, it's very exciting. And long overdue. Hey, Grace? There's a couple of things I want to talk to you about. Mainly about Jennings."

"You know," she said, as if she hadn't heard me, "when no one paid the slightest attention to what I did in the studio, I thought of the pieces as having infinite value. No one was offering a hundred dollars for one of them, so I could imagine them being worth a million. But now they're in the realm of reality, money reality. Do you understand? Of course you do, you of all people. Once the pieces have prices on them, you're put into a slot. Selling a piece for five thousand dollars destroys the dream of selling it for a million. The money bullies you, it's defining somehow, it tells you who you are. And you know what's so strange? I'm sorry, I know I'm going on and on, but it's so weird. Now that money is attached to the work, I don't feel it's really mine. The money's nice, but it sort of wrecks everything, too."

"It shouldn't," I said.

"I know. But money leaves a smell."

"I'm happy for you, Grace. You've worked long and hard and you deserve all these good things that are starting to happen."

She gave me a searching look. Grace Cornell of Eau Claire, Wisconsin, was always capable of frisking you with her pale green eyes. "You had a front-row seat for the whole sad spectacle," she said, her smile cold and candid. "I can still see the look on your face when we first came to New York, me and Thaddeus, and he showed you one of my drawings."

"I remember. It was of Franz Kafka. So. Back to Jennings, if we could."

"I could tell you weren't exactly head over heels about that drawing. You held it between your thumb and your forefinger, like some dead thing you picked up off the side of the road."

"You might have read too much into that, Grace."

"Oh, it doesn't matter. I was probably being . . ." She shook her head. "We came to New York so convinced we were going to be great artists but my good old reliable self-doubt kicked in as soon as the plane landed and on the ride in from the airport it got worse, and by the time we reached your apartment I felt this big." She described an inch with her thumb and forefinger.

"But look at what you've accomplished," I said.

She knitted her brows, tilted her head back, gave me one of those looks.

"Beautiful house," I persisted.

She tonged fresh ice cubes out of the bucket and plunked them down into her glass, poured a ridiculous amount of vodka over them.

"Thaddeus and I don't exactly feel the same way about Orkney, but don't get me wrong—I love it. I never had anything really nice until we bought that house. But there's always something wrong with it, not just with the house, which is a constant money-suck, but the idea of the place. It was like Thaddeus's castle and he *put* me there, like Rapunzel. Now he's frantic about keeping Orkney as a way of keeping me."

"Why would he worry about that, Grace?"

"Who knows?" she said. "But now you're a part of it. Did you ever think of that? Your money is helping him keep Orkney, which is his way of keeping me." She made a laugh that had as much to do with true merriment as falling down the stairs has to do with dancing.

"Don't you want the place?" I asked, wondering if she knew what I had given Thaddeus at the Paris Commune. But of course she did, she must have. And the ease with which she concealed her knowledge put me on alert.

"I think we should sell it," she was saying. "If things keep going for me like this, I want to move back here. I want to be where it's happening. Jennings said there's a place like ours about five miles south of Orkney that sold for a whole lot of money."

"Jennings is a real estate expert now?" I said.

"You know what? Anyone who looks down on Jennings is making a huge mistake. I sure don't. He believed in my work a hell of a lot more than anyone else, including my husband."

"You two drove your work to Florida, right? In a truck, the two of you."

"I couldn't possibly have done that alone. All that loading, all that driving. A truck? Forget it. Why do you ask?"

"That was generous of him."

"It certainly was."

"Grace, I should tell you—Jennings told me something about Emma."

She thought about this for a moment. I let the silence do what silence can do.

"Really?" she said. "About Emma?"

The sentence was formed in my mind—he has all but told me he is Emma's father—and it rested there, as hard and snug as a bullet in its chamber. Yet something held me back. Friendship, loyalty, fear, cunning. But why? Grace and I had never formed a true friendship. She was a part of my life, as I was of hers. Could it have been as simple and sad as that? Maybe it was just good manners. Whatever the impediment, I hesitated.

But I could not retreat.

"He says—"

"Jennings?"

"Yes. He has all but said he's Emma's father."

She did not laugh. She did not wave her hand as if I'd said something absurd. She did not flash anger. She did not accuse me of a willingness to give credence to an obvious lie, to a veritable hallucination. And she did not suggest I was making the entire thing up. There were no histrionics. No shaking of the head or exasperated sighs. There was only a long, long, searching look. Her color had darkened when Jennings's name came up, but now Grace settled down and became placid, the way a pond startled by a stone will gradually regain its glassy composure.

"I don't see what that has to do with you, Kip. I really don't."

"I didn't want to be a part of it," I said. Yet as soon as the words left my mouth, their very insufficiency acted as a goad, and I began to recover some courage. "Our lives are mixed together, Grace, and they have been for a long time. You first came to New York, you stayed with me. You needed jobs, I got you interviews. You got married, I put the wedding together. And I bought those acres from you so you wouldn't lose Orkney."

"Yes, I know, you're a hero," she said.

"That's not the point. I know I'm not a hero."

"All those things, those lovely gestures, so helpful—and don't think I wasn't grateful, I was and I am—but it was all for Thaddeus. Every bit of it."

"I'm asking you something very simple here, Grace," I said. "It isn't rocket science."

"What are you asking me, Kip? Be straight."

Hmm. But I let it pass.

"I'm asking if you're involved with Jennings."

"Now?"

"Jesus, Grace. Really."

"It's really none of your business, but I'm not."

"Okay, let me ask you this. Is Emma—"

"Jennings dumped me. A long time ago." She sat back with a look that suggested she'd just seen something humorous. "Oh, Kip, you poor thing, the expression on your face! This is a bit much for you, isn't it?"

"How can you be so awful to someone who loves you?" I asked.

"Thaddeus and I understand each other. And I promise you he doesn't want to talk about paternity tests or go snooping around anyone's DNA. He adores Emma and he would do any-thing to protect her and keep her safe and happy and secure. And you know what? As far as I'm concerned, that makes him Emma's father."

Andrew and Hunter, who lived on the first floor of my build-ing, were in the courtyard sharing a late night cigarette, and the scent of it, acrid as burning dirt yet somehow pleasing, wafted through my open window. The couple—Andrew, my age, an intellectual property attorney, and Hunter, consider-ably younger, some kind of freelance graphic designer—had re-cently adopted a baby from China, and now they had to smoke outside. They waved the smoke away from the baby monitor between them, the sound of their murmurings like the word-less warbles of doves.

"I don't see how you could have done this," I said. "And to sustain it for all these years."

"You know how it is," Grace said, her tone casual and instructive. "You tell a lie and then you have to tell another lie to cover the first lie and oops here comes another one to shore up the first two, and before you know it you're so wrapped up in your little stories and your evasions that it's easier just to keep things as they are and not try to figure out how to undo all your cover stories. You're stuck. Anyhow, my life was never really my own. I was sort of dragged along and tried to make the best of it. That's going to change. It's already changing."

She folded her hands, the hands of a woman many years older, dry and cracked, all those solvents, all that worry. I could feel her deciding what she would say and what she would keep to herself, and her thoughts were as present in the room as the whir of the fans.

"Have you ever wanted someone to just beat the living shit out of you?" she asked. She tapped her finger against the side of her glass of vodka, moving it closer to her inch by inch.

For a moment, I wondered if I'd heard her correctly. "Not really," I murmured. "It sounds painful."

"Sometimes it's just what the doctor ordered," Grace said.

Maybe she was deliberately trying to shock me into subservience, her way of putting me in my place, her version of Lyndon Johnson calling his aides into the bathroom so he could give them orders while he emptied his bowels. How could she have said something so personal, so intimate to me? I had never even seen her in a bathing suit. I'd never heard her sneeze. And now she was telling me she needed pain to connect to her body? She *had* to be running a number on me. But I never knew for certain; this was really the last time we ever spoke.

"Were you beaten as a child?" I asked. My voice was muddy and uncertain. "Spanked?"

"No. Never. It's not that. My father ditched us and Mom clung to me as if I were the adult who would protect her." Grace looked at me appraisingly. "My family didn't abuse me, unless you call embarrassment a form of abuse. If you want to know, I had bad experiences with men when I was a teenager. Not really men. Boys. College boys. Fraternity boys. I was in high school and I knew where all the parties were. And boy was I ever welcome. It wasn't rape or anything. But it was kind of ugly. Sometimes I was drunk, and sometimes I was pretending to be a lot more drunk than I really was. No one forced me. I was into it. It wasn't exactly fun but it was fascinating, and I felt powerful. But then something changed. I don't know what it was, not really. Suddenly it all seemed so sad and disgusting. I hated men and I hated me. And I went dead inside. Not really dead. Hibernation. I could still feel something, that didn't go away, but some other part of me was always separate and watching. Do you understand? Sometimes I feel separated from my own body. Things don't link up the way they need to if you're going to be happy, or even just okay. There's a gap. There's a missing piece and pain fills it in. Pain brings it all together." Her tone was matter-of-fact. "Thaddeus knows this. He knew it from the beginning. But it was understood between us that he was always going to be gentle. And I was fine with that. No problem. I always felt secure with him because he loves me so much. And he's safe. He's totally safe. And gentle is good. Don't you think so?" She looked at me inquisitively, as if truly soliciting my opinion, as if it mattered to her what I thought about her tastes and needs. But after a moment, she closed her eyes; she seemed to be summonsing a memory. "Yes. It can be so lovely, so, so lovely. But there are times when . . . when I need . . ." She made a fist and shook her head. "But Thaddeus is so gentle."

"You make it sound like a failing." I kept clearing my throat.

"It can be. He doesn't understand how awful it is to feel separated from your body, and he doesn't get it that the pain makes it better; it puts you in the moment and gets you out of your head."

"And Jennings is so accommodating, right?"

"Oh, the look on your face, Kip. You think it's so terrible? You think I'm so terrible? Or unusual? A lot of people are like I am. Not everyone wants vanilla ice cream for dessert." She sniffed the air. "You wouldn't have a cigarette around, would you?"

I walked to the window and looked at my neighbors in the courtyard. Thin clouds covered the full moon like bars over a window, and Andrew and Hunter were barely visible. The happy couple. Or so I imagined them to be. Free of shame, free of constraints, sharing so much more than that midnight Marlboro. Hunter dragged deeply on the cigarette and passed it to Andrew, who first tidied it up, flicking the ash, rotating it between his fingers to even out the burn. They had been tested, they were in the open, their brothers and sisters, their parents, their colleagues, everyone knew. They would be known as I would never be known. Known to the world, known to each other. I would die a stranger. The cigarette was smoked nearly down to the filter. Hunter snubbed it on the sole of his slipper and then offered his hand to Andrew, who allowed himself to be pulled out of his chair.

When I finally turned around, Grace had already gone to bed.

CHAPTER 24

Harmonic Convergence

Using the wisdom and technique of all the 12-step programs, I kept away from the Kaufman-Cornells one day at a time. They may have been steering clear of me, too, but more likely they were too busy with their fucked-up lives to give me much thought, while the nature of my fucked-up life was that I was always to one degree or another thinking about them—not just Thaddeus but the lot of them, even the dogs and cats.

Largely on my recommendation, Adler Associates was completely divested of our Sears holdings, and as a reward for all the dull places I traveled to during the Sears investigation Ken dispatched me to Amsterdam toward the end of the year. He wanted me to talk to the principals of a company called Windmolen, which manufactured electricity-generating turbines, and sold them all over Europe, especially in France and Spain. We didn't ordinarily invest in offshore companies. Our clients were satisfied with modest returns generated by companies like General Motors, Eastman Kodak, Xerox, and Alcoa—if they wanted to take a flier on something riskier, they made those investments elsewhere. I appreciated Ken's generosity, his distracted, muted, but always affectionate treatment of me, and by the time Amsterdam was offered I no longer felt guilty or nervous in his presence—Thaddeus had tiptoed in and out of Johnson & Johnson and no one was hurt.

The trip was poorly planned. Most of the Windmolen employees were off for the Christmas holidays, and the factory that assembled the gorgeous titanium windmills was down to a skeleton crew, which left me with the Windmolen president and several lesser executives, including a sister and brother duo who were the entire public relations department of the firm. My first night, they took me to dinner at a newly opened Tex-Mex restaurant, where the Indonesian waitstaff was dressed in blue jeans, checked shirts, and neckerchiefs, and where the food was just about as Tex-Mex as the people serving it. The next day, we visited the Windmolen offices on Prinsengracht, in one of those narrow, immemorial Amsterdam houses, tobacco-colored stone, tall windows, the glass cataracted with age. Later, the brother and sister drove me about fifty miles out of town, through a monotonous and flat landscape, where the frozen stubble of the tulip fields abruptly ended at the gray horizon, and where, suddenly, the factory sprang into view, looming over the landscape as if it had arrived from outer space.

When we returned to Amsterdam they took me to a party for a tall, pretty woman and an even taller, prettier man, who were both on the Windmolen board and who were celebrating their engagement to be married. The party was in the boardroom and everyone there wore glasses with frames not yet available in the States, and spoke perfect BBC-inflected English. The guests drank as if there were some prize to be given to the first person to pass out, though the Dutch never really lose self-control. Amsterdam was a city rife with jazz, hash, and whores, but most people continue to live bewilderingly orderly lives. Tonight, the men wore bright, flowery, unserious ties. The women were more formal, and in the minority, maybe one for every three men. The few people I'd already met did their best to keep an eye on me, introducing me around—This is our American friend Christopher, from the Adler group—but I could tell no one knew what the Adler group meant. We were financial small fry and even if I were to recommend to Ken that we bet on Windmolen (which I did), our purchase of shares wouldn't mean all that much. It wasn't as if I were here representing Lehman Brothers or some other investment bank ready to plunk down $100 million. After an hour had passed, my handlers left me to my own devices. And between slight jet lag and my own Christmas-is-hell state of mind, I was soon floating in a wandering trance of loneliness, patrolling the party's periphery until I found an inconspicuous place to stand, near a rented piano being played by an American jazz musician who was joined by a middle-aged singer named Anneke Gronloh. She was popular in Holland in the early sixties, probably a great favorite of the guests' parents, and, impish and ample, she sang a Middle Eastern–inflected song while rotating her hips. The guests enjoyed her performance but in a way that exuded irony and the sense of superiority that is often at irony's core, clapping their hands in rhythm and stomping their feet with such force that the room shook and the bulbs in the starburst chandelier flickered off and on as I slipped out of the party.

The canal along Prinsengracht was the dark clay color of Grace's Weimaraners; pale yellow lights from the huddled houseboats trembled in the rippling water. The air was cold, heavy, and damp, and the sidewalk was deserted. I thought of Amsterdam as a late late night city. Had they all forsaken the dicey nightlife to stay home and wrap presents? I glanced at my watch, feeling that horribly familiar panic—all the time that was being wasted, utterly wasted, the hours, the months, and finally the years.

It was eleven o'clock on Prinsengracht, and five in the afternoon in Leyden, and Thaddeus was with his family, including Sam and Libby, visiting for the first time since a year after Thaddeus and Grace bought Orkney. That first visit, they had been curious to see what their son's new riches had brought him, probably expecting that it would prove to be closer to a cabin than the palace he burbled on about over the telephone.

"Where did you find this place?" Libby had asked as Thaddeus showed them the rooms, the wide plank floors, the fireplaces, the stained glass. "I mean it, Thaddeus. Where in the world did you find this place?" He laughed and tried to rationalize her question, reminding himself that Libby and Sam were parochial, and the house must have seemed foreign to them, overwhelming. Nevertheless, he suspected that what Libby really meant was not how did he find the place but how did he come to buy it? How did a little schlepper who never had two nickels to rub together suddenly own eighteen rooms and a million trees? The suggestion that Orkney was out of his league ought to have insulted him, but at the time the money protected his feelings. He was flush, his confidence was soaring—that career-derailing mimosa was years from being handed to him, and the money was pouring in. My occasional reminders that the movie business was notoriously fickle did nothing more than annoy him.

Years had gone by without the Kaufmans coming east again. They would have been virtual strangers to David and Emma had Thaddeus and Grace not brought them to Chicago every other year—Grace's mother had quit the city and lived with Grace's brother outside of San Diego, and regularly sent boxes of presents to the children. For Sam and Libby, however, doing the Grammy and Grampy thing was of little interest. Neither of them had met their own grandparents, and they assumed that children would have no interest in and possibly even shrink away from the elderly. Most of Sam and Libby's extended family had perished in the European holocaust, and their own parents had died young, stateside, leaving both Sam and Libby to cobble together a life for themselves, relying on the short-lived support of comrades and the unshakable connection to each other.

The Kaufmans hadn't come east to see their son and their grandchildren. A man named Barry Horowitz, one of the small handful of ex-Trotskyists with whom the Kaufmans had remained in contact, had vanished about six months ago. His children and the police had searched for him, but to no avail, until his body was found in the weeds not more than a hundred yards from his house in Wilkes-Barre, Pennsylvania. Apparently, he had been on his way to a nearby patch of woods after having taken a lethal dose of sleeping pills, had stumbled, and died where he hit the ground. The memorial service had been in the city. Afterward, the Kaufmans rode up to Leyden with Thaddeus, who'd picked them up on the Upper West Side before they could flee.

During their night at Orkney, the senior Kaufmans mainly

stayed in their room, emerging only to ask if Thaddeus could possibly make it a bit warmer. He was able to lure them down for dinner, where David and Emma viewed them somewhat fearfully, and Thaddeus—over the silent veto of Grace's frown—reverted to his childhood compulsion to raise their spirits, topping off their wineglasses as soon as they took the tiniest sip, urging them to eat, smiling adoringly at them, cracking jokes. In his childhood, he used to sing and dance for them—his stage was the two inches of wooden floor between the fringes of the red and purple Persian rug and the light brown baseboard, that little strip of naked wood upon which he could clatter his heels in an approximation of tap dancing, whirling his arms around as if he were fighting off a swarm of hornets. As a child, he was never successful in jollying them out of their crepuscular blahs, and now thirty years later his efforts fell just as flat.

On the second day of the Kaufman visit, they were all invited to a pre-Christmas party at Sequana, a nearby estate, this one owned by a music producer named Pete Marino. Marino was waiting until spring to unload the property, convinced that, despite all of the opposition, the cement plant was going to be constructed on the river, forever despoiling the view from the mansion's windows. Without that view, the value of Sequana would be cut in half, since the kind of buyer who would want such an estate, and who could absorb the expenses that came with the property, would surely not want to be anywhere near much less look at smokestacks and conveyor belts. Even the sight of another house was a deal breaker for the people who were estate shopping in Windsor County.

Many of the people Marino had formed social relations with since buying Sequana were wintering in Palm Beach or

St. Maarten or simply staying in the city, choosing to avoid the county's ice and snow. Marino, dressed in a blazer and freshly pressed jeans, his wrists and fingers adorned with silver and turquoise, nevertheless held court from his favorite chair near the largest of Sequana's hearths. He was boyish at fifty, with rosy lips and merry blue eyes.

Thaddeus stayed at his parents' side, introducing them, escorting them to the bar area, encouraging them to help themselves to the appetizers the catering staff was circulating. Sam and Libby had dressed for the party as they had for the memorial service, Libby in a floor-length green dress with long sleeves, Sam in a sober gray suit, white shirt, and gray tie. Hoping to strike an alliance with his parents by indicating that he was *in* but not *of* this party, Thaddeus said, "Look at this, a Christmas party with no kids. It's just ridiculous."

"Oh, you and kids," Libby said. "You make such a fetish of it. You wait on them hand and foot."

I'll give you hand and foot, he thought. He was growing weary of explaining away his mother's tepid feelings toward him. He was tired of telling himself the story of her bad luck, her suffering, tired of excusing his father. Losing that child. Coming home and finding their happy, clueless little boy watching TV and spooning peanut butter out of the jar. He was sick of doing the emotional arithmetic for them. The wan smiles, the benign neglect, the skepticism—these were their rituals of mourning, their offerings to poor little Hannah. They would not play favorites—if both children could not be adored equally, then neither would be adored.

But at that moment, Thaddeus's wrathful musings were cut short by something he noticed: his father was rubbing his eye with the heel of his hand. His mouth was half open and he seemed confused, like a child waking in a strange bed. The eye he'd been worrying drooped like a deflated balloon. Nightmare image out of Francis Bacon.

"Dad?" Thaddeus said.

By way of an answer, Sam fell to the floor as if dropped from the jaws of a crane.

———

The snowflakes on Prinsengracht were large and fluffy and seemed to ride the breeze, hovering over the pavement for extra moments before dissolving upon landing. Of course I know that the fact that it was snowing as I stood outside the Windmolen office, and that it was also snowing in Leyden as Sam lay dying on the floor of Sequana had nothing to do with me or with love or fate or destiny. It's all longitude and latitude and the earth chugging along on its appointed rounds. And yet. The heart, malnourished, fearful of dying of starvation, seizes whatever it can, knowing how to live on coincidences and trivialities, gathering and gobbling all the little morsels of meaning, and making a meal of them.

Through the dark Amsterdam night a man emerged with his head down, wearing a watch cap, a long coat, boots. An unlit cigarette was in his mouth. As he drew closer to me I turned away, checked the roadway, pretending to look for a car that was on its way to pick me up. The stranger stopped and asked me if I had a light, and when I made a confused gesture he asked me again, in English.

I decided it was no accident, his stopping to speak to me. He wanted something beyond a light for his cigarette. In a burst of daring, I said, "Oh, sorry, don't smoke."

"That's good," he said. "Filthy habit."

"Oh, I've got plenty of those."

He laughed appreciatively.

"You're American, yeah?" he said.

"Guilty," I said. And then, with ten times the confidence I would ever have on native soil, I said, "Hey, you know what? There are matches in my hotel, which is about two minutes' walk from here."

"In your hotel?"

"Yes, it's quite nice." My heart raced and rumbled like wooden wheels over cobblestones. "I'm here on business and they've given me the Olivier Van Noort suite. Of course I have no idea who he is or was."

"He was an explorer. He sailed everywhere. Hundreds of years ago."

"I see. Well, that makes sense. At first I thought they'd given me the Oliver North suite. That would have been strange."

I began to walk and he walked with me. I turned up the collar of my overcoat and he turned up the collar of his. He told me his name was Mees, and he made sure I pronounced it correctly—May-es.

I wondered what he was like. There was a time when I could not stop myself from wondering who was packing what in their shorts. I had developed my curiosity into a kind of horny science. Like so: using a combination of my paid-for personal experience, time in the locker rooms of various health clubs around the world, and pornography, I had accrued a database of genitals, cut and uncut, massive and modest, chunky and sleek, and I had correlated this knowledge with certain facts about the owners of the genitalia to the point where I believed I could form a fairly accurate picture of what a guy was keeping in his equipment shed not only by the size of his fingers and feet but by his posture, his height and weight, Adam's apple, and voice. Some of my theories were quite theoretical. Even for theories they were theoretical, and I would have been the first to admit they might not stand up to rigorous testing. For example, I believed that blond guys often had stout, furious-looking penises, and that Slavs were never entirely flaccid and their members dangled in a kind of erotic indeterminacy, hanging midair like a wind sock in a faint breeze.

I told him my name was Christopher but that most people who knew me called me Kip. My mood brightened. It was the first time I'd given my real name to someone with whom I was going to have sex.

———

David used his cell phone to call 911, but other than that everyone was useless. No one present knew any first aid. They didn't know if they should pick Sam up or leave him undisturbed. "Is he breathing?" Thaddeus asked, his gaze going from one person to the next. His mother was glaring at him, furiously.

"What's the address here?" David called out.

"Sequana!" yelled Marino.

David told the emergency operator the name of the estate but she insisted upon an address.

"We don't have an address," Marino said. "Will you give me . . ." He pulled the phone out of David's hand. "We're at Sequana on Riverview Road," he growled into the phone. "And we've got an elderly man here who has lost consciousness. Okay? With all due respect, may I suggest you get an ambulance here immediately."

"I think we should call a New York hospital," David said. "The places up here don't know anything about anything. Remember when I got so sick in Italy and the guy at the embassy said the best thing would be to take me to Germany?"

"But we didn't do that, David," Grace said.

"You should have. It was just luck that I got better. I could have died."

"You had the flu," said Thaddeus.

"I had a temperature of one oh three!"

"Is Grandpa dying?" Emma asked Grace.

"He'll be okay," Thaddeus said, rising from his crouch. He staggered for a moment, almost stepping on his father. He looked at his watch; two minutes had gone by.

And by now I was back at the Hotel de l'Europe, accompanied by Mees. The clerks behind the check-in desk wore blue suits with boutonnieres. Mees and I made our way across the lobby beneath the gaze of giant faux Dutch master paintings of sixteenth-century burghers in various poses of self-possession, with their neck ruffles and arch little smiles. My key was waiting for me, saving me from having to say my name. Oh, the deep discretion of the Dutch! And the deep discretion of high-priced hotels. It's that master-of-the-manor treatment you pay for, more important than the room itself. I scooped up the key, and the clerk and I gave that tight-lipped little nod men give to suggest the best of intentions.

"Very nice," Mees said, surveying my room. "Permission to smoke?"

I tossed him the small box of matches that had been placed

in a ceramic ashtray and I pulled a split of Piper-Heidsieck out of the minibar.

"I love hotels," I said.

"Here my father-in-law rests when he comes for business," Mees said.

"Oh? You're married?"

"Not so much anymore."

"Ah, yes," I said. "I know. I'm in the same boat. I'm recently divorced." Even in front of a stranger, a man I would in all likelihood never see again after this night, I could not be truthful. The elation I'd felt when I gave my real name was officially over. I opened the champagne. The festive pop, the cobra curl of vapor rising. We did not toast each other or clink the rims of our glasses. We just downed the Piper and when our glasses were empty I filled them again.

"Shall we?" I said, gesturing to the bed in the adjoining room, with its salmon and silver bedspread and profusion of pillows. There is an assumption shared by luxury hotels that guests want as many pillows as possible, that if four pillows on a bed is comfortable, eight must be twice as comfortable, and sixteen a preview of heaven.

"That's what beds are for," Mees said, in a singsong voice you'd use on a child. I think he was having a moment of shyness.

"I need to ask you something," I said.

"I practice safe sex, if that's your question," he said.

"Oh god, no. Of course. Me, too. Definitely. Very safe. What I want to ask you—please don't be offended—is whether you are expecting money." I pointed to myself, the bed, and myself again.

"Money?"

"That's what they call it."

"If you have extra money you don't want, then give it to me. By all means. Are you asking me if I work as a prostitute?"

"Yes. I'm sorry. This is more about me than about you. You understand?"

"Do I seem like a prostitute? Because I was walking at night? If you want to know, I am a teacher. I am a full professor of sociology at the University of Amsterdam, which I am sure you must be familiar with because we have been in operation since four hundred fifty years."

"I'm sorry if I've offended you. Most of my experiences with men have been paid for," I said. "As I said, it's not anything about you."

"Well, if your money is burning holes in your wallet, I can always use some." He stepped forward, put me on alert with a glance, and kissed me. His breath tasted of spearmint; without my seeing it, he must have slipped a lozenge into his mouth to dispel the taste of tobacco. The excitement of it made me whimper for a moment. I kissed him back, but really I was suddenly out of my depth and the ardency I meant to communicate came off more like wildness, violence.

"This is going to be good," Mees said. "I'd like to visit the W.C. To wash off." He chucked me under the chin and winked, which was too bad, but nobody's perfect.

———

Thaddeus was alone on the curved front porch, bundled against the cold, and staring furiously through the snow at the estate's winding driveway, waiting to see the headlights of an approaching ambulance. His consciousness was fixed on the outer world, knowing that even a moment's reflection would bring back the memory of Sam's stunned, frightened expression, right before he fell. Yet there came a sharp stinging moment of remembrance, a gasp of memory, crushing and quotidian, devastating in its apparent lack of significance and demanding attention by its mere presence. Thaddeus, his fourteenth summer, having fallen asleep listening to *The Midnight Special* on the FM radio, stretched out on the sofa in the apartment's front room. Etched into the darkness was a deeper darkness, his father's form, standing over the radio, briefly illuminated by the light of the radio's complicated dial, with its profusion of useless hash marks. The radio was silenced, the New Lost City Ramblers disappeared. "We don't want to wake your mother," Sam whispered. He was in boxer shorts that somehow looked government issued. "That's the last thing we need, right?" He stood, waiting for Thaddeus to get off the sofa. "You like sleeping out here near the air conditioner?" Thaddeus made a little grunt of assent. "It ain't such a bad deal in this outfit, isn't that right? I mean, who's got it better than us?" Thaddeus didn't know what to say. All his life he had felt protective of his parents, protective of their moods. He wanted to reassure his father—but of what? Sam smelled of bed, and toothpaste, and the Mercurochrome he swabbed between his toes every night, a cure for athlete's foot that never seemed to work. Fuck you and the horse you rode in on, Thaddeus said to himself, and Sam stumbled, as if pushed, as if he had read his son's mind, or perhaps in his half-asleep state Thaddeus had accidentally said the words aloud. "I guess it can get kind of lonely here sometimes," Sam said, before leaving the room. The floors were carpeted and from the front of the apartment, down the corridor to the bedrooms, the sad father's footsteps were as silent as the stars. Thaddeus wasn't even certain he had left until he heard the click of the bedroom door closing.

Thaddeus had already checked twice with Marino to make sure the gate had been opened, but now he was thinking it might make sense to run the half mile to the gate and see for himself. Why trust the remote opening of the security gate when the ambulance might be waiting right there while Sam's life slipped away? He trotted through the darkness and the cold air filled his lungs like broken glass. When Marino bought Sequana, the driveway was a bucolic slurry of dirt and pebbles; paving it had been his first order of business. But now a thin sheen of ice covered it, making it treacherous, and Thaddeus lost his footing for a moment, waved his arms for balance. The world was silent save for the creak of empty trees enduring the wind.

The gate to Sequana's driveway was wide open. The weather had not closed Riverview Road. A car streamed by, its headlights boring into the darkness, and music trailing behind it. *We will we will rock you.* He waited at the gate, thinking the rescue team would be there at any moment. And then suddenly it seemed to him that it was utter foolishness to be at the gate, that he should be at his father's side, or his mother's, his children's, what was he doing? Shirking? Hiding? He felt the familiar flurries of self-doubt. He headed back to the house, walking quickly at first, and then running, running as fast as he could, the cold air stabbing into his lungs. The mansion emerged from the darkness like a sunken ship suddenly rising from the sea. Perhaps the EMTs had found another way onto the property? Was there another way in? Maybe there was, maybe there was. . . . His mind habitually searched for the benign explanation. He could almost see it: his father safely strapped onto the gurney, the EMT workers wheeling him to the open doors of their vehicle, Sam's eyes slowly opening, smiling, giving everyone an embarrassed thumbs-up.

But instead of that tableau of rescue, what Thaddeus found when he entered the house was a raging Pete Marino. "How hard is it?" he asked no one in particular. "You get in your little truck and you go where you are fucking needed, you dumb stupid motherfucking knuckle-dragging idiots. Jesus Christ. Where are they?"

Libby was on the floor, her husband's head in her lap. She stroked his hair. David and Emma stood next to her, their heads bowed. Grace stood at a window, peering out at the unyielding darkness.

"They're not here?" Thaddeus asked.

"No, they're not," Marino said. "And don't tell me it's not deliberate. Who are these people? They're the same ones who cause all the trouble here. They're throwing their goddamned blocks of cement, and starting fires, and doing whatever the fuck they can to make life impossible. And now this? This? Deliberately dragging their asses because the call came in from a house they don't approve of? That's murder."

Thaddeus crouched near Libby, who was still on the floor with Sam's head in her lap.

"Not now," Libby said.

"I want to talk to him."

"Does he look like he wants to talk? Will you please grow up?"

As she said those words, the sound of a siren emerged from the wintry night.

"They're here!" Emma said, racing to her mother's side at the window.

Thaddeus checked his watch. Eighteen minutes had passed since David had called for help. If you were eighteen minutes into a screenplay, you already had introduced all the major characters. If you were in a plane, eighteen minutes would take you from Albany to New York City, passing over a million rooftops, farms and condos, cows and crack dens, mansions, tenements, swimming pools, prisons—eighteen minutes and everything our country had to offer would glide by.

Thaddeus and Marino stood at the open front door, shoulder to shoulder, glaring, sighing, making gestures of impatience as the EMTs moved with what struck them both as pathological caution. They had brought two vehicles, an ambulance and a pickup truck. Their hazard lights throbbed in the darkness, illuminating the silver plumes of exhaust pouring out of the tailpipes.

———

Mees emerged from the bathroom nonchalantly naked. I had correctly anticipated what was going on underneath his clothes, his ruddy genitalia was what I had assumed, though the prominent ridge of flesh separating the ventricles of his scrotum was something of a curious surprise. He had powerful legs, covered in blond hair that grew in tight larval coils. He left the door open and urged me in with a wave of his arm. "You are next," he said with great cheer. Sensing some resistance on my part, he added, "You'll be glad you did, I promise you."

How do you not wash when someone directly asks you to? I

closed the door behind me, locked it, got into the shower, and used the wand. As often occurred when I was about to have sex, my mind was slowly going blank. I soaped, rinsed, stood there staring at the tiles. Lust and revulsion did their familiar pas de deux.

"Well, here we are," I said, falling onto the bed. Mees had not bothered to pull the cover down and the bedspread's harsh golden threads irritated my nakedness. I lay on my back with my hands behind my head. I did what was necessary to keep my body in good shape and showing it off was an agreeable experience. In America I was homely, but abroad that was not what people saw, not right away. Abroad, I was first and foremost an American.

I rolled onto my side, pressed my hardness against him, kissed his cheek, forehead, right eye, left. For a moment, I loved him, frantically, insanely, it was like wandering through a dark house and suddenly opening a door to blinding sunlight.

"I've been thinking about you," I whispered.

I could not keep myself from noticing the look of uncertainty on his face; he waited for his misgivings to subside and finally said, "Yes. I know."

"All this time apart," I said. "Wasted years."

"Not good," he said. He kissed me on the mouth. His tongue was hefty, vaguely bumpy, like a washcloth. He wanted me to stop talking. And then he ravaged me. Meaningless sex has a bad reputation, but unless you have a heart made of granite there's actually no such thing as meaningless sex. Before he left, I got him to give me his full name and address. He wrote it down for me in a very careful hand, and left soon after, without asking me for mine.

He smiled in a kindly way and said, "Sweet dreams, Mr. You."

————————

"You think you could move any slower, you stupid jerks?" Marino said, more or less under his breath, but willing to be overheard.

"Guys," Thaddeus called out. "We're losing him." He tried to strike a collegial tone.

There were six EMT volunteers, including Jennings, dressed in a tan Carhartt jacket, jeans. He was wearing rubber flip-flops, his feet bare, as if he had been on his way to a shower when the call came in. The nail on his large toe, right foot, was black and appeared to be dying.

"Who's hurt?" he asked Thaddeus.

"It's my father," Thaddeus said. "I think he's had a stroke or a heart attack."

"Why is this taking so long?" Marino asked, making no attempt to hide his disapproval.

"Well, let me walk you through this, Mr. Marino," Jennings said. He said "Mr." as if it were a taunt. "We're volunteers. The call comes in. Each of us in our own home. We drop whatever it is we're doing, if we're sleeping, or eating, or changing a diaper, we drop it as soon we hear there's an emergency some-where, and we get in our own private vehicle and drive as fast as we can to the garage where this here meat wagon is wait-ing for us, and we get the address where we're supposed to be going. You did not even give an address so that slowed things down."

"Can we *not* talk about this now?" Thaddeus said, his voice rising.

"I'm with you," Jennings said, patting Thaddeus on the shoulder. "Let me see what I can do to get things rolling here. Okay?"

Of the six EMT workers, one was a woman who years before had worked at Orkney as a nanny. She was delivering information to the hospital through a walkie-talkie but it appeared not to be working. She spoke and then held it away from herself and shook her head. She had once commented upon Grace's work, calling them "pitchers," and David, not even four years old, had corrected her pronunciation. Thaddeus had admonished the boy but that had made matters worse.

"Hey, Laura," Thaddeus called out, raising a hand in greeting but either she didn't hear him or she chose not to reciprocate.

Two of the other volunteers were taking the gurney out of the back of the truck. One of them pulled it by the grips while the other stood to one side. There seemed some impediment to getting the gurney out and the second volunteer watched while the first tried to shake it loose.

"What in the fuck are they doing?" Marino said.

"I don't know, I don't know," Thaddeus whispered.

The second volunteer got into the back of the wagon. "Give her a yank," he called out, and a moment later the gurney was on the ground, its back wheels spinning.

As yet, none of the EMT workers had set foot in the house. The gurney was righted, the straps tightened, though the usefulness of that was mysterious since they would only have to be unbuckled again. There seemed to be certain procedures and they went through them, as impervious to logic or human need as the ticking of a clock. Before the gurney was picked up, both volunteers put on their gloves, tugging at them carefully. "It would have made me laugh if I hadn't wanted to strangle him," Thaddeus later told me. Another of the volunteers, a ponytailed guy in his thirties with an orthopedic boot on his left foot, was peering into an enormous bag of medical supplies, and doing seemingly meaningless things, like picking up a roll of gauze, holding it to the light, turning it this way and that, and dropping it back into the bag. Next came a towel, scissors, a suction bulb, on and on, each viewed for a moment before being dropped back into the bag. Finally, he fished out a stethoscope and looped it around his neck. The volunteer who had driven the ambulance walked over to the gurney and engaged in a brief conversation with the two in charge of getting it into the house. For the life of him Thaddeus could not understand what needed to be said, or why this was taking so long. Were the EMT workers taunting him? Was this some kind of slow-down strike, like baggage handlers at the Rome airport?

Marino muttered, "This is like a slow-motion murder," and began to shout at the EMT workers. "Hey, you guys, there is an old man in there on my floor. On my floor! And you're standing around with your dicks in your hands."

None of the volunteers gave the slightest indication of having heard Marino. They spoke quietly to one another as they filed into the house, gazing up and around for a moment to take in the splendor.

Jennings was the last one in. He clapped Thaddeus's shoulder and said, "Don't worry, we got this." He paused, and gestured toward one of the EMT workers—the one with the stethoscope. "You know Larry, right?"

Thaddeus shook his head no.

"Oh man, you do, you do. He's been over to the property a

million times." He called out to his old friend Larry Sassone. "Hey, Larry. Come here for a sec."

"I can't now, Jennings." He unzipped his jacket and tucked in the chest piece of his stethoscope.

"Does he know what he's doing?" Thaddeus asked.

"Nope. We're just a bunch of good old country boys who like driving that truck and whooping the siren."

The metal guardrail of the gurney clipped the dark blue molding around the doorway and a little chunk of wood dislodged like a peach pit spit onto the floor.

"Oh, for fuck's sake," said Marino, but no one paid attention to him. Shaking his head and making no attempt to conceal his extravagant frown, he took his place with his guests as they silently watched Sam being lifted onto the gurney. For the moment, the EMT workers seemed at last efficient. Larry Sassone listened for his heartbeat as Sam was being strapped securely in. Marino's cook emerged from the kitchen, drying her hands on a dish towel. She was a prim-looking woman in her fifties; blind in one eye, she moved her head in odd angles, to take in the room.

"Hi, Mom," said the EMT worker who was steadying the back end of the gurney.

"You drive carefully," the cook said. "The roads are a mess."

"Don't worry, Mom. See you later tonight, okay? Love you."

Grace gestured with her eyes, letting Thaddeus know that he needed to follow behind the gurney and get into the ambulance with his father.

"What are you doing?" cried Libby, to no one and everyone. "Can't you see? He's already dead. He's gone, he's gone. This is ridiculous." She gripped the back of a chair for balance. She breathed heavily but her face was neutral. She surveyed everything that was happening in front of her as if she were watching a film of it for the fifth time, looking for little details she might have missed.

Jennings, noticing Grace's gesture, told Thaddeus he could ride along with them.

"I want to come, too," Emma said. "With Grandpa."

"You can't," David was quick to say.

"Listen to your brother," Jennings said. He pulled off his glove and lifted Emma's chin with two fingers, peered into her eyes. "You stay right here, okay?"

"Okay," she said, in an obedient whisper.

Thaddeus followed Jennings outside and waited while they put Sam in, secured him. When it was time, Thaddeus climbed in, trying to ignore Jennings's helpful hand on his elbow. In his cashmere coat and loafers, he felt foolish. It was not easy to climb in. He had to get on his knees; the icy metal floor radiated through his trousers.

Here in the back of an ambulance, with its oxygen tanks from which the green paint was flaking, and the ominous coils of amber tubing hanging from the ceiling, and the discarded blood pressure cuff on the floor, and the metal containers of medical supplies bolted to the metal walls, here in this box of disaster and its aftermath was the unlovely strenuous and terminal truth of the world.

Jennings and Larry Sassone hoisted themselves in and pulled the doors shut with a mighty boom. Thaddeus found a place to sit that minimized the chances of his being in the way, while Sassone hovered over Sam, replacing the oxygen mask and then carefully turning on one of the tanks.

"Is he breathing?" Thaddeus asked. "He doesn't seem to be breathing."

"We don't do final assess. We deliver the patient."

Jennings sat next to Thaddeus and patted his arm. "Hang in there, buddy," he said.

Thaddeus was acutely aware they were not yet moving. They were parked in front of Sequana like a bookmobile. What was keeping them? He heard voices and then the sound of a truck's door closing. More voices. Laughter. Another door slamming shut.

"You start the tanks yet, Itchy?" Jennings asked Sassone.

Jennings calling Sassone Itchy jogged Thaddeus's memory. Of course! Him. He had already closed the door in Sassone's face. Jennings had brought him around. Jennings had always been good about keeping hunters off Orkney's grounds, but he had asked for special dispensation for Sassone, who was called Itchy because in high school Sassone had loved Nietzsche and his friends had gleefully corrupted the weird name to a comic book handle. At the time, Thaddeus had decided not to make an exception to the no-hunting rule, and he had given the matter no further thought until this very moment, when it struck him that in all likelihood Itchy had hated him ever since and this was Sassone's revenge for being deprived of his two does and a buck. Yet there was more to it. Sassone alone hadn't manufactured the delay. They were all in it, the lot of them.

"You sitting there?" Sassone asked Thaddeus.

"Yeah. Is that okay?"

"Sure. I'll ride up front." He stooped as he walked to the front end of the interior. He must have realized how he looked because he turned toward Thaddeus and dangled his arms and made ape noises. Laughing, he turned away and banged his elbow twice against the glass, letting know whoever was in the cab that he was sitting up front.

"Thank you," Thaddeus muttered as Sassone left the back of the truck. But thought, *for nothing, you sack of dirt.*

Sassone slammed the double door behind him and Jennings began to cough, suddenly, violently. He opened his mouth and, bowing, shook his head, as if trying to dislodge a stinging insect caught at the back of his throat. A strand of spittle hung from his mouth, swinging back and forth like a trapeze ring after the acrobat has fallen. He gathered it in with his fingers, looked at it for a moment through narrowed eyes, before rubbing it into the rough weave of his trousers.

Where he had expected to find pity or at least concern for his old friend, Thaddeus found only anger. Not just with Jennings, but for all of them, the entire crew. Knuckle-dragging fucking bastards, he thought. He hated the tenor of his own mind, but it was too late to silence it. All the time wasted while the life drained from Sam. The murderous meandering even after they arrived. Marino was right, it was a slow-motion homicide. And Jennings was at fault as much as any of them.

Finally the ambulance started to roll, very slowly at first, the gears grinding. Sam's stretcher began to roll but it had been tethered to metal rings on the wall and it only moved an inch before suddenly jerking to a halt.

"Is that all right?" Thaddeus asked.

"No problem," said Jennings.

"How come no siren?" Thaddeus asked, but he was unable to wait for an answer. His stomach churned. "And what the fuck, Jennings. What the fuck. It took you forever to get there—and now look at him."

Jennings glanced toward Sam, shrugged. He reached back and fished out the ends of his seat belt, fastened it. "Belt up, Thaddeus. We'll be picking up speed."

"If he dies, it's on you," Thaddeus said. He waited for a response. The siren whooped on and then off. It grated on Thaddeus. The siren burst sounded celebratory. Who were these men? Really, truly. Who were they? Jennings's silence, rather than coaxing Thaddeus into silence himself, only served to goad him. He looked at his hands. They seemed to belong to someone else. As did his mind, his thoughts, his fury.

Thaddeus stood just as the ambulance was making a turn and he stumbled forward. He wanted to take the oxygen mask off his father. It was absurd, it was a mockery, like putting a hat on a dog. But was he dead? How could you tell for sure? How, he wondered, how in the world can I be a man who does not know for sure if his own father has died?

Sam's lips were parted, and Thaddeus could see the pale gray tip of his tongue, lifeless as a bookmark.

"Hey, Pop," he said. "Pop?"

The EMT truck took another sudden turn. Thaddeus was in too much disarray to maintain his balance and he tripped over his own feet and fell directly onto his father. The skin was cold and oddly sticky, like unbaked bread slowly rising in its tin. Thaddeus made a desperate sound.

"Sit down, Thaddeus," Jennings said. "We're almost there. Take it easy."

"Take it easy? Really? Is that your suggestion? Can I ask you something? What were you doing all that time while he was just lying there on the floor?"

"I could ask you that, too. What were you doing?"

"Waiting for you," he said, reattaching his seat belt.

Jennings had the slow, easy smile of a gambler who knows he is just about to show winning cards. "Yeah, I guess you were. We're just lowly volunteers, brother. We don't get paid. You know that, don't you? We just do it best we can. We're not doctors or race car drivers. We hammer things and fix things. You know. I don't have to tell you."

"You're all murderers, and I swear to God, Jennings, I don't care what kind of history we've got, or how many times our kids played together, none of that means anything to me anymore."

Furiously, Thaddeus undid his seat belt and Jennings undid his, and they did their best to stand and face each other. The ambulance made a turn and they staggered, trying to keep their balance. They were practically touching. Jennings placed his hands on Thaddeus's shoulders. And that's when Thaddeus tried to hit him, as much to his own surprise as to Jennings's. When was the last time he had hit a human being? The main reason he knew how to make a proper fist was that he'd researched it for a screenplay. He closed both of his hands, squeezed and squeezed until his thumbs touched the knuckles of his ring fingers. But the blows never landed. Jennings swatted the first swing away and quickly closed the space between Thaddeus and himself and enveloped Thaddeus in an overpowering embrace.

"Shhh, it's okay, it's okay, shhhh shhh shh," he whispered, as if to calm a spooked horse, a frightened child.

Thaddeus slowly unfurled his fists, dropped his hands so they hung at his sides.

"I know," Jennings whispered. "There's nothing like a father."

They both shifted their weight to keep balance as the EMT truck made another turn and picked up speed.

"You were good to my father, Thaddeus. And I would never hurt yours. You know that, don't you? We understand each other, right?"

Thaddeus's shoulders were shaking.

"Neighbor," Jennings said, in his deep voice. And then he whispered it over and over. "Neighbor, neighbor."

Thaddeus took a deep breath.

"It's okay," Jennings said. "Let it out. You have to let it out."

Thaddeus took a step back. He grabbed his hair, pulled it. "Fuck."

"I know, man. Your dad."

"My dad."

"I know."

"That sweet, sad man. He never raised his voice to me. When he was pissed off he'd sigh and puff out his cheeks."

"You're going to fall if you don't sit down, Thaddeus."

"He hated bullies. And cheaters. He wanted life to be fair."

"He seemed like a real nice guy, Thaddeus. He's with God, no bullies there, no cheaters."

"He had these eyes, dark, sad eyes. I can't believe I'm never going to see them again."

"Your eyes are just like his." He placed a steadying hand on Thaddeus's shoulder. "And David's got them, too."

"I tried to make him happy, you know, I tried and I tried."

"Look at what you've done with your life, man. He must have been so proud."

"You think?" said Thaddeus. He eked out the smile of a man who never really expected things to go his way. "Well, I guess that's that." Or maybe he said, Oh well, or So it goes, fuck me with a chain saw. Whatever he said, there was some little verbal flag of surrender before he could take the advice that Jennings had offered and then he let it out, yes he did, he let it all out, and Jennings gathered him in and held him securely as Thaddeus wept, sobbing out the grief that came

from the very core of him, a grief and an aloneness that had
no beginning and no end.

———

At which point, Mees was gone and I could no longer bear being in the
bed I had briefly shared with him. I made my way to the sofa.
The chilly satin upholstery came as a small relief. As I drifted
off, I thought, *This isn't even a sofa; it's a fucking love seat.*

CHAPTER 25

Places, Everyone!

Jennings and Muriel along with Jewel and Henry were in their small yellow house, one chimney, one bath. Thaddeus and his family were in the mansion, five chimneys, six baths. Jennings left a basket of apples from the mini-orchard on the porch of the big house. Muriel, in her worn jeans and flowing Indian blouses, scoured forest and field for little objects with which to decorate cakes for a local baker, her hair pinned up in those Princess Leia buns that look like earphones. Every now and then she'd leave one of the bakery's concoctions in the foyer of the main house, which made Grace furious, mainly because she didn't want Emma to have cake. Thaddeus was not so lost in his fraternal fantasies to fail to notice that when an old locust tree uprooted after a soaking rain and took off a portion of porch as it fell, it was Jennings and Henry who dragged the tree away and cut it into lengths so it could season and be used in the future for fence posts.

About three months after Sam's death, in the raw snowy week around Passover and Easter, Muriel and Jewel came to Orkney's front door. They both wore pink puffy ski jackets and gray caps bearing the name of Jennings's company, Windsor Asbestos Solutions. Muriel's old, temperamental Taurus was behind them, trembling as it idled, with exhaust pouring out of the tailpipe like water out of a fire hose.

"Hey, gang, what's up?" Thaddeus said. Though he was working on the outline for a new script, he did his best to sound welcoming.

"We've come to wash your feet," Muriel said. She was smiling radiantly. Her eyelashes glistened with melting snow. Jewel was holding a woven wicker basket like the one Muriel carried in the summer when she walked the property gathering wildflowers. Today the basket contained several individually wrapped baby wipes.

"My feet?" Thaddeus said, embarrassed and laughing.

Muriel glanced at Jewel, who took one of the baby wipes out of her basket and handed it to her mother while saying, "Jesus said I have washed your feet. . . ." She stopped for a moment and Muriel patted her arm. "So you should wash one another's feet. I made—"

"Set," said Muriel.

"I set an example—"

"Set *you* an example," said Muriel.

". . . that you should do as I have done for you."

"Perfect, sweet pea, perfect," said Muriel. Then, to Thaddeus, "May we come in?"

On the advice of one of Jennings's old friends, a former prison guard and now a deputy sheriff, both Jennings and Muriel had been ordained as ministers in what seemed to me a somewhat dubious religious order called I, John Charismatic Church of the Redeemer, and now the two of them held services in the house on Wednesday nights and Sunday mornings.

It was enough to have the yellow house classified as a place of worship and just that week it had been taken off Leyden's tax rolls. Today they were making the rounds washing feet, as were the other fourteen members of their church. Jewel seemed a little embarrassed, but Muriel was serene. Now that she and Jennings no longer had the expense of real estate taxes to worry about, they had something that Thaddeus and Grace did not—they lived in a house they could easily afford.

CHAPTER 26

Fresh Deck, Same Hand, New Jury, Same Verdict

On December 6, I came to work straight from Newark Airport, after having spent the weekend in Orlando. I'd had dinner Saturday night with one of our clients with whom I had a presumed friendship, and Sunday was storming everywhere and my flight was canceled and I couldn't book another one. I ended up at the nearest Hilton, a quick shuttle from the Orlando airport, where I ate room service chicken, watched television, and ended up so lonely and grumpy that I called in for sex, choosing someone virtually at random by Googling "Orlando male escort." The lad they sent over looked to be sixteen years old, though he insisted he was twenty-eight. Nevertheless, I was afraid it was some sort of sting operation and I paid him to go home, after which I ravaged the minibar and then myself.

Monday, when I finally reached the office it was nearly noon. My assistant said that Ken had come by twice looking for me and wanted to see me as soon as I came in. She looked worried. I closed the door behind me and sat at my desk for a few moments, gathering myself. I could feel some unspecified danger, its closeness, its implacability, its mercilessness. It was like being in a dark woods and hearing the snap of a twig.

"Oh, there you are," Ken said, entering my office without knocking, closing the door behind him but without taking his eyes off me. Ken had barely aged. His wife grew stout, his parents died, his children went to college, Europe, rehab, and on to careers, but Ken's face, round and untroubled, remained resistant to the passage of time and to the stresses of our profession. It was like an artist's initial sketch, before the cross-hatching and the shadowing. His hair was an exuberant swirl of kinks, like a black sea with spumes rising from its surface. Today—as was increasingly his habit—he was dressed as if for a weekend on Martha's Vineyard, in faded jeans, loafers, and a souvenir sweatshirt from the High Sierra Music Festival. Ken rarely saw the public. As AA grew, Ken conducted most of his business over the phone or on his laptop. Over the past year or so, I had wondered if Ken's disengagement from the day-to-day operations of the company was a sign that he was going to retire. I worried over the prospect of losing my connection to the man who valued what I turned out to be good at—writing concise, upbeat reports for our investors, maintaining my faux friendships, and spotting what was strong and what was weak in any company we might invest in. I worried that without Ken I might not be able to work at my profession, and as he sat opposite me, languidly scratching his belly underneath his sweatshirt, I felt an overpowering wave of sorrow, and regret over my foolishness.

But Ken hadn't come to fire me or even to warn me. Instead, he was offering me a chance to get out of New York for a while. He wondered if I would consider relocating to San Francisco for a year or two, and I agreed to do so before he could even fully explain the purpose of the move, which was actually occasioned by our taking a big loss on IBM and a smaller—but still significant—loss on AOL. Ken was still investing conservatively but it was starting to hurt us.

Ken wasn't beguiled by the dot-com bubble when everything connected to the internet or to wireless communication was treated as if it cured cancer or enabled time travel. Such was the finale of the twentieth century, and the end of that exuberance was not in sight. Ken was willing to put some of the firm's money into a start-up, if the right opportunity came along. Nearly all of AA's clients were based in New York, the Carolinas, or Florida, and they viewed the rise of Silicon Valley as if it were taking place in a foreign country. I was going to generate a bimonthly newsletter called "The View from the West," which would be, in Ken's words, "sent to our clients free of charge," which nearly made me laugh since nothing we did was gratis. Everything was in the service of maximizing our take, which was fine with me—our clients only cared about maximizing *their* take.

Other than business trips and an occasional holiday abroad, I had been living in New York City continuously since graduating college. I had dated about seventy women in that time, changed address five times. I had probably spent a million dollars on restaurant food, and if you were to categorize everything from theater tickets to hand jobs as entertainment, I had spent another million either entertaining myself or relieving myself of a loneliness so deep and so ferocious that I think I would have otherwise gone mad.

In New York, I was known and not known by the same people. Some of the women I dated conversed among themselves and saw "remarkable similarities" in their experience with me. The best I could have hoped for out of those comparisons of notes was their coming to a collective conclusion that I was a Real Gentleman. I certainly wasn't "handsy," as I heard one of my co-workers described. I certainly didn't act as if allowing me to take care of the check or buy the tickets entitled me to intimate contact. If any of the women had expected real physical pleasure or perhaps even a lasting relationship, they may have felt some disappointment and irritation. By and large the women with whom I shared dinners and day trips, visits to museums, botanical gardens, flea markets, street fairs, lectures, readings, plays, concerts, and cozy evenings at home trying out recipes and watching movies were themselves highly desirable, busy and very accomplished—writers, film editors, actresses, lawyers, bankers, journalists—with no pressing need for me or anyone to save or shape their lives. I was quite sure they were as content as I was to enjoy the time we spent together and part friends before anything romantic occurred. I suspected that a few of them had similar agendas to mine, were closeted or otherwise conflicted, and wanted someone of the opposite gender to be seen with at one of New York's innumerable fund-raising dinners. I was a presentable escort to sit with at the table their company purchased to support some worthy cause, such as cancer research or the Central Park Conservancy. My company regularly bought two tables for ten to support the American Heart Association (Adler's father had died at the age of forty-two of heart failure), as well as galas for *The Paris Review,* cystic fibrosis, the Alvin Ailey dance company, and Meals on Wheels, paying as much as $50,000 per table. We at Adler were expected to fill the twenty seats with our spouses or significant others. I have to admit that for those evenings—and there were many of them, many—I took pains to be seen with a woman who was not only accomplished and vivacious, but who had a shot of being the most beautiful woman in the room.

The thing about New York is that when you first move there, it seems like an impossibly immense place with so many lives simultaneously unspooling, so many conflicting realities, that if you don't do anything wildly strange and egregious you can live your life for the most part rather privately. And then one day New York doesn't seem nearly so huge and complex and the thousands upon thousands who passed through your life, people you would in all likelihood never see again, start to appear a second time, and a third—the cabdriver seems familiar, the fellow delivering your take-out lunch calls you by your first name, and Sean Tee, whose ad you saw in *The Village Voice*, comes to your apartment and you both realize he's been there before, the previous time as Billy McDougal.

Wasn't San Francisco the gayest city in the country, possibly the gayest in the world? Home of Harvey Milk, the Castro, a total bacchanal of a Halloween parade that made the one in New York seem discreet. Once, crossing Bleecker Street carrying home in an insulated sack a rotisserie chicken from Jefferson Market, I had to contend with the parade as it rainbowed and glittered by a mere block from my apartment. I waited for a break in the procession of leather and feather and cowboy hats, Tin Men, Glendas, Spocks, and throngs of happy homosexuals who had not bothered to don their gay apparel but just enjoyed strolling through the city streets with twenty thousand of their closest friends, all to the accompaniment of drums and police whistles, tambourines and cheers. Freedom was in the air, freedom and joy and sorrow and survival.

History was passing me by.

I kept my head down, but my face must have betrayed me. A tall parader made even taller in high heels, fishnet stockings, spangled miniskirt, and a headdress spewing feathers stepped out of the parade's flow and touched me on the elbow. A giant, something out of the Bread and Puppet Theater.

"Come on, honey," he said. "Don't be shy. Join the fun."

What drew him to me? I was not the only one watching the parade from the curbside. There were thousands of us along Bleecker Street, fathers with kids riding their shoulders, old gay men wiping away tears, tourists with their cameras. But this towering marcher in a spangled skirt touched *me* with his long blue fingernail.

No thank you, I tried to say, but all I could do was shake my head no. He gave me a look—Really? Are you sure?—and on an impulse I stepped off the curb and fell in behind him, joining the weirdly holy procession, swinging my insulated bag of take-out chicken like a censer. I kept my eyes on my recruiter's back. His dark skin glistened with sweat and glitter. My heart felt as if it were looking for a way out of my chest. I told myself I would take ten steps and then bail, cut through the marchers and go home, but ten steps turned into twenty, and twenty into thirty, and before I could peel away I had walked from Tenth Street to Perry on the gushing artery of Bleecker Street. At last, I said goodbye to the man in front of me with a quick light tap on his shoulder blade and cut a pathway through the parade, muttering my excuses as I made my way onto the sidewalk.

And so, I moved to San Francisco, into a lovely house in Pacific Heights, on Jackson Street, right across from Alta Plaza Park.

The house was rented and furnished for me by a company called Exec-locate.

It didn't take me long to realize I would be no freer in California than I had been in Michigan, or New York.

In fact, the crushing realization was almost immediate. I'd been met at my new place by two men from Exec-locate, two guys about ten years my junior, one of whom looked as if he was torn between becoming a pirate or a personal trainer, the other dressed like a banker, self-contained and opaque in his London tailoring and wire-rim glasses. They dropped by to see if everything was to my liking and to discuss changes I might want. It was mine for the asking, from furniture to artwork to yanking out the vinca ground cover in the back garden and replacing it with a medley of wild grasses. There was, however, nothing I cared to modify, not at that point; I felt about the place the way I felt about the nice hotels AA booked for me, content to relax and do my work in the posh anonymity of the Royal This or the Palace That. Failing to interest me in redecorating my news digs, the two men wanted to inform me about all the goods and services and events in my new neighborhood. I wasn't sure if they were running a gaydar test, or if they flat-out assumed I was gay. Some of their welcome to the neighborhood suggestions were boilerplate—best place for smoothies, jogging paths, health clubs, sushi—but quite a few were pointedly on the lavender side of the street, such as the Harvey Milk Bar, which hosted the West Coast's premiere karaoke nights every Sunday, a boutique specializing in cowboy attire called Sons of the Pioneers, which the pirate/personal trainer's brother owned, and where I would be given a 20 percent discount, and an upcoming Fight for a Cure march convening at the Transamerica Pyramid the next evening at 6 P.M.

"I'm afraid my marching days are behind me," I said. "Not exactly my thing." I believe my face was dead neutral, but it was as if a sudden wind had blown through my new rooms slamming shut every door. The two men did their best to keep the mood cheerful; they may have thought me a coward, but I was still a customer.

"Well, I was going to say, if you decide to make that march, we're having people over afterward," said the suited one. Upton. His name was Upton Hayes. I wondered if he was named after Upton Sinclair, who had run for governor in California sixty years before. Thaddeus's parents had once sold Upton Sinclair's entire Lanny Budd series to Studs Terkel, who gave their store a nice mention on his radio show the next day. But I didn't ask Upton about his name. I had lost the right to ask any questions by saying the AIDS march was "not really my thing." I had surrendered my right to say anything. I wanted them both to leave. I wanted to be alone. And there, at last, we had some real reciprocity going. They, too, wanted me to be alone.

CHAPTER 27

California Street

Time passed in San Francisco. Much happened, little changed. The team Adler had assembled to run the West Coast AA was a much more agreeable group than the New York office. If my San Francisco colleagues were into titty bars and coke, they kept it to themselves, or at least they kept it from me. We were on California Street, in the Bank of America building. Our office was spare and stylish. We all had computers, of course, and there were television sets in two of the corners, one playing CNN, the other tuned to CNBC, but if you wandered in you might think we were an architecture firm, or maybe a think tank. Bare floors, Stickley furniture. There were but eight of us, plus a steady stream of temps, and two interns. We were diverse, one guy from Singapore, one from Jaipur, a gay woman from Des Moines, a wheelchair-bound math genius from Bogotá. Average age thirty-two, average vibe arty. In fact, the only one of us who appeared to have stepped out of the past and fit the description of a finance guy from the *Man in the Gray Flannel Suit* 1950s was me, the gentile from Michigan, which I eventually found amusing, in a private, bitter way, since my self-presentation was at its core an impersonation. As it happened—I don't know why I couldn't have predicted this—the farther I lived from Thaddeus, the more he occupied my thoughts, and now added to the familiar obsessions over what is he doing, what is he wearing, eating, saying, laughing about, thinking, there was another litany, this one based purely on worry. I fretted over his actual safety, his health, his mental stability, as if by depriving him of my proximity I had somehow cast him into imminent danger of cracking up.

Thaddeus and I emailed each other, and he told me he had been campaigning for his mother to move east, but that so far she was showing only irritation at the suggestion. "I'm not going to be some little widow taking care of her grandchildren," Libby had said, but Thaddeus persisted. I doubt he really wanted her to be nearer to him, much less live at Orkney, but he was duty bound to try. And then, of course, of course, a thousand times of course, there was his need to be admired, especially by Libby, the alpha and omega of his desire to please. And yet: everything he had ever done to make himself admirable to her had failed, often miserably. His whirling arms and legs as he danced for Libby and Sam at the dining table, leaving his food to grow cold on the plate, led not to the eventual laughter he had hoped for, nor to the lightening of the mood, and certainly not to applause. His performances elicited admonishment and lectures about trying too hard and making a fool of yourself. His declaration of devoting his life to literature was a bone to drop at Sam and Libby's feet, and his sudden success was devalued in his own mind by the suspicion that his parents thought that a talent falling far short of being an author might be perfect for the smart-alecky skills of a movie guy. His hope that Orkney might impress them was soon reduced to a hope that they would limit the disparaging things they said about the house—its isolation, its upkeep, the snobby neighbors, the difficult stairs, the biting wind. Thaddeus's attempt to honor their expired socialist values by giving Jennings's father that yellow house and a few acres had been greeted with tut-tuts from Sam and unmasked fury from Libby. "I assume you know the difference between a big shot and a big idiot?" she declared. And now the truth, the undisclosed truth of Leyden had swallowed Libby's husband whole, had left him to die like an animal on some millionaire's cold floor while the local lumpen dragged their heels in an act of rebellion that was, in Libby's view, as overt as the storming of the Bastille.

The week I'd arrived, Thaddeus offered to come to San Francisco and help me get used to my new city. "We can figure the place out," he said. "It's tough being in a new place, even for a seasoned traveler like you. Lonely, I bet. Are you?" I foolishly said—far, far too quickly—that I was fine and there was no need, and the offer evaporated. Time passed. We rarely spoke on the telephone. After the Bush-Gore election, there was a flurry of calls during the maddening week or so in Florida when it was still undecided which candidate had carried the state. The TV cameras were watching the election officials inspecting the iffy ballots, while throngs of young Republicans in blazers and khakis pounded on the doors, demanding that Florida be called for Bush. The fate of humanity was at stake, though of course we could not know that the winner would con us into war in the Middle East.

"I blame Mrs. Gore for this entire mess," Thaddeus said. It was three in the afternoon in Leyden, noon for me. Foggy and clammy outside, diamond bright and cool in the office. Hearing his voice, I hated San Francisco.

"How is she responsible?" I asked.

"Gore couldn't embrace the Clinton legacy because Tipper is such a hard-charging prude and now we're all going to have this incurious brat in the White House."

Maybe three months after I started in SF, Thaddeus had written me, *Just to let you know, I am steadfastly resisting asking for any more of your—shall we say?—guidance.* Even a relatively innocuous remark like that made me furious—and frightened. Did he not understand what peril he was putting me in? Had he missed the story in the morning paper about the insider-trading fool being perp-walked out of his office on Beaver Street and his partner busted in his showcase home in Greenwich, dragged out in handcuffs while his wife and his two children looked on? But if Thaddeus had missed the story in the Monday newspaper, there would likely be another similar one on Friday, and in case he missed that there would be another soon after. Doing jail time was to some people in my business merely a part of the job's risk, bending the rules was how the alpha males played to win. Of course, as it was in domestic life, most people who cheated on Wall Street got away with it, but whenever I read about somebody getting caught at something as premeditated as a pyramid scheme, or as stupidly spontaneous as revealing privileged information at a bachelor party, my commitment to obeying the law only intensified.

One cloudy cast-iron Tuesday—San Francisco without sun can be tough—I came to the office directly from a tedious breakfast meeting with a man named Michael Tischler. Tischler's company was called PhoneClad, which designed and retailed protective covers for mobile phones. You could get your favorite sports team, your favorite breed of dog, the *Mona Lisa*, the Three Stooges, an Escher-like swirl of spiral staircases, polka dots, Saturn, and on and on. PhoneClad's stock was flat and Adler was considering taking a position in it, but before Ken invested he wanted to be reassured PhoneClad wasn't this year's Tawk. I thought the product was of limited value and since I was paying for breakfast I was blunt with Tischler. "So what do you think is happening here?" I asked. "People buying a phone, that is rational, that makes sense as a sustainable income flow. But people buying smart little jackets for their phones, dressing them up like Barbie dolls? That's where I get a little confused."

Tischler shrugged, feigned nonchalance. He was handsome, with smoochy dark eyes and a cleft chin. "Up to you. People want to protect their investment and for a lot of people out there the phone is a significant investment. You don't see it? Others will. But I'll tell you what, since you're paying for the eggs Benedict, I'll let you know I'm a sprinter not a miler and when Nokia makes me an offer to take over—which they are going to do, by the way—I will sell the company to them, and a lot of smart people are going to get very, very, very rich."

Oh, will they now, I wanted to say. I supposed he was just swaggering to save face, but we both knew he was coloring well outside of the lines to suggest there was an impending takeover of his company. Perhaps I was being hypervigilant, and I was still feeling that excess of caution when, later that day, I opened a long email from Thaddeus.

> *Hey man! I was trying to walk off today's edition of Poor Poor Thaddeus's Desperation and found myself on your corner of the property. Look, I don't want to wave my own*

feelings as if it was a flag everyone is supposed to salute.
But I have to tell you just being there made me realize what
an amazing true blue friend you are. I just totally miss the
hell out of you man if you want to know the honest truth.
I've had easy access to you for a long time and I guess I got
spoiled. You have no idea how many times I've gone onto
the internet to see what it would cost to jump on a plane
and come out to SF to visit you. You're my best friend in this
horribly imperfect world and there is no one in second place.
I totally fucking miss you. . . .

I read this a second time, and a third, and was getting ready
to print it while maintaining what I hoped was a neutral expression in our open-space offices at 555 California. The con-
ference room had a door you could close and the bathrooms
were private, but other than that we were in a hive. Everything
was shared. My face was scalding and when I glanced to check
if I was being watched, I saw that CNN was broadcasting footage of a derailed Amtrak train somewhere alongside the Hudson River.

CHAPTER 28

The Segment

REPORTER: As part of our ongoing series America in Depth, we are taking a look at what some are insisting is the work of one or two mentally unstable individuals, but what others are warning us may be the opening volleys in the next American civil war.

Continue on Amtrak train. Shattered windows. Dented sides.

AMTRAK PASSENGER—MALE, 50S: I heard some of the trains were experiencing attacks, but no I didn't figure it happening to a train I was on. (Gestures half humorously, half helplessly.) I guess that's just how we are, humans, you know. By the time we get things figured out, it's usually too late.

AMTRAK PASSENGER—FEMALE, 30S: I thought it was a landslide. I was on a trek in the Andes a month ago so I guess landslides were on my mind. (Laughs.) I guess I was sort of relieved it was just people throwing rocks. But the people on the train were very upset, even the regulars.

Footage of Amtrak train heading north, following the river,
pulling into the Leyden station. Uniformed Amtrak employees
helping passengers disembark. Passengers have festive air,
expensive luggage, are well-dressed, well-to-do urban types
streaming toward camera. . . .

AMTRAK OFFICIAL (V.O.): The safety and comfort of our
passengers is our number one priority, and we take
these incidents very seriously. It may be the case
that whoever is responsible for the attacks on our
Hudson River line is not aware that our trains are
the property of the United States of America and
acts of violence or vandalism is a federal offense. Be
that as it may, I can promise you this—whoever is
responsible for this will be caught and prosecuted to
the fullest extent of the law.

Shots of damaged Amtrak cars: shattered windows,
dented sides, a completely collapsed roof interior. Amtrak
headquarters, Washington, D.C., middle-aged man in suit
and tie, 1890s-style mustache, muttonchop whiskers.

AMTRAK OFFICIAL: I really don't understand who would
want to do something so cowardly as this. The trains
belong to all Americans. And we love our trains, don't
we? At first, we thought it was just stupid kids, but,
unfortunately, this seems to go a bit deeper. . . .

Shots of river. Sailboats. Swans. Reflected sunset.

REPORTER (V.O.): Historians tell us that the crucial
battles between the British and the colonists during

the American Revolution were over control of the mighty Hudson River.

Shots of Broadway, Leyden, New York—the two-block main street, cute little shops, high-end coffee house, shoppers enjoying a beautiful Saturday afternoon.

REPORTER (V.O.): But in this Hudson River town, one hundred miles from Midtown Manhattan, there has been a second battle for the Hudson River, largely unseen, unheralded, and unreported.

Shot of storefront: the Rural Gourmet, with a huge X made of tape, holding in the shattered storefront window.

Shot of charred remains of a gazebo.

Shot of dark green Jaguar, pummeled by cement blocks, the hood collapsed, the windshield destroyed.

Shot of white stone driveway leading to an estate. An immense pile of shattered cement blocks has been dumped in front of the iron gate.

REPORTER: And it's not just the trains coming in and out of this once bucolic community that have come under attack.

Shot of trailer park: proliferation of signs printed to look like American flags, with the word Jobs! *superimposed over the stars and stripes.*

Shot of cloverleaf cul-de-sac lined with six-room ranch-style homes, lawn signs: Jobs! and Cement Plant = Rock-Solid

Jobs. One handmade sign shows a serpent coiled on a hard hat and ready to strike: Don't Effing Tread on Me.

Shot of reporter—Cal Brunswick—telegenic in his blue blazer suit, youthful smile, standing in front of a Huguenot stone house across from the Leyden cemetery.

REPORTER: This house, known locally as the DeWilde Tavern, was first constructed in 1721 and is now the unofficial headquarters of Windsor County Greenwatch, an organization that has been fighting the construction of a cement plant in their community since plans were first announced five years ago.

The reporter sits with Latham Winters, a praying mantis of a man, in the Greenwatch offices—low ceilings, cast-off furniture, not a penny wasted. Gorgeous photos of the river everywhere—sunsets, waterfowl, sailboats, reflections. . . .

WINTERS: I think it comes down to this—why are we here, and what is our responsibility? Are we here to put up satellite dishes and feed our own faces, or are we here as custodians to unparalleled and irreplaceable natural wonders?

Shot of Amtrak train running alongside the river. As it nears the Leyden station, the train whistle emits a series of sonic blasts.

The blasts are slowly replaced by the music of birdsong and the bucolic sight of a man strolling through high grass. A hazy smudge of mountains in the background, the silvery flash of the river. The reporter and a couple of bounding dogs follow along—and the unseen camera crew.

REPORTER (V.O.): Some residents find themselves caught in the middle of a fight over historic preservation and economic growth. I spoke with Thaddeus Kaufman, a riverfront dweller for the past twenty years.

Shot of Thaddeus Kaufman—in his late 40s, maybe early 50s; graying hair. He wears jeans, a Yankees baseball cap, a pair of horn-rimmed glasses dangling from a colorful eyeglass cord.

THADDEUS KAUFMAN: I see it from both sides. My wife and I—she's an amazing painter—moved up here because of the natural beauty. But we have a lot of friends who would love to see that cement plant and there's no question but that its existence would be something of an eyesore. But you have to ask yourself—does an eyesore outweigh giving people decent jobs? I love the river and I love the people of this town and what I really would like to see is for everyone to get what they want.

Thaddeus Kaufman crouches, scratching a dog behind the ears.

Shot of Thaddeus Kaufman walking back toward his house, a large Hudson River mansion with one of its shutters dangling and a pile of roofing shingles standing on a pallet on the front lawn.

REPORTER (V.O.): Later, I had a chance to ask Thaddeus if his house or land had been the target of any of the recent attacks. He shook his head and waved off the question, but he did say that he had taken steps to ensure his family's safety. This is Cal Brunswick reporting from Leyden, New York.

CHAPTER 29

About Face

By the time the segment was over and the ad for Lipitor was running, I was standing at the center of the office with tears streaming down my face. When I realized I might be making a spectacle of myself, I reversed my steps and retreated to my work area, dabbing at my eyes with the heels of my hands, doing my best to regain my composure.

A few moments later, Stephanie Buchsbaum was standing before me, her eyes calm and kind behind her squared-off black and turquoise eyeglasses. Stephanie was Midwestern—Des Moines—and knew how to express and perform concern while maintaining strict personal boundaries. "Hanging in there, Kip?" she asked.

"Ah," I said, with a wave of my hand. "Aging parents."

As soon as she left, I reached for my phone. I listened for a moment to the dial tone and took a deep, steadying breath. Just as receding floodwaters can reveal a radically altered landscape, the intricate network of barricades and blind alleys with which I had for virtually my entire life hidden my nature had been up-ended by the shock of seeing Thaddeus on TV, and I knew with a certainty that shared a border with mania that today was the day and this was the hour, the minute, and the moment I would say to Thaddeus what I had been thus far unable to say. I dialed the first digit of his number, the second, the third, and then I hung up the phone, no more able to make that call than I was twenty minutes ago, twenty months ago, or twenty years ago.

Make the call, you coward, make the call. And yet I waited. I was used to calling myself names. Self-loathing barely fazed; I had self-loathing for breakfast. I picked the phone up again. Put it down. Waited to get back to my apartment. Tried to make the call from there, a little vodka, a little Verdi to ease things along. Failed. Almost tried it again the next night, but had forgotten to factor in the three-hour time difference, and hung up mid-dial. A month passed. I tried to force myself to make the call. I couldn't do it. I couldn't do it drunk and I couldn't do it sober. A year passed. Ken persuaded me to stay on in the Bay Area. The Twin Towers had been turned into a crematorium. I was more than glad to stay where I was. Now that I wasn't calling Thaddeus, I couldn't help noticing that he wasn't calling me. It made me wonder if I'd been supplying all of the fuel for our friendship all along. We'd had a few jokey emails, but no conversation. When I had to go to New York, either to meet with the team, or deal with my sublet apartment, I didn't try to fit in a dinner with Thaddeus, or even call him. You'd think obsession would simply wither and die, but you'd be wrong. Hopeless love thrives in silence and darkness. Silence and darkness are its food and water, its soldier's joy.

There was work, of course, and often work helped. While many in the business succumbed to panic trading after 9/11, AA had kept its powder dry and now a year later we were in better shape than ever. Feeling flush and on top of his game, Ken was looking to make a much larger investment than had been his long-standing strategy up until now, and he was soliciting all of us for ideas. To my annoyance, Ken was still interested in PhoneClad, a company I found absurd, run by that hot-air factory Michael Tischler. Tischler had already told me Nokia was one of its suitors, but now there seemed to be others.

And then, on October 9, 2002, at 3:15 Pacific Daylight Saving Time my intern buzzed through to tell me that Thaddeus Kaufman was on the line.

CHAPTER 30

Seconal

I knew from the moment he said hello that he was suffering, though he made every effort to sound calm, even a little remote. "How are you, Kip? How's San Francisco?" San Francisco was okay. "Good. Good good good. Sorry to call you at the office." He ought not to worry about things like that. "Right. Right." And what about you? I asked. And that's when he got around to telling me. Libby was dead.

"She took her own life," he said. Here, he pressed on, but in a sideways direction, reverting to literary references—Camus insisting that suicide was the only philosophical question worth perusing, Woolf filling her pockets with stones, the powder burns left on Hemingway, Plath turning her kitchen into her own private Auschwitz, the whole condolence card catalog of writers ending their life. When I asked him what had happened, meaning, of course, how did she accomplish the end, he fell silent for a moment, and another moment after that, and another.

"Sleeping pills," he finally said. "They found her there, in fucking Four Freedoms, right on the floor. But the little pharmacy bottle—what are those things called? It's not a bottle.

It has a name. The little amber plastic . . . Well, whatever. But what is it called? It's driving me crazy. You don't call it a bottle. Oh, never mind. It was in her hand. She wanted everyone to know. My guess is she was trying to make sure there was no autopsy. She really didn't want to be cut open. That's Mom for you, right? Very private to the end. A closed book. A locked door. You knew her. Isn't that how you saw her? Or did I just somehow miss the whole thing?"

"Oh, Thaddeus . . ."

"No, it's okay. It was what she wanted. She didn't suffer, that's what I'm telling myself. The thing about sleeping pills is if you don't fuck it up, it's a pretty good way to go. And she didn't fuck it up. She did a good job. And if you're that un- happy? Who's to argue? I guess she didn't have anything to look forward to. And with Dad gone . . . I guess she was done. She was completely done."

What about her son? Did she not have grandchildren? Was her situation really so desperate? Could she not put food on her table and a roof over her head? But of course I could not, would not, would never say these things to Thaddeus. "When did this happen?" I asked.

"Saturday night."

"Saturday night?"

"I'm just now finding out about it, Kip. It took this long. They found her Monday morning. Someone peeked in and saw her feet and then they came back a little later and saw them again, and put it together and called the police. I don't know anyone who knows her and no one who knows her knows me. She brought a note with her to the fucking store. Instructions about what to do with her. Which was to bring her body to this place called Chicagoland Cremation Society. Which I know all about because she was really upset that we had Dad cremated out here. Which was her decision, too, mainly because of the expense and the incredible hassle of shipping his body back to Chicago. She sent me a copy of the contract they'd signed with the place. It was all prepaid. She even underlined the part about the urn. Mom was very urn-est about things like that. About not wasting hard-urned money."

He was silent, either admonishing himself for making a joke about it or waiting for me to laugh.

"And the other thing she brought with her was a three-by-five card with my name on it and the word *son*. No address, no phone number, nothing. Just *son*. The word. Not even my whole fucking name. The police were actually conscientious about it and looked for me. They tried a bunch of Kaufmans in Chicago, and at one point they even tried New York. They even went to Mom's apartment to see if they could figure out who this mysterious son was and where he lived. It was insane. And you want to know how they finally found me? My parents—this sort of kills me—there was a videotape of *Hostages* propped up on the bookshelf, very prominently, apparently. As if it were a book and I was the featured author. Anyhow, it made one of the cops curious and she picked it up and read all the credits and saw my name and that was actually the first real lead. She called Fox but of course no one who was there when *Hostages* came out is still around. But they told the cop she could check with the Writers Guild, which she did, and of course I'm pretty much a dead letter at the guild, but it is a union, and therefore capable of human decency, so whoever took the call said they'd do a little poking around and they found Josh's number, my old agent, who knew where I lived, and the rest, as they say, is show business history."

"So now what happens?" I asked.

"I go to Chicago. And then I don't know. I can't figure it out. When Dad died, my mother handled everything. I don't know what I'm supposed to do. I feel like asking around but it's so embarrassing to ask *Hey, what are you supposed to do when your mother dies?* See to her cremation, I guess. And I suppose there's a will. And the apartment. The store."

"Is everyone going with you?"

"No, no. No. David's in school, and Emma just had her appendix taken out, speaking of timing. Grace is staying with her."

"I'll meet you in Chicago."

"It's okay."

"Thaddeus, come on. You're not doing this alone."

Silence.

"Really?" he said at last. "Are you sure? Do you have the time?"

"Of course."

The line was silent again. And in that silence I was able somehow to think for a moment or two that he believed what I believed—which is that each of us, whether we know it or not, is allotted one person who loves us without question, without reason, without recourse, and with nothing to gain, and for him, for Thaddeus, for my poor broken-hearted friend, that person was me. "I knew this would happen," he finally said, through tears. "I knew if I talked to you, it would all come busting loose."

———

I left early the next morning. I wanted to be on the first plane out of SFO, but we had to wait on the tarmac for the early morning fog to burn off. These delays normally made me sick with impatience, but this day I was glad to have the extra time. I had brought my PhoneClad paperwork with me, and I was in the middle of composing a long memo to Ken about the company. I'd had a couple more meetings with Michael Tischler, and the sense of his arrogance and untruthfulness I'd gleaned during our initial breakfast had deepened. I thought he was basically a snake-oil salesman and I also was convinced that PhoneClad itself was fated for Chapter 11. Nevertheless, my dislike for the man and my skepticism about the durability of his business were offset by the knowledge that there was definite interest in acquiring PhoneClad, in which case there was real money to be pocketed. Ken was eager to make a decision.

We had another variable to factor in: George Bush's team had gotten their resolution before Congress, one that would give the president the right to bomb the hell out of Iraq and this was the day the resolution was coming up for a vote. Hans Blix and the U.N. inspectors were still looking around Iraq in search of evidence that Sadaam Hussein was hiding his weapons of mass destruction, but everyone knew it was just a matter of time before we went to war with or without the evidence.

I had offered to meet Thaddeus in Hyde Park at his parents' apartment on Ellis Avenue, but he didn't have the key. I suggested perhaps then we could meet at the bookshop but he didn't have the key to Four Freedoms, either. Perhaps then his parents' lawyer? He didn't know the name of their lawyer, and wasn't sure they had had one. He only had the phone numbers of a couple of survivors of Sam and Libby's old circle of friends. Illness, death, Florida, bitter disagreements about social issues such as feminism, gay rights, and legalization of marijuana, as well as the ferocious quarrels about international issues like who to support in a border conflict between India and China, the role of violence in the struggle against apartheid, the end of communism in Russia, the bombing of Serbia, and the war in Afghanistan had all but obliterated the old bunch, and the few people Thaddeus was able to reach sounded surprised but not acutely distraught over the news of Libby's death. Whichever way he turned, Thaddeus was met with indifference. It was as if his parents were strangers and their deaths were not really his business. As he was in life, so he remained in death: excluded.

He reserved adjoining rooms at the Palmer House, the hotel where Grace was clerking when he first met her in 1976. She had sneaked them into an unoccupied room, and it had been Thaddeus's first time in a fancy hotel. It had seemed like a palace of unsurpassable grandeur—the Moorish lobby, the uniformed bellmen, the Egyptian cotton sheets, the deveined shrimp, the place was his undoing. He remembered that afternoon the way an addict recalls that first inner warmth, the sweet syrupy pleasure. The passion of being with Grace melded with the spacious bed, the immense towels, the inlay, the gold leaf, the sconces.

I had over the years heard so much from him about this hotel, which continued to exist in Thaddeus's mind as the pinnacle of luxury, despite his having stayed in far pricier places during his years working in the movie business. Perhaps the place had fallen on hard times, but it seemed ordinary and just a little shabby to me—the carpets worn, no bellmen in sight, people in shirtsleeves and cargo shorts milling around the lobby, the check-in desk understaffed, a smell of disinfectant in the air, a coffee urn stuck in a corner next to a tower of disposable cups, and the announcement board welcoming the Great Lakes Payday Loan Association.

Thaddeus had paid for my room and was waiting for me by the elevators when I reached the fifteenth floor. He looked the way you look when you have flown eight hundred miles a few hours after learning your mother has died from a deliberate overdose of sleeping pills—frightened, disheveled, maybe a bit drunk. He had the eyes of a spooked horse, and he needed a shave.

He took my carry-on from me and reached for my briefcase, too, but I held on to it.

"Top secret?" he asked.

"Work," I said. "Boring. Look, you don't have to be strong or anything. This is a total nightmare. I know Clinton ruined this forever, but I actually *do* feel your pain."

"It's okay."

"No, it's not. It's not." I stood in the doorway of my unlit room. "It's not okay at all."

"Are you ever moving back to New York?" he asked.

"I guess. Not sure exactly when. Soon, I suppose."

"Some people are afraid of New York now. Prices have gone way up in Windsor County, so many people wanting to leave the city."

"I like California. But I miss New York." I thought I might say I miss you, but I let it pass.

"I almost wished I was there when it happened," Thaddeus said. "Stupid, I know. But just to be a part of something. Something to sink my teeth into. Maybe do some good. Save someone, or help someone. Give blood. Sweep up the mess. Just for a while to be part of something bigger."

"Well, it was big all right."

"Those men used the Hudson River to navigate their way from Boston to the Twin Towers and they flew right past Orkney." He looked wistful, like a child fantasizing some gaudy act of heroism. It seemed ridiculous to me. Who would want to be close to that catastrophe? He quickly changed the subject. "Hey, you probably want to freshen up, as my mother used to say. And I'm going to call home and see how Emma's doing. Poor Emma. She was pretty wiped out but she really wanted to come here with me. She's completely bedridden and in pain but she was so worried about me."

"She's a great kid."

"The best. So kind, so good, such a beautiful soul. Hey, did I even remember to thank you for being here, Kip? You're true blue, man. *Friend* seems like such a meager word. And so does *grateful.* Where would I be without you, Kip? Where in the fuck would I be?"

CHAPTER 31

Naked Lunch

So far, Thaddeus's planning had not extended beyond coming to Chicago and booking two rooms at a hotel. Without a key to his parents' apartment—as he had lacked since the night Sam and Libby came home to find sixteen-year-old Thaddeus playing host to about thirty friends from Hyde Park High—and without the keys to Four Freedoms—which he wasn't given even when he worked there—his only access to his mother's life was the name of the cremation society. In truth, there were few things I enjoyed as much as making myself useful to Thaddeus, and after I took a quick shower I found the phone number for the cremation society, as well as their address, and learned they were open until 7 P.M. From the cremators, I was also able to get the name and address of Libby's attorney.

Jill Zolitor answered her own phone, in a sour voice, as if she were getting a lot of crank calls and hang-ups. I explained to her that I was calling about Libby Kaufman and I was in town with her son. "Her son?" she said, a sine wave of incredulity in her tone. "Well, let's see now, let us see, let us see," she went on, in that familiar way so many lawyers have of never saying in three words what can be expressed in twenty. "All right. Here we go. If you can . . . You say you're close by. Oh, this heat, this heat, this crazy October heat. Let me see. Let me . . . Okay. If you can be here at four thirty. Please bring proper ID. You understand, of course. I have a copy of your mother's will—"

I was being driven to such distraction by her prattling on that I didn't even bother to remind her that we weren't talking about *my* mother.

". . . and I have other things you will want, I mean that you will be, um, um, interested in. Specifically, here we are talking about keys to the apartment on Ellis Avenue and a set of keys to, uh, uh, the bookstore. And we also have here a copy of your mother's will, which I . . . which you know, but it bears repeating . . . Um, can you wait, can you hold on for a moment, there's someone at the door. . . ."

Armed with the information I had collected in a mere five minutes, I knocked on Thaddeus's door. "It's unlocked," he called out. "I'm just getting out of the shower."

I let myself in. His suitcase was open on the bed. A little can of peanuts and an open beer were on the bedside table. Lemon-scented steam wafted through the open bathroom door. I sat in the room's only chair as Thaddeus emerged from his shower, naked, towel-drying his hair. Turkish slippers of inky hair under his arms, a bit of eczema on one of his elbows. There was no place on earth I would have rather been than in that room.

"Are you okay?" Thaddeus asked me, continuing to vigorously dry his hair. His flesh jiggled slightly. His genitals pitched left and right. His dick—hello!—was broad and sturdy, a kind of proletarian genital, the glans a hard hat, the nut sack a lunch pail. He cupped his balls, flipped them up, and let them drop, as if they were comatose and he needed to revive them.

Why was he doing this to me? I remembered Morris's cautionary words: *He will destroy you, Kip. He will. He might not want to. But he will. He will destroy you.*

And yet. I was not a child, I was not a boy, I was a man, a grown unhappy man, and I thought: fuck this. If he wants to put on a little show, I will be a very willing audience. I considered putting my hands on him. For all I knew, he was inviting me to do so. He might have—must have—sensed my interest. He looked down at himself.

"Maybe if I had a much bigger dick I wouldn't have ever needed such a big house," he said.

"You're fine," I said. "Happy medium and all that."

"Based on? Oh right, all those afternoons in the Downtown Athletic Club locker room, with all the other masters of the universe changing into their squash shorts."

I was tempted. Certain phrases presented themselves, such as I've seen more dicks than I've seen sitcoms. I had built a penitentiary made brick by brick and bar by bar of pure unadulterated silence and I knew how to keep order in it, but suddenly a bit of truth escaped and I blurted out, "Let's not forget that that thing has been in my mouth."

Oh! The leap, the terrifying sensation of everything familiar suddenly gone. I grinned and wagged my finger at Thaddeus, but it might have been—must have been—too late. He was giving me one of those *what have we here?* looks.

But then, his gaze was not quite so inquisitive. His eyes softened. "Ah," he said, "so you remember that."

"Sure," I said. "Of course."

"I was really all over the map those days, wasn't I?"

"I wasn't sure you'd even remember it."

He laughed. "These things do blur, that's true."

"I guess you wanted everyone to love you," I said.

"Yeah. I suppose."

"I remember it," I said.

"It's not as if I forgot all about it," he said.

I went to the window and gazed out over Grant Park. The unseasonable heat hadn't tempted anyone out to enjoy the greenery and the lake view except for one lone bicyclist pedaling through on a silver racing bike, looking like a medieval knight with his long hair flowing from the back and sides of his safety helmet. He had a rainbow flag fixed to the back of his seat. How could he be so free of fear and shame? It made me frightened for him. What if he were set upon by teenagers who needed to prove their masculinity by kicking the shit out of a fag? What if his boss saw him, or his neighbor, or his sister, or his father? I kept my back to Thaddeus. I heard the minibar open, and the tinkle of all the miniature bottles of booze inside. The bicyclist pedaled out of sight. The sky was lowering and the choppy gray and white waves made Lake Michigan look like the runway in a cluster-bombed airport. I finally dared to turn around. Thaddeus had put on his pants. He was still barefoot and without a shirt. He looked like a middle-aged man who ate what he wanted and exercised when he damn well felt like it. For this I had thrown away half of my life? For this? For him? For Thaddeus Kaufman?

Short answer: yes, if it pleases the Court. Further elucidation, Your Honor: I'd do it all again.

"I need to call home," he announced, as if I required more proof that I had wasted my life.

He sat on the edge of the bed and dialed out on the landline. I pointed to myself and then gestured toward the door, raising my eyebrows to indicate my willingness to leave and give him some privacy, but he shook his head no, and made a face that meant Don't be ridiculous.

And here is what I heard.

"Ah, so you're home. (*Pause.*) No, I wasn't. I'm just saying you're home. (*Pause.*) I realize that. It's not as if I wish I were here. (*Pause.*) Yes, well, my understanding was that they kind of waive visiting hours for parents when it's a sick kid. (*Long pause.*) Okay, fine. It's fine. Just—how is she? (*Pause.*) Seriously? She just had her appendix yanked out of her and you're talking about her weight? (*Pause.*) What I'm trying to say—(*Pause.*) No you don't, you don't know what I'm trying to say. (*Pause.*) Fine, fruits and vegetables are good for everyone. But high fiber doesn't prevent appendicitis. (*Pause.*) But where did you read it? (*Pause.*) *Prevention* magazine is not a reliable source. It's one of those cider-vinegar-and-organic-honey-cures-cancer magazines. This is our daughter, for crying out loud. And she's just been through hell. I'm not going to let some nut bar from the Rodale Press advise us on what's best for her. (*Pause.*) Anyhow, she's recuperating so that's good. So can we let her eat whatever she wants? At least for now? And we can worry about her weight some other time. Or, preferably, stop worrying about her weight starting now? (*Pause.*) Okay, sure. See who it is."

He stood up, moved the phone away from his reddened ear, and paced. He glanced at me apologetically a couple of times, until it became clear that whether or not someone had called in on Grace's other line or was or was not knocking on Orkney's door, Grace had no intention of continuing talking to Thaddeus. "Oh come on," he muttered, and very carefully placed the receiver back in its cradle.

"Everything okay?" I asked. I had to say something.

"I don't know," he said, glancing at me and then looking away. I could feel his embarrassment; his wife had for all intents and purposes hung up on him. He was back to the minibar, this time pulling out two little bottles of Smirnoff. "A voice inside me tells me this is what I must do to get through today."

"I'll join you."

"Thank you, my brother. Vodka okay?"

"Whatever. Maybe a whiskey?"

He crouched before the minibar, pulled out a little squared-off bottle of Jack Daniel's. He handed it to me, we clinked bottles, guzzled.

"Tell me something," he said.

"Like what?"

"Anything. Get my mind off of . . . all this shit."

"You're a good person," I said. "Better than you think."

He nodded, as if I'd said, Hey, do you think it might rain? "Back at you, Kip," he casually said. He opened his second Smirnoff.

"We should go," I said. "I found Libby's lawyer and her office is just a couple of blocks from here. She said she would see us right away."

"How'd you find her?"

"From the cremation people." I checked my watch. "We should go now. She has keys to the apartment and the store, and she has your mom's will."

CHAPTER 32

Jackson and Wabash

Jill Zolitor's office was in a shabby, narrow building in the Loop, wedged between a vacant shoe store and a defunct cafeteria. It took only a few minutes to walk from the hotel but the air was dense and hot and Thaddeus and I were perspiring as we pushed our way into the empty lobby, lit by two flickering fluorescents. The building had but one elevator and we stood before its banged-up doors listening to the Marley's Ghost rattle of chains as it made its way down to the lobby.

"What is that smell?" Thaddeus asked.

"Wet newspaper? Mildew? Failure?"

"It's not failure," he said. "That's one smell I'd recognize. Hey, wouldn't it be weird if today's the day I learn my parents were sitting on a boatload of cash?"

"What are the odds?"

"Very long, my brother. Very long indeed."

The door to Zolitor's office was locked. I rapped against the milk glass. Thaddeus looked grim, as if preparing for bad news, though I couldn't imagine what he might be worried about—hadn't the worst already occurred?

"Who's there?" a porous, smoky voice called out.

"It's Thaddeus Kaufman," I said.

"Oh, okay, okay." The scrape of chair legs, the sound of a desk drawer being shut, the shuffle of feet. Zolitor was an extensive woman in her late forties, tall and broad. Her right ankle was wrapped in a compression bandage. Though her face was heavy, her features were sharp, like a wicked jack-o'-lantern.

"Oh, there's two of you," she said, warily.

"Yes, I'm Christopher Woods," I said. "I contacted you? And this is Thaddeus Kaufman."

She frowned, looked us over, and evidently found us both harmless enough to allow in. Her office was small. Glass-front bookshelves, metal filing cabinets, a wrinkled poster of a unicorn leaping over a rainbow. Her one window was open and a large fan was facing out, removing cigarette smoke from her office. She seated herself in a high-backed leather chair—the only place to sit.

"Sorry. I killed my ankle over the weekend and I'm on painkillers. Tell me again—which one of you is Thaddeus Kaufman?" she asked.

"I am," Thaddeus said.

"I'm very sorry for your loss, Mr. Kaufman. I didn't know your mother very well, but she seemed like very special people. This world isn't always hospitable to special people." She made a *what are you gonna do* gesture.

"May I ask how long you were the Kaufmans' attorney?" I said.

She had a portable TV on her desk, tuned to C-SPAN. The House of Representatives was voting on the Iraq resolution and the yeas were comfortably ahead.

"Now, that's an interesting story," Zolitor said, brightening at the question, glancing at the TV and then back at us. "Libby and I met . . . hmm. Give me a sec and I can actually give you an exact date." She yanked open a desk drawer, pulled out a calendar, turned the pages. "Oh, here it is. Good thing I wrote it down. There's nothing like good old pen and paper. I would have guessed January. And you want to know why? Because I remember the snow. Big storm. Two feet of snow. The wet kind. The backbreaking kind. But here it is. It was April. That's Chicago for you. Hot summer days in the middle of October and snow in the springtime. April second. Right in the shop, Four Freedoms. My apartment is only a block away, but it was my first time in." She made a wave, as if the busyness of her life swirled directly above her head. "I had recently inherited my brother's collection of Samuel Clemens, who wrote, as you know, under the name Mark Twain. A nautical term. Well, be that as it may . . ."

She cut her eyes toward me, hearing me sigh. She wasn't billing by the quarter hour but nevertheless she was undeterred and rambled on—Libby came to her apartment, looked at the books, made an offer, they talked, hit it off, and on and on, the details of their interaction both trivial and horrifying, overflowing with detail that had no purpose or meaning except that the story would eventually culminate in a broken-hearted woman of seventy-four swallowing sleeping pills in her place of business.

The phone rang and the lawyer grabbed it. "Jill Zolitor's office. Oh! Look, I'm going to have to call you back." She listened, smiling at us apologetically. "Yes. The ones I would worry about are in the back of the refrigerator. Second shelf. What? No. Just throw them away. Gar-bage. Okay? Yeah, I'm watching. Jesse Jackson voted against the president. Big surprise. So did Jerry Costello—he can kiss his career goodbye. He's an idiot. Look, I'm here with a nice couple who have come to see about some very sad business so I have to go. Bye. Yeah. Love you, too."

Nice couple? I stood: shoulders back, eyes front, like a Beefeater in front of the Tower of London.

"Maybe I should have guessed," Zolitor continued, back to the nice couple before the receiver was asleep in its cradle. "Libby came in. . . . I think it was . . ." Again the calendar was consulted, the pages turned in a fairly leisurely fashion. "Oh my, it was the last day of June." She smiled at us, why I'll never know: perhaps she was mentally ill. "She and her late husband had a joint last will and testament, which they made many years ago, but now her circumstances were different." She made a small deferential bow in my direction, still, apparently, under the impression that Libby was my mother. "She brought me a"—Zolitor breathed in deeply and slowly exhaled—"full inventory of the bookshop, very detailed, Libby was very detail oriented. And other information I would need in order to make a new will, which—"

Here Thaddeus jumped in. "Yes, the will. I'd like to see it."

"Wills are made public after their submission to probate court," Zolitor said. "Quite a few of us in the profession would like to do away with that step. It's really quite unnecessary in most cases. Back in . . . I think it was 1992, '93 perhaps. One of those two. Anyhow, I was in a working group of attorneys and we were putting together a proposal we wanted to take down to Springfield, a way of streamlining the probate process. But you put fifteen lawyers in a room and it's . . . what can I say? This one says this, this one objects, this, that, on and on. We got nowhere. Anyhow. I meant to walk Libby's will over to the court this morning, but things have been kind of crazy around here. I have a client who is trying to close on a building on Clark Street and it's just been a comedy of errors. Plus my ankle, I've got a real situation going with this damn ankle."

"Awfully sorry about that ankle," Thaddeus said, "but I'd like to have a look at her will." He made a slow, broad smile, like easing the pin out of a hand grenade.

I understood that beneath Thaddeus's well-tended exterior there was an element of rage. It can be assumed: we're human, after all. "If you can't look like Cary Grant," he once declared, "at least do your best to act like him." And he did, he did his best. Even when he called me to say he was going to lose Orkney, a certain graciousness was maintained. Even when he let me know his suspicions about Emma, there was a bit of humor. Yet here in Zolitor's ten-by-ten office he was suddenly no more able to temper his fury than a child lashed to the saddle can control the frantic gallop of a runaway horse. He pressed against her desk, jutted his chin, and pointed. "Give me that will," he said, his voice boiling over—it was almost comical, like seeing someone you know overact in a community theater production. "I want it right now. You understand me? Right now."

Zolitor did not find it amusing. Her eyes radiated pure animal fear, the paralyzing kind—one of evolution's perplexing moves, in which prey gives predator an extra moment or two to strike. Finally, she was able to say, "I would be in violation . . ."

"Look here," Thaddeus said. "My parents are dead. My mother killed herself. I have no idea why. And at this point, I don't much care. What I care about is what is in that will. For me at this point there is nothing else. I want to know what she had, and where it's going. And if you think for one minute I am going to allow you to keep this information from me—you're so wrong, you could not be wronger."

"It's not here," Zolitor said.

"You already told me that your ankle hurt too much for you to get my mother's will filed. So it's here. It's on your desk, or in a drawer. And I want to see it."

"Thaddeus," I said, rubbing his back, hoping to calm him as you would soothe a dog being driven mad by thunder. "It can wait."

"She was broke, Mr. Kaufman," Zolitor said. She coughed onto the back of her hand; her fingers were trembling. "They were in debt, deeply in debt when your father passed and things only got worse. If it's money you're after, I'm afraid your mother's will is going to be a disappointment."

"Here's some good advice—and I think you should take it. For your own peace of mind. Understand? Do not cross me, and don't get in my way. Give me the will, right now. I'm not interested in your little summary. I want to see it." He grabbed six or seven or eight of the manila folders haphazardly stacked on her haphazard desk in this haphazard excuse for a lawyer's office, and raised them above his head, brandishing them for a moment before slamming them down.

My work often brought me into rooms where the tension was palpable, but normally the rules of social etiquette were followed. Smiles were smiled, nods were nodded, voices remained modulated. (Businessmen in dramas deliver hysterical orations, but really they tend to be circumspect, evasive, untruthful, and their antipathies as well as strategies remain hidden.) But here in Zolitor's claustrophobic office what was often on the inside of a negotiation was on full display—it was like the Pompidou

Center, where the building's infrastructure wraps around the edifice like vines around a tree. Zolitor took a few moments to recover from the shock at being aggressed upon, but I have to hand it to her: she calmed quickly. She rose from her chair and the same hand that moments before had been fluttering nervously now yanked open the bottom right drawer of her old oak desk. She pulled out an old manila envelope, which had been reused several times—three sets of names had been crossed out; "Elizabeth Kaufman" was printed in ink, the letters slanting far to the right. She tossed the envelope across the desk toward Thaddeus with a snort of contempt.

"I billed for two hundred dollars and believe me this has been from the outset more trouble than it's worth. I am sorry for your loss, Mr. Kaufman, but there is no excuse for your behavior here."

"Fuck yourself," Thaddeus said, reaching for the envelope. He tore it open and two sets of keys fell to the floor. He put them in his pocket and turned to leave, reading his parents' will as we headed for the door.

I could hear the congressmen and congresswomen cheering the passage of the resolution.

CHAPTER 33

The World as Will and Idea

A renter her whole life, eschewing jewelry, furs, antiques, and anything that could be construed as luxury, Libby died owning very little. At first glance (which turned out to be accurate), whatever money she had was in four separate checking accounts, a strategy based on her fear of bank failures, though each of the accounts held sums that were monetary miles under what would be covered by the FDIC.

Her will was brief; devoid of boilerplate, it was just a couple of pages. Thaddeus had begun reading it in the elevator and by the time we were in the lobby whatever lingering hopes he had of being rescued by some marvelous legacy were gone. Even as I avoided looking directly into his face, I could see his disappointment in the slump of his shoulders, the clouding of his eyes, the wince. Libby had chosen a different beneficiary for each of the checking accounts. Her former cleaning woman, Margaret Thomas, was to receive whatever was in Libby's account at the Hyde Park Savings Bank. "I was never really sure what her first name was. Margaret," Thaddeus said. "We called her Mrs. Thomas. You know, in honor of the civil rights movement and all. Anyhow, I think she died about ten years ago, so I have no idea what the hell she's doing in my mother's will. I would have to say that money will go back into the estate. Yes? And this one, at Woodlawn Savings and Loan, it's earmarked for Uncle Morris. Who needs the money like Christ needs a bicycle. Anyhow, I called him. He was really shocked when I told him what happened and said he was coming out here."

"Ah. It'll be good to see him."

"Right. I forget that you and he became great friends. And look at this, she's got Committee for a Sane Nuclear Policy in the will. Do they even exist anymore? Didn't they just sort of fade away at some point?" His expression was furious and confused.

"I don't know," I said.

"Well, let's say they don't exist anymore. If that's the case, what happens to the money at"—he glanced at the will—"the Amalgamated Bank of Chicago?"

"It'll be complicated."

I was going to add that probably we were not talking about a great deal of money, but I decided not to. An elderly man in a porkpie hat and white plastic shoes came into the lobby, his unhappy face beaded with perspiration. He had to maneuver sideways through the door because he was wearing a Cash for Your Jewelry sandwich board, with a picture of a diamond ring on one side and a watch on the other. I guessed his shift was over and he was going to drop the sandwich board off, maybe get paid, and then deal with whatever the rest of the day might bring.

"Well, at least I'm in the will," Thaddeus said, as oblivious to the old man as the old man was to us. "I'll take some relief in that. No mention of David or Emma, of course. Big sur-

prise. I get whatever's in her checking account at Republic."
He squinted. "Oh Christ. She has me living on Twenty-Third
Street. I doubt that building is still standing. Did she really not
know where I lived? Or did everything that's happened in my
life since moving to New York seem ridiculous to her? I guess
my life lacked gravitas." He said the word as if there were something loathsome about it.

We left the building. Heat radiated everywhere, the sidewalk, the street, the buildings, the passersby, all of whom had
grim expressions, even the children. Cars were barely moving. A Trailways bus disgorged clouds of foul exhaust while
the driver tapped his fingers against the steering wheel. Near
Wabash, jackhammers were tearing up the road. There is a
special kind of misery when cities are hot, a kind of fren-
zied stasis, stubborn and hopeless. A glance toward heaven
made matters worse. How did we ever make the world so
filthy? Where were our damn manners? This was really not
the planet we had evolved to inhabit. We were not built to
breathe this kind of air, or to hear this level of noise, or to live
beneath a sky that looked like the top of a plastic container in
which mysterious leftovers are stored.

Thaddeus showed me the keys to his parents' bookshop.
"I'm going. Who knows? Maybe there's something there."

"Right. Who knows?"

"Do you want to come with me?"

"Of course."

He folded the will and put it in his back pocket, and let out
a long sigh.

"I feel humiliated," he said.

"This is so terrible," I said. "But it's so good to see you
again."

"Let's walk over to Michigan," he said. "Maybe things are moving a bit better there."

We hailed a cab on Michigan Avenue and headed to the South Side. The driver was a middle-aged woman, gaunt, her face as narrow as a crescent moon. Ready for the war that was by now certain to come, she had lashed a small American flag to her side-view mirror. She blinked her eyes rapidly and continually, her long white lashes fluttering like the wings of a hummingbird. Thaddeus and I sat on opposite ends of the backseat, gathering our thoughts as the taxi crawled through traffic on the way out of the Loop and onto the Outer Drive. Suddenly, it began to rain, a pelting downpour that struck the roof of the cab and the windshield, each individual raindrop large and heavy.

We passed McCormick Place, monumental in a kind of Midwest Mussolini way—yet it brought to life a lovely memory: here was where Thaddeus and I saw the Stevie Wonder concert more than twenty-five years ago. In some live concert recordings you can hear one guy in the audience who seems almost unhinged by how much he is loving what he's hearing, shouting "Yeah" and whooping like a mounted soldier. Well, that evening at the Stevie Wonder show, Thaddeus was that person. He leapt from his seat, he shouted out requests, he screamed Stevie's name, and I looked on in amazement, wondering if I had pinned all of my hopes for human happiness on someone who might be a bit of an exhibitionist, a tiny bit gross, silly, too, and maybe even a click or two out of his mind, like those guys who went to our college's football game with their bare chests painted blue and yellow.

"Hey, look," I said to him in the taxi. "Remember when we saw Stevie Wonder there?"

"Sort of," he said, "but not really."

McCormick Place was behind us, and now we were passing a landscape of weeds and cruddy trees and train tracks, with a backdrop of public housing, that Chicago mix of prairie and blight.

Thaddeus rapped his knuckle against his window. "Look at this place."

"Grim."

"You could make a movie about East Germany, 1970, right here," he said.

"You could make a movie about here here," I said.

The downpour had stopped by the time we arrived at Four Freedoms. Its long front window was streaked with rain but the books displayed were still visible, standing there with a desultory air of abandonment hanging over them. A daddy longlegs was making its sideways skitter from head cap to head cap in search of sustenance or a resting place, from Carl Sandburg's *Lincoln: The Prairie Years* to *The Collected Works of Karen Horney* to *The Family of Man*, where it turned itself in a half circle and seemed to be facing me. Meanwhile, Thaddeus had gotten the door open and I followed him in, glancing a last time at the spider, who raced from book to book, urgently following my movements.

CHAPTER 34

Four Freedoms

It was almost dark and very hot inside the shop, an assaultive heat drenched with the smell of death. Thaddeus switched on the lights and stood there with his arms folded over his chest, surveying the place, an expression of pain twisting his face. Clearly, Libby had begun to decompose before her body was taken away. The store reeked like rotted meat upon which someone had frantically sprayed the most horrible perfume, a smell that even days after her removal plunged us into a kind of terror and revulsion. We shrank from it as from a raging fire and fought the impulse to flee.

He was sweating through the back of his shirt, a straight line of darkness along his spine, and two round blotches of darkness around his nascent love handles. His hair glistened. How I wanted to stand close to him, and, yes, what an impulse to put my arms around him. As if I had the power to make him feel less awful. It was a kind of arrogance—desire can bleed into megalomania, of course it can. I know it now, but I knew it then, too. The mind presents a sobering fact, the body rejects it. I stood closer to him. Touched him lightly on the arm.

"You all right?" I asked.

"Look at this place," he said, gesturing with his right hand, while bringing his left wrist up to his face to cover his nose and mouth. Before us were a thousand square feet of inventory, books books books, old and new, shelved by category in eight-foot-high gray metal shelves. Each aisle was denoted by a five-by-seven card, which years before Libby had constructed using letters cut out of magazines, as if they were ransom notes. History, Economics, Music, Literature, Women's Studies, Chicago. "Here is where books come to die," Thaddeus said. His arm dropped to his side and he breathed deeply, forcing himself to consume the wretched reality of what had happened here days before.

"I think we should get out of here."

"I need to look around."

"I'll open the door, let some air in."

"No, don't. People will come in."

"We wouldn't want that."

"No books on the floor," he said. "I take that to mean her dying was a smooth journey. She wasn't clawing at anything or struggling. Just sort of went to sleep, nice and easy."

"Yes, I think you're right."

"All these books are just garbage now. There's no way to get the smell out of them. Or if there is, it would be so expensive, no way it would be worth it." His voice wavered and he was silent for a moment. "So that's that."

He walked through the rows of bookshelves, glancing at the spines, while I stood where I was, near the counter in front. I waited, and a minute or two later he walked behind the counter. He found the switch for the air-conditioning and the unit came on with a sound like tennis shoes tumbling around a dryer. There was a stack of books on the end of the counter, maybe twenty of them, all with yellow Post-its on them, noting for whom they'd been put aside—they were like remnants of a lost civilization. There was a six-pack of little cans of Sacramento tomato juice. A credit card reader, disconnected, with the cord neatly wrapped around it.

Thaddeus tried to open the wooden cabinet under the counter, casually at first, jiggling it, and then with mounting irritation. But the door did not succumb to force, and soon he turned his attention to the cash register. "I never could figure out how to open this fucking thing," he said. He pressed buttons, seemingly at random, until he hit the drawer with the heel of his hand, and the drawer popped open. His face lit up for a moment, but the register was completely empty, not a dollar, not a dime. "Fuck," he said. He glanced at me, sheepishly, as if I'd witnessed him doing something gross, which I suppose I had, though it didn't bother me. Reality is essentially gross. So, yes, show me, show me everything. The grosser the better, really. Show me what is unfiltered, accidental, and true.

"Maybe we should go," I said.

He gave no indication of having heard me. He'd found a letter opener and he was using it, trying again to open that locked cabinet. He jammed the blade into the narrow space between the door and its frame and he worked it back and forth until the tip of the letter opener snapped off. Furious now, he kicked at the door, turning his back to it and ramming his feet into the wood like a donkey trying to escape its stall. At last, the wood gave way and Thaddeus started breaking off pieces of it and throwing them over his shoulder until he had created an opening large enough to reach through. He pulled out a gray metal box, which he slammed onto the counter. He rested his hands on the box and closed his eyes, and the relief he felt at that moment flowed into me.

"Cash?" I asked.

"Usually."

"Is it locked?"

"Combination lock. But I think I remember it." He took a deep breath, rubbed his hands together. On the first try, the box opened and there *was* money in it. His haul was maybe fifty dollars' worth of ones and fives. He jammed the bills into his pants pocket. "I can't believe you had to watch this," he said.

"It's fine, it's okay. I get it."

"Do you?"

"You're going to get through this," I said. "You will, I promise."

"If you're a mother and your son is still alive and you have grandchildren? Who does that?"

"Somebody so unhappy they can't control themselves."

His face reddened and his eyes lost their focus.

"Yeah," he said, at last. "Thanks. I might need you to remind me of that from time to time. Right now I hate her. I don't want to."

"Let's get out of here, Thaddeus. Come on. Let's go."

"Okay. But one more thing." He walked out from behind the counter. "I've always wanted to do this."

The bookcases in Four Freedoms were arranged with just enough space between them to make an aisle for customers to walk through and browse. The aisles were narrow, so narrow that two people could not stand in front of the same book. If Ken Adler had sent me here to evaluate the health of the business I'd say from the looks of it Four Freedoms was stagnating, taking in more inventory than they were moving out. Thaddeus walked to the aisle directly across from the checkout counter—Archaeology and the Ancient World. It ran two-thirds the width of the store—the other third was a carpeted area, with four upholstered chairs and small tables with lamps, a reading area for the customers. Thaddeus placed his hands against the books in the middle of the row that was about chest-high to him and gave them an exploratory push. The books slid away from him, but only by an inch or two. The shelves at Four Freedoms were deep enough to hold two rows of books, one south facing, the other north. Here Archaeology and the Ancient World faced south and Anthropology and Art History faced north. Thaddeus kept his hands on the five or six books he had pushed back, bent his elbows, curved his back, bared his teeth—he looked savage, mad, accountable to no one but himself—and quickly, vigorously straightened his arms. The shelf, holding hundreds of books, tottered. He shoved it again and again it tottered. Art history books on the other side were tumbling onto the floor, in twos and threes. Large and small, used and remaindered.

"Fuck you!" he shouted, and shoved again, this time with such force that he almost landed on the bookcase himself. "Fuck books, fuck Four Freedoms, fuck everything." The shelf fell away from him and he stepped back as it hit the next shelf, and that shelf, unable to resist the force of the blow, also fell, knocking over the next. The shrieking crash of the metal shelves toppling like dominoes, the thudding rain of books.

Thaddeus's hands curled into fists and he raised them above his head and pumped them triumphantly up and down as if he'd just won Olympic gold.

CHAPTER 35

Deeper Than Ever

It was as hot on Fifty-Fifth Street as it was in the store, and nearly as foul. A road crew, all of them sweating profusely, was making rushed repairs to the street, slathering tar onto the surface like army medics patching up the wounded with Super Glue. The sky was filthy gray and trembling. University of Chicago students, slender and tan and seemingly oblivious to the threat of a storm, glided by on their bicycles. It was six in the evening and from somewhere nearby a church bell rang the hours, each peal reverberating in the heavy air.

"I know it's wrong to ask," Thaddeus said. "But I do wonder for whom that bell is tolling."

I smiled but was not amused. From someone no longer an undergraduate and given the circumstances, the joke seemed pretentious and pathetic. Thaddeus shifted his gaze toward me and tried to ascertain whether my smile was genuine or forced. Oh, how he needed that little droplet of dopamine that came from human approval, his drug of choice. He had sweated through his shirt, his deodorant, and the last vestiges of his beautiful youth. He was as rank as an abandoned old

man. I avoided his eyes and felt something odd and unprec-
edented. I don't know how to describe it. It was fleeting. It was
as if I were wandering around a house I knew as well as any
place on earth and suddenly found myself in a cold, unfamiliar
room. What was this room, who was this man? It was not just a
mental sensation, it was physical, too. I could feel love wilting,
crumbling, dying. I didn't actually know if love was dying, or
if it was me. I was not going toward the light, but toward darkness. I wondered if I had ever really loved Thaddeus at all, or if
I had spent half my life caught in a lie I'd told myself.

He sensed me slipping away. My failure to laugh at his joke?
Or to meet his gaze? Something alerted him. His nervous system reacted to the tiniest titrations of human attention. And
his need to be liked, loved, included, appreciated—oh my god,
it was bottomless. He put his arm over my shoulders, like a
ten-year-old boy nominating you to be his best friend. A smell
like rust and onions emanated from within him, mixing with
the smell of Libby's decomposition on our clothes. My own
fragrance was probably no less repellent, but we forgive it in
ourselves.

I shrugged away from his arm and walked as far from him
as the width of the sidewalk would allow. He looked confused,
hurt. Oh no, I thought. Oh no. And I reached for my old feelings like a sleeper who imagines he is falling grasps blindly for
the edge of the bed.

When Proust's Swann finally realizes not only that Odette
does not love him but that she is not, in truth, really his type,
the reader feels relief, understanding that at last the fever has
broken and Swann is to that extent a free man. My fever had
broken, too, but it lurked within me. It was like what pharma-
cists say about taking the entire course of antibiotics and not

being beguiled by the first signs of health—the contagion is still there and the symptoms will return if you don't take all twenty-eight pills. By the time we reached Ellis Avenue and we stood there for a moment looking up at the Kaufmans' darkened windows, and Thaddeus took a deep breath and let it out slowly, slowly, slowly, transmitting his emotions directly to me, and I felt his resentment, his loneliness, and his pain, and I knew he was wondering what it was going to feel like stepping foot in that sepulchral apartment, in what could not have been more than eight, maybe nine beats of the heart, I was more or less right back where I started.

CHAPTER 36

Here It Was

The door to the Kaufmans' apartment had a tricky lock, but Thaddeus remembered what it required. He put the key in, jiggled it back and forth, until the lock surrendered. He took a deep breath and opened the door. The entrance hall smelled of floor wax. Thaddeus flicked on the light, and the hallway gave a little jump, as if we were intruders.

We were eye level with an old poster, tan and black, a woodcut image of Leon Trotsky, his icy beard and pitiless eyes that looked at you with what Sam and Libby believed held some hidden store of *menschkeit*—until they no longer believed in him, or socialism, or progress, or any other incarnation of the happy ending. The poster advertised a John Dewey lecture given in 1937 in the Town Hall in New York, sponsored by the Commission of Inquiry into the Charges Made Against Leon Trotsky in the Moscow Trials. I imagined it was the place to see and be seen if you were an anti-Soviet left intellectual with a couple of bucks to spare.

"That poster is not a reproduction," Thaddeus said.

"I know."

"You've seen it before, right?"

"Yes. It's always been here. Same spot."

"They weren't big on change." The poster was about two feet wide and four feet high, and it was matted, framed, and placed under glass. Thaddeus took the frame from the bottom corners and lifted it off the makeshift hook, which was just a heavy black nail someone had hammered into one of the wall studs. The weight of the thing surprised him and he staggered back before he righted himself and leaned the poster against the wall.

"It's mine, I guess."

"I don't know. Contents of the house. I suppose. Was it mentioned in the will?"

"I bet this thing is worth money."

"I don't know."

"I have an instinct. I bet this Trotsky at Town Hall poster is worth many many thousands of dollars."

"You may be right," I said.

"I'm kind of making you sick, aren't I?"

"It's okay."

"I'm sorry. I know I'm behaving abominably."

"Well, we all have things inside of us we like to keep hidden."

He nodded and gazed at me with a frankness that was almost rude.

"I'm going to sell this," he said, turning back to the poster. "Some rich former Trot who's probably now raking it in at some right-wing think tank will buy it. Those old Trots, man. They all hated Stalin so much that they were more anti-Communist than any conservative, which proves, I guess, that hate lasts, hate has real legs, and it's a fuck of a lot more powerful than love. Love is like a little boy lost in the woods, and hate is the wolf."

I followed him into the dining room. He switched on the

light, and the pale green walls, and the long Formica dining table emerged from the darkness. Next, he turned on the air conditioner, which years ago had been poorly installed, with pieces of foam and what appeared to be a pair of socks jammed into the gap between the machine and the window frame. The old GE sounded like a cement mixer as it slowly came to life. Thaddeus turned it off again.

"I can't stand that sound," he said. "I've become phobic about noise. It's so quiet at Orkney. You know, except for the sound of me going broke."

As the air conditioner slowly rumbled to a halt, the stillness in the room seemed to thicken.

"Are you okay being here?" I asked.

"Here? I'm always here."

I presumed he meant that these rooms were so much on his mind that he was occupying them emotionally, whether or not he was physically here, so I nodded, as if I understood, and pointed to the table.

"That's where your uncle Morris was sitting when I first met him."

"That's where everyone sits who ever came here. You sat on one of these chairs and they fed you. They didn't encourage you to go into any other room because then they might have to talk to you. They actually liked visitors but they didn't want to talk to anyone. So, yeah, this is where he'd have been when you first met him. The start of a beautiful friendship."

"He's a great guy. When do you think he'll arrive?"

"No idea. He and Mom weren't close. No one in my family is close or ever has been. We're all ships in the night. Except for me. I do closeness. I do extreme closeness—according to Grace, I do suffocating closeness."

So much of conversation is a kind of under-the-table tug-of-war, with one person hoping to pull the conversation in one direction while the other is trying to implement an entirely different agenda, and I suppose smooth relations depend upon our ability to wage this tug-of-war without it becoming overt. My courage was building to the extent I *wanted* to talk about meeting Morris, knowing full well that any careful examination of my relationship to the old pediatrician would eventually reveal all we had in common, but Thaddeus had redirected the conversation's flow, and I lacked the stamina and the daring to insist we pursue a topic that might lead us to discuss things I had spent the better part of my life concealing.

He paced through the apartment. I sensed he would not want me to follow him so I sat at the long dining table, waiting. The dining room was on one end of the apartment, adjacent to the gloomy, spotless kitchen. A long, minimally lit corridor led to the living room, with its two sofas and four chairs, each turned in such a way that you would have to crane your neck to make eye contact with whoever was sharing the room with you.

Thaddeus's first stop was what had once been his bedroom, but was now completely empty. Long stripes of different shades of blue had been rolled onto the pale brown walls, suggesting that Libby had at some point been contemplating having the room repainted but had not decided on a color. "Oh Jesus," I heard him mutter.

Sweat dripped down my spine, and the closeness of the room was getting to me. I was losing track of who I was, and with the next breath the whole *concept* of knowing who you are seemed dubious. Maybe there is no such thing as the real you, some essence that travels through a lifetime. Maybe who you are is just what you happen to be doing at any given moment.

And I suppose what frightened me was not having any clear idea, or really any idea at all, what I would do next.

He went to his parents' bedroom, and I heard the sound of ransacking as he opened dresser drawers and tore through the contents. Could he really have been so deranged at this moment as to believe there would be treasures hidden among the neatly folded blouses and underthings? Libby didn't have money, I was sure of it. She had been collecting Social Security and probably living on—what? Fifteen hundred bucks a month? Every day I was surrounded by people who made that much every hour. Those were the creatures in my neck of the woods, me of all people! What was I doing there among them? I was suddenly filled with a loathing for money and the hierarchies it creates and sustains, a loathing so sudden and fierce that it practically felt like panic. Libby and her thousand dollars a month. I tried to imagine how she budgeted that out. So much for rent, food, medicine, gauze, toothpicks, bathroom tissue, soap, sugarless gum, there she was, day after day, trapped in a world utterly ruled by money. But then so was I. Can you imagine a world without money? I couldn't. I tried but it was beyond me. It was easier to imagine the end of the world, the polar caps melting, the rain forests barren and bald, the last surviving humans with totemic tattoos and Mohawk haircuts, slaughtering one another for the last bits of organic matter. These things seemed vaguely plausible. These were things I could envision. But a world without money? That was remote, that was a dream within a dream. How would a world without money work? What would that mean? A barter economy? A trust economy? No economy whatsoever, just a lot of hunting and gathering? The various hypotheses were invisible behind a blizzard of what-ifs, every possible escape route from money was blocked by theories of so-called human nature. Could it possibly be true that society without money as its governing principle is completely impossible? Were we created by God or, taking God out of the discussion, by millions of years of evolution so we could spend our moment on earth trying to accumulate money? Was there really no other way? Isn't it largely accepted that there is no transaction or interaction that is not darkened and damaged once money is involved? What if we were all equal, and no one was better than anybody else? Was that kind of world truly impossible? Was disharmony as intrinsic to existence as night and day and gravitational force? I realized as I mused that I was having the thoughts of a fifteen-year-old, but that didn't seem to refute the basic idea, which is that money ruins just about everything, and even as we acknowledge its poisonous nature we continue to pursue it and continue to celebrate and display it, like a wolf rolling in the rotting flesh of something dead, trying to slather its fur with the scent of decay.

I was sweltering in this Tomb of the Unknown Socialist while the person I cared for more than any other pillaged his mother's bedroom looking for checkbooks, cash, or any other sign of money. At this point, I think he would have let out a whoop of triumph if he came upon a Mason jar filled with dimes.

Thaddeus emerged from the bedroom with a black three-ring binder under his arm. At first I thought it might hold the Kaufmans' financial records but it was an expandable photo album, with five snapshots per plastic page. He walked with it to the front of the apartment and I followed after, and when he sat in a mustard yellow armchair more or less in front of their old console TV in its faux Mediterranean cabinet, I sat on a gray and black sofa, with its depleted pillows and stout legs. I folded my hands between my knees, and made as much eye contact with him as the feng shui of the room allowed.

I was by now sweating so profusely that my clothes felt as if they were made out of drool. Thaddeus was doing no better than I; in fact, he was probably worse. Those round rosy blushes of his that had always symbolized readiness for merriment, connection, and love, those two badges of persisting youth were now subsumed by a redness that had swept across his face like a tide, leaving only the orbits below his eyes deathly white, and making the eyes themselves look haunted, hopeless, and mad.

"Here," he said. "This is what I found."

He tossed the binder to me. My hands were sweaty and I muffed the catch. I retrieved it from the floor and opened it. The first pages were black and white three-by-five snapshots of Thaddeus from his very first days up to about his third birthday. He was a worried-looking child, with a beseeching smile that persisted to this day, although not right now. The snaps were standard: several of baby T in a crib asleep—it's a certain kind of parent who can love their child the most when it is sleeping. But there were others: standing, holding the top of the crib for balance, a little Gandhi with his spindly legs and loose diaper. And there he was in the very chair in which he now sat, an infant in shorts and blue sneakers holding an upside-down copy of *The Tawny Scrawny Lion*. He might have been two years old in the picture, his hair was long and dark, swept back like a stylish Italian banker. The album held two more pages of Thaddeus before switching to Hannah, though these, of course, never recorded anything beyond infancy. She was serene, plump, with little wisps of dark hair growing every which way. Hannah in arms, Hannah swaddled. Hannah on Sam's lap. Thaddeus on his toes peeking into her crib as she slept. Libby pushing Hannah down Fifty-Fifth Street in a gloomy funereal carriage such as the one that clattered down the Odessa steps in *Potemkin*. After four pages of Hannah there were no more pictures of children. The next page held but two photographs, both crooked in their plastic sleeves. The first was taken outside of Four Freedoms with the blurred images of passersby, as if they couldn't get out of there fast enough. The second was of Sam and Libby standing at the counter of their store, unsmiling, in a pose that made Grant Wood's farm couple seem like a pair of total goofballs. And after that there were no more pictures whatsoever. Nothing and no one. Birthdays, graduation, their son's wedding, their grandchildren. Nothing they cared to record, nothing they cared to remember.

"This is sad," I said.

"I know," said Thaddeus.

I tried to hand the album back to him but he shook his head. I placed the album next to me on the sofa.

"Aren't you going to take it with you?" I asked. "You must. You can't leave it behind." But even as I said it, I thought, Who would want these sad snapshots, these photographs of emptiness?

Thaddeus folded his arms across his chest and pressed his lips together. By now, he had expended his fury and right behind it was grief—it had been lingering there patiently like a parent waiting for a toddler's tantrum to subside.

"I think this is where I was sitting when they came back from the hospital, after Hannah died," Thaddeus said. He ran his hand over the arm of the chair, back and forth, back and forth. "I woke up that morning. Alone. I don't think I was alarmed. I just assumed that everything was the same only different. I don't remember feeling any alarm at all. I turned on the TV. I ate. I was enjoying myself. That was my big mistake.

The unforgivable thing. When they got home from the hospital, they found me right here."

"You were a little kid. They left you alone for hours. What were they thinking?"

"Maybe they expected they'd be able to get back home before I woke up. That's probably what they expected."

He shifted his gaze from me to the bookshelves that went floor to ceiling on the south wall of the room. "All these books here? I doubt they read more than twenty of them. And the books in Four Freedoms? Forget it. Zero. They had three semesters of college between them. But that didn't stop them from giving me grief for not having the grades to get into the University of Chicago." He went back to rubbing his hand against the fabric of the upholstered arm. "What's wrong with me?" he asked. "I have no right to say these things. I'm sorry. I must really be trying your patience."

"Not at all."

"They were so unhappy, Kip. That's what I can't stand. I could never. I would have done anything to make them smile. But they were . . ." His voice splintered. "They were so unhappy."

He covered his face with his hands and sobbed. A minute passed and the seconds carried their burden of meaning slowly, deliberately. It was like being in a car that has careened out of control, how in the moment before impact the world slows down and you see the finch bobbing at the end of a branch, and the frilly remains of a sticker that has been peeled off the stop sign and a squashed Coke can in the weeds along the side of the road. I listened to Thaddeus cry and heard his breath moving through him, saw the silvery whiteness of his scalp between the waves of his hair.

He lowered his hands and waited to compose himself. He seemed unaware of my presence, until he said, "Tell me something."

"What do you want to know?"

"I don't care. Anything. Just tell me something."

I had not imagined that my moment would arrive in this suffocating apartment. I had not factored in both of us reeking, both of us exhausted.

"All right," I said. "I'll tell you something. But this is probably not the time or the place and you will almost certainly not want to hear it."

He looked alarmed. "Perfect," he said. "Just what the doctor ordered."

"I'm so glad we're in each other's lives, Thaddeus."

It was as far as I could go, as close to what I wanted to say as bending one slat of the venetian blind to peek outside is to actually leaving the house. I couldn't say now what I ought to have said twenty years before, or ten, or even five. Had the time ever been right? Timing is everything—isn't that the truth? It's what we believe, at any rate. It was too late for me to change the course of my life. I would need to accept who I was. A person who had chosen early on not to be known. I wasn't brave. Most people are not. That's why we have a word for the people who are. My life was already half over. It was probably too late for a new one. Probably. Too. Late. Hemingway boasted about telling his sad story in six words. I could do mine in three. Actually: two.

"Thanks, man," he said. He rose from the yellow chair and walked down the hall to the back of the apartment. Like a dog, I followed him. Like a dog. He went to the kitchen to get a butter knife and then to the entrance where he lay the poster announcing the John Dewey lecture on the floor. Using the knife as a tool, he unfastened the clips on the back of the frame. He carefully removed Trotsky's apocalyptic portrait and rolled it up tightly. Rising again, he was momentarily overcome with dizziness; he staggered and I caught him by the arm.

"I always thought you loved me," he said. Sweat was pouring off him. "Wherever I was, whatever I was up to, I always kind of assumed you were out there, thinking about me. Was it just a story I was telling myself?"

I was lost. I didn't know if he was trying to humiliate me, or seduce me, or if he was so completely spent that he was just telling the plain truth, falling into it like a runner whose race is over.

"Oh, I love you all right," I said, trying to sound cheerful. "That's never been in question, has it?"

We left the apartment. Thaddeus locked the door and I followed behind him as we descended the stairs to the ground floor. He drummed the rolled-up poster against his open hand as he walked, as if the thing was a bat he intended to use on somebody's skull.

I was a few steps behind him and I said in a soft voice, not a whisper, but quietly—letting chance decide if my words would be heard—"I mean it. I do love you. If I spent the rest of my life with you, I'd consider myself the most fortunate person in the world."

Maybe it was a whisper. He didn't turn around. Maybe I never said it at all. I'd imagined saying those words to him or words to that effect so many times over so many years— maybe this was just more of the same. But maybe I said them. Maybe this was the time. And maybe he heard them. But he didn't turn around and he continued to thwack that poster into his hand until we reached the oak and glass door in the little lobby, at which point he turned around and said, "Thanks for doing this with me, Kip. You're true blue."

"Aye aye, captain," I said, saluting. "Wherever our journey takes us."

CHAPTER 37

I Was Warned

We rode in relative silence from Hyde Park back to the Palmer House. Thaddeus drummed the rolled-up poster against his knee while he stared at the lake. The thwack of it kept time with my heart, and presumably with his. It was growing dark. The silvery lights of the city shone against the slate sky. In front of our hotel, I tried to pay the driver, but Thaddeus would have none of it. His manner was gruff, and his gestures were emphatic, impatient, as if by trying to pay for a goddamned twelve-dollar taxi ride I was trying to gain some advantage.

We made our way through the lobby. One of the ballrooms was being used for a *quinceañera* and the guests were milling around, the teenage girls like gauzy birds of paradise, beaming with panicked joy in their pink organza and yellow tulle dresses, and the boys self-serious in tight-fitting gray suits, white shirts, and bow ties. Parents, uncles and aunts, friends, leaned on one another, tipsy and loose, laughing, embracing, like revelers on a gently rocking party boat.

The sounds followed us into the elevator, but once the doors slid shut we were in silence, and we began our slow rise.

"I thought you loved me, Kip."

"I do," I quickly answered. "Of course. How can you even wonder?"

"Then save me, man. You called me 'captain.' You're my captain, too. You said we're on this journey together. Right? Didn't you? Then why don't you fucking save me?"

But from what? Did he want to be saved from a marriage to someone who had kept such a foundational secret from him? Or did he want to be saved from having to live the rest of his life without me? Yes, it's what I wondered, because the body is a chemistry set and the element of ego is volatile, and a few drops of hope create a compound that can overwhelm the nervous system. Or was he merely hoping I would share privileged information with him about a stock? Was that going to be our arrangement? Me risking the loss of my job, and maybe my freedom, and he deigning to renew my season ticket for a ringside seat to the ongoing drama of Life at Orkney? Teeth clenched, Thaddeus shook his head, and in the awkward and painful silence I heard Jennings in the woods years ago saying *money money money,* the mockery in his voice, the despair, and the knowingness. As the elevator rose it vibrated slightly, and I thought I heard the metal frame of the car hit against something—brick or metal—ever so slightly. Perhaps the mechanics of the building were starting to slip. The river of fashion had changed direction and the money that had once poured into this business had gone elsewhere. Someone always has to lose, that's the economic model, that's our system, that's the truth no one can hide. *The money the money.*

We arrived at our floor. We stepped out of the elevator and the doors slid closed and opened again, slid closed a second time and opened yet again, and did this a third time, too. When I think of that evening at the Palmer House, I remember those ominous stuttering doors so clearly. I stood there, unable to move for the moment, and realized that whatever became of what was left of our time in Chicago, I would never be able to return to my familiar spot at the edge of his life.

"Hey," Thaddeus said, "at least let me buy you dinner."

"Sounds good," I murmured.

He plucked at his shirt. "I'm a mess," he said. "I need a cold shower and then a hot shower. Wash, rinse, repeat."

"As well," I said.

"We can go to Bruna's," he said. "You know it? Oh, it's good. Old-style red sauce, garlic bread, southern Italian. Comfort food for the weary."

"Whatever you say. It's your town."

"If only. I never should have left. Chicago . . . I don't know. Chicago is comfortable. I mean compared to New York. You can be yourself here. You don't feel like you're missing the point if you're not rich."

"You're exhausted," I said. "You don't have to entertain me. You can just rest if you want to."

"I don't want to rest. I'll clean up and call you in thirty minutes." He looked at his watch, an old square-faced Longines. I'd been with him when he bought it from an antique watch dealer in the diamond district on Forty-Seventh Street. We joked about it over lunch. He said, *This watch is an heirloom. It's been in my family for more than an hour.*

"I'm going to have to do a little work," I said. "My phone has been buzzing all day and I'm going to have to deal with a few things. Is that okay, captain?"

"I like this 'captain' thing," he said, smiling. "Okay. I've got calls, too. Mine will be quick, most likely. Come and collect me when you're ready and I'll be all yours."

Hmm.

At the time my mobile phone was a BlackBerry, using technology developed by RIM, Research in Motion, a firm whose call letters were a source of compulsive riffing in both Adler offices. Maybe it was paranoia, but it was hard for me to believe that those jokes about rimming and rim jobs weren't somehow meant to lure me into the open, a kind of duck call like my sporting grandfather used to entice the gorgeous mallards he wished to kill. Why someone would want to shoot or even annoy a beautiful care-free duck is beyond me, but at any rate Ken Adler loved BlackBerry and we'd done well buying shares in it, coming in fairly strongly at around two bucks a share and even after the panic following 9/11 we were still in the solid black on it. Adler eventually got out in 2004 at thirty dollars a share, a very substantial profit, but by that time someone else was doing my job. Some people made a great deal of money— the stock eventually went to over a hundred bucks a share. And some people got screwed, royally, as the stock went out of favor and tanked. That's Capitalism 101—if somebody is throwing their hat up in the air and shouting yippee, someone else is crying in their beer. If everybody wins, the game's over.

The messages waiting for me were PhoneClad related— Tischler's insanely inessential and ridiculous company was really in play, and Ken, usually wary of getting involved with the tulip fever that more and more accompanied IPOs and takeover rumors, was keenly interested in getting involved. Beginning when my plane was nosing through the fog at SFO, and continuing throughout the day, Ken and our compliance officer, Dave Solomon, and a young woman named Laura Mills, who was so fresh out of Harvard that she was still getting her mail forwarded from Cambridge, had all kept a stream of emails coming my way, apparently undaunted by my not having replied to a single one of them. Their interest in PhoneClad seemed to grow like mushrooms in the cave of my silence, and by the time I skimmed through the nearly fifty emails coming out of the New York office their interest had grown into eagerness and I was starting to doubt my own low appraisal. Tischler was a smoke-and-mirrors man, and his product was essentially nonsense, on a par with the pet rock (I was wrong about this), and his ability to run a large company was severely compromised by his focus on making a quick killing (there I was quite right).

After showering and putting on a change of clothes, I wrote to Ken and the others. My response to their wanting to bet on PhoneClad was too nuanced (okay: equivocal) to peck out on my BlackBerry. I wanted to register my hesitations without getting in the way of Ken's enthusiasm, and I also wanted to touch on some of the perils I perceived—mainly having to do with Tischler's character. I suspected he was a maestro of the faux leak. When I had breakfast with him, he had bragged about Nokia wanting to buy PhoneClad, and when I saw him again at an Amnesty International fund-raiser in Tiburon he took me aside as if we were buddies and had some quid pro quo relationship, telling me that not only Nokia but Motorola and Circuit City were expressing keen interest in acquiring the company.

Who knew? The stock market had already recovered from the sell-off after 9/11 and an appetite for big paydays was rampant. It was possible that Tischler was not completely full of crap and would be able to unload PhoneClad, with its six hundred outlets and its three-year deal with Costco, at some staggering multiple of earnings. I indicated this in my email to

Ken and company, after writing it out by hand on a legal pad whose pale yellow surface and twenty sea green lines still exists in my memory as a warning flag waving urgently as I sped around the most perilous turn in the roadway.

It was how I was spending my one and only life, and as I wrote out my memo, the words *the money the money* chugged like an old-fashioned steam engine through my mind. Everybody wanted money and now that communism was dead, the Russians and the Chinese were also in on the hunt. *The money the money the money.* The world was going mad over money. We were choking on it, burning from it, drowning in it, killing each other and ourselves.

Moments after I finally sent my long email, Thaddeus was at my door, dressed in clean clothes—gray slacks and a blue shirt, both wrinkled. He never really could do a decent job packing a suitcase. He was showered, shaved, and wearing his woodsy scent—Pino Silvestre, which I also kept on hand back home.

He noticed my phone and the legal pad on the desk. "I shouldn't be bothering you. Looks like you're still working."

"No, no. It's fine. I just pressed send."

He watched with an interest that I found disturbingly keen as I put my phone and my legal pad into my briefcase. I closed the bronze clasp and it made a loud, unpleasant sound, sickening and final, like the snapped spine of a small animal. I put the briefcase on the upholstered bench at the end of the bed. Beyond the window, the darkness was obdurate, as if the building had been covered by a tarp. There was not a star, not a flickering light. The world beyond this room seemed to have disappeared.

"I called home," Thaddeus said. "No answer." He sat and he

seemed to be looking at the briefcase more than he was looking at me. "Maybe there was a complication? I called the hospital. It just rang and rang. Rinky-dink little hospital. We should
have taken Emma to New York, even for something routine. As
if cutting someone open could ever be routine."

"Maybe try again." *Stop looking at that briefcase*, I thought.
Stop it right now.

"I left a message. Grace is awful about phone calls. Phobic."
He lifted his chin, indicating my briefcase on the bench. "Very
impressive, Kip. All your top secrets, secure in your satchel like
the nuclear codes." Laughing, he made a move, as if to dash
over and grab the briefcase, though he did not get out of his
chair.

Where were we seated exactly? Was I here, was he there,
how close, how far? I would have to navigate through all those
forensic inquiries, as if how we got from where we were to
where we were going could be measured, or mapped out. In
court, what I could have said, should have said, was We were
seated on the edge of an abyss.

What I did say was this: Thaddeus sat on the hard chair
near the room's desk and I sat in the bergère chair. He shifted
his position so we were facing each other, with about four feet
of pale jade carpeting between us. I was clenching my hands
together so tightly that when I relaxed them they ached.

"You know what?" he said. "You've gotten handsomer as
you've aged."

"Hmm. Maybe you've just gotten more tolerant as *you've*
aged."

"Well, that could be. But the years have been good to you.
You've definitely improved."

"I could take that as a bit of a knock," I said.

"How?"

"Well, what does it say about how I used to look back in the day?"

"I don't mean it that way."

"Really?"

He laughed. "No, darling, you were stunning, simply gorgeous." In the voice of a wrecked southern belle. Limp-wristed, he touched his chest with his fingertips, rolled his eyes. Total camp.

I felt sick.

The TV was on. "Is that C-SPAN? You actually watch that? I thought cable companies had to carry C-SPAN because the law requires it."

"The Senate is voting on the Iraq thing." For a moment I couldn't look at him. I forced myself. He'd meant no harm. He had only been trying to be amusing. It was humor, good old-fashioned straight down the middle of Main Street humor.

"I'll bet you a million dollars they authorize," he was saying. "And I'll bet you another million Saddam doesn't have those weapons of mass destruction."

"I don't have a million dollars."

"Maybe they'll bring back the draft."

"I doubt it. There's enough poor kids out there; they won't need to."

"I can't even imagine my kids going into the military. It would never cross their minds. It would be like deciding to be a rodeo clown or allowing their bodies to be used in some medical experiment."

"I'm glad. They're not poor. You were able to give them that. They're privileged. I know, it sort of stinks, but it also means they won't have to kill anyone or get killed."

Thaddeus nodded. I could feel him weighing what he was going to say next. "Do you remember after the closing on that land we went for drinks and I was talking about Emma—"

"Yes, of course. I remember." I didn't want him to have to say it again.

"Well, here's the thing—I shouldn't have said that. Whatever the truth is—and I don't know the truth, I don't think anyone does—but Emma's mine. There's no question about that. It's not up for debate. The child becomes your own as you raise it. It took me a while to understand that. What I should have said then and what I can say now is that Emma is my daughter. And my love for her is unconditional and forever."

"I know. She's yours." My legs were cramping. I had to stand. Out of some instinctual caution, I grabbed my briefcase off the bench at the end of the bed and put it on the floor of the closet. I could feel Thaddeus's eyes on me.

"Wow," he said. "Must be top top secret."

"Don't," I said. "Really. Please. I need my job. It's all I've got right now."

I walked to the window and stood staring at my own reflection superimposed on the glass.

"I need a drink," I said.

"Oh," said Thaddeus. "I thought you'd never ask."

I grabbed several little bottles from the minibar and removed the fluted paper covers from the tops of two glasses.

"We don't need to bother with ice," said Thaddeus.

"Grace had no right to treat you that way," I said.

"We never speak of it. That was the agreement without an actual agreement. Those are the ones that really stick. And once that was in place we couldn't undo it without everything falling apart. And we were never sure, neither of us. But before we more or less agreed to just let the whole thing go, she admitted it happened once between her and Jennings. Once. That seems a bit unlikely to me. Sleeping with someone just once isn't how things normally go. Once that line is crossed, people tend to let things play out. Don't you think? But I'm not going to argue numbers with her."

"At least she admitted it," I said.

"She had all that artwork just piling up and piling up in her studio. And Jennings flattered the hell out of her. Maybe it wasn't flattery. Maybe he was a huge fan of her work, which is very seductive. And he was around. Let's not forget that unlike some of us he was there every day and every night. Front and center. Working the property, fixing this or that, turning that old piggery into a studio—like she really needed a studio with all those empty rooms inside of Orkney. But I went along with it." He mimed writing a check, ending with a flourish that left his hand high in the air. "I think I felt guilty because a part of me didn't believe in Grace—a rather large part, if you want to know the truth. I think I wanted her to put the brushes away and just . . . I don't know. Enjoy life?"

"So where is it now?" I asked.

"With Jennings?" Thaddeus looked stricken for a moment, old and alone. He tried to cover it with a smile, making matters so much worse.

I could not protect him. All I could do was say, "We don't have to talk about it."

"She slept with him. Fucked him, or he fucked her. They fucked. I have conjugated that copulating verb many times, believe me. At least they had the goodness to do it in her studio, and not inside the house. He probably built the studio with that in mind. Who knows? I don't need or want the whole truth. What would it do for me? Would I leave her if I knew for sure? No, I would not. I don't want that. This is bad enough. Being without her and breaking up my family? That would make everything much much worse."

"I never understood why you didn't get a DNA test," I said, with my back to him.

"I've thought about it. Often."

"And?"

"I don't want to know things just for the sake of knowing them. And I don't want Grace to leave me."

"You'd be leaving her."

"What's the difference? Everything would still be wrecked. I don't know what's going to happen to us. She's making money now, not money money, but money. Maybe there's more coming. I don't understand the art world. It seems insane to me. But I think if she ever really hit it big, she might leave me. I don't know."

"Because of money?"

"Grace does whatever she wants. She's selfish, if you want to know. But to me there's something so magical and true about her selfishness, and I like to be around it. She grew up feeling disliked and she got used to it. It doesn't really bother her. She might not even be that *nice*. You understand? I mean, the way nice people care what other people think and feel and kind of work around it. She really doesn't care. It's one of the things that draws me to her. I find it . . . thrilling, to be honest with you. I realize this all sounds rather abject. But it's not really love unless there's something abject in it. Don't you think?"

"Me? I guess so. I don't really know. Maybe. But wait. I have a question. Where's Jennings in all this?"

"I don't know what he thinks."

"He thinks he's Emma's father. That I can tell you."

"Obviously, it's not something we discuss."

"Maybe you should."

"I have to get along with him. I used to think that maybe I'd buy the place back from him. But with what money? Anyhow, he's dug in. He was raised in that house. And now that they've taken it off the tax rolls by saying it's some kind of church—which it's not, by the way—they can stay there stress-free. I think that was Muriel's scheme. She walks around with her basket of flowers and she says very little, but she's actually very clever."

I turned to face him, but he was already standing just inches away from me. Remember this, I urged myself. Remember every moment of it.

"What are you looking at out there?" he asked, peering past me.

"And what about Emma," I said. "Does she know anything about any of this?"

"It's just darkness, isn't it. You're staring out at the darkness." He put his hand on my shoulder.

"Don't," I said. "Please. The way you feel about Grace? That's how I feel about you."

CHAPTER 38

Second Half

And so began the second half of my life. How did I feel as it commenced?
Just as a survivor of a suicidal jump off the George Washington
Bridge reported in a story I'd read the week previous: *Oh shit,*
he said, *I think this was a big mistake.* The jumper was about my
age, a jazz saxophonist living alone in Fort Lee, New Jersey. He
was about to be evicted from his apartment, he was unable to
afford his many medications, and now that he was hospitalized
with a multitude of broken bones, a swollen brain, two crushed
feet, an eye that burst like a soap bubble, an exploded bladder,
and a ruptured spleen it was doubtful his financial problems
were going to get better anytime soon. *You know when you fall
two hundred feet, the water is like a cement floor,* he said.

Did his life flash before him? the writer wanted to know.
Did he have what scientists call the LRE—the Life Review Experience? The jumper said he was overcome with memories of
his mother and father, and of his first day at school, his first
saxophone, the magical time he wandered into a late night
jam session at Small's and got to play "Angel Eyes" with Tommy
Flanagan at the piano and Cecil McBee on the double bass.

For me, the leap off the bridge of lies and silence was different. It's wrong—it may even be *grotesque*—to compare my confession and the terror it struck in me to the annihilating despair that the saxophonist from Fort Lee must have been feeling, but in the long interval of silence separating my declaration from Thaddeus's response, or reaction, or whatever one can call what happened next, in that looping Einsteinian eternity I could only wonder what the fuck I had just done.

And yet, as if to cushion the blow when the free fall was complete and I hit the ground naked and unmasked, memories *did* flood in. It was like an infusion of an anesthetic, lessening the terror—maybe that's why we are deluged with scenes from our life as it ends, to distract us from contemplating what is coming next. Whatever the cause, there I was, sobbing in Dr. Wessler's office, grabbing tissue after tissue. And there I was, leaving Morris and Robbie's apartment and lingering at the door after they closed it behind me and hearing Robbie call out to Morris, "Honey, can you come here for a sec?" Soothing myself in bed, with the scent of Pino Silvestre rising up from the sheets. Like so many of the things we do when we are unobserved, there was something small and embarrassing in pretending that bottled scent was somehow Thaddeus, hoping only to drain desire out of myself as if it were an infection. But I knew I was but one of many. I knew as the day broke there were millions more or less like me, waking up alone or next to the wrong person. I have learned one of the lessons of loneliness, one of its shocking side effects: when you are in a state of longing, desire goes on and on and on, like an ocean without a shore. So there I was, on a flight to Denver, sitting two rows behind a man who from the back looked quite a bit like Thaddeus—his height, his build, the slope of his skull—

and spending four airborne hours convinced it was Thaddeus yet not once getting up to make sure because I wanted to preserve the fantasy. Don't awaken me, let me dream. Love like mine is really just a dream, and here is what Aristotle says: in dreams the element of judgment is absent. But the morning always arrives, here it comes step by step, the pitiless jailer coming closer to inspect your cell. The horrible mornings. All of them compressed into one scented pillow flung blindly across one room, whether it was in Ann Arbor or New York or Denver or San Francisco, or Athens, or Key Biscayne. Okay, important to note what I did not allow myself to do. I did not subject another human being to my obsession. I knew I was unavailable and I never allowed anyone to think otherwise. No one wasted their love on me, or their time. No human placebo for me. I did not want one person to stand in for the person I really wanted. I did not stoop to convenience. And as for Thaddeus, I restrained myself, even if it meant breaking my own spirit. I did not stalk, I did not peek and hide, I did not beg, I did not dial the phone just to hear his voice. When we dined together, I did not order the second bottle of wine so he'd miss the train to Leyden. I did not bury my face in the sheets of the bed he slept in. When I was alone in his house I did not scour the premises looking for secrets, and I did not try to sow discord in his married life—in fact, I tried to help him shore things up. I only wanted what was best for him.

Thaddeus cleared his throat, and after that took a deep breath. I could feel his center of gravity moving infinitesimally toward me. Which brings me, Your Honor, to Emily Dickinson. Hope is that thing with feathers? Perhaps for her hope chirped bravely through life's storms and never asked for even a crumb, but if my hope was a bird it was a bird that flapped wildly, a bird that devoured common sense, which it would tear to shreds.

But my hope wasn't a bird. It was a moon rock or some other alien element with a magnetism that completely subverted my internal compass, spinning the needle like a helicopter blade.

Or would you accept hope was dope, and I was addicted?

No. Hope was a prison. Here's a proposal, Your Honor. Time served?

"Sorry," I said to Thaddeus, not because I was sorry I had finally declared myself but to get him to say something, anything. And as the silence continued, I added, "Not the most opportune time to bring them up. My feelings and all."

"Yeah," he said. His hand was still touching my shoulder, weightless, a lost glove.

"Did you know all along?"

"It's . . ." He shook his head. "It's very flattering."

I thought about hitting him. "I'm not trying to fucking flatter you," I managed to say.

"I know, I know," he said, quick as always to make amends. He was the handyman of his own life, patching it up here, patching it up there, never a moment's rest.

"Do you even understand what I'm saying?" I asked.

"Yes, I think I do. I do. Of course I do."

The heavy air that had blocked the view from my window began to dissipate, and as we spoke I could gradually make out little pinpricks of starlight in the sky and the diffuse smudge of the streetlights around Grant Park. The change disturbed me, I'm not sure why. I think it suggested we were moving through space, through time, just as you can be sitting on an airplane and trying to relax in your seat with a drink and a bowl of microwaved mixed nuts, and then suddenly something happens and you notice the clouds are streaming madly by and it strikes you in the most disquieting way that you are in a machine hurtling through the sky at six hundred miles an hour.

"I don't know what to say, Kip. Everything seems to be in the wrong place. But maybe everything is right where it belongs."

"Really, everything?" I said. "Isn't that like saying God doesn't give you any problems bigger than you can handle?"

"When a door closes, a window opens?" offered Thaddeus.

"If God opens this window, I think I'll jump out of it."

"I'm sorry, Kip."

"It's not your fault. All you ever did was be yourself. I was in hiding before we ever met. It was actually better once I met you. I could imagine a happy ending."

He took his hand off my shoulder. And ran that same hand through his hair and put it back on my shoulder, and—because it was my nature, because I could not stop from wondering, could not wriggle free from the cat's cradle of absurd interpretations that had bound me all these years—I wondered if what he was doing was putting a part of himself on me, a DNA transfer, as if the hand that had touched his hair and was now on my shoulder was a kind of kiss, or a pre-kiss, or something else for which I had no name but was meant to bring us closer. Though I did understand that if something has no word to describe it, that probably means it doesn't exist.

CHAPTER 39

To My Great Surprise, He Pressed Charges

"We'd better eat something or we're going to get drunk," I said. "Maybe some Pringles."

We had finished our drinks and refilled our glasses.

"I'm not eating Pringles," he said.

"I forgot how elegant you are."

"Yeah, it's one of the things about me that people forget. We're going to miss our reservation at Bruna's. Do you care?"

"No, not really."

"Good. We'll stay here. Do you have more work to do?"

"There's always more. But I'm done."

We clinked glasses.

"That thing in the elevator, Kip. About saving me. I'm sorry. That was a wrong thing to say. You've done so much and I know if you could help me here you would."

"Well, we've both said inappropriate things. I called you 'captain,' so we can call it even."

"'Captain' works for me," said Thaddeus. "I like it. As in *O Captain! my Captain! our fearful trip is done.*"

We clinked glasses again. We stood in the middle of the room. This chair, that chair, everything seemed wrong.

"Can I ask you something?" Thaddeus said.

"No."

He smiled. "You go out with all these amazing women."

"Oh my god, Thaddeus. Are you really asking me this?"

"So have you always really been into men?"

"I've always really been into you."

"Grace always said you were gay."

"It sickens me to even think I'm being discussed like that."

"It must have been awful, Kip. So many lies. You lied, Kip. You lied to everyone. Or was it just to us?"

Us. He was an us. I didn't much care for the us-es of the world, with their you-wash-and-I'll-dry lives, their horrible little hikes through the Cinque Terre, their depressing codependency, the constant phoning—I'm at the grocery store, I'm at the hardware store, I'm stuck in traffic, I'm at the gynecologist, I'm at the urologist, I'm having a colonoscopy and there's a camera up my ass.

"No," I said. "Not just to you. I'm very private."

"But you lied. I mean . . . people come out all the time. Why didn't you?"

"What do you think? That just because gay pride becomes a thing, then every closet in the world is emptied? It doesn't work like that. For every person who decides to go public with their private life, there's another person who decides not to. I didn't want to be a minority. It never felt right to me, or safe. I didn't want people to think about what I did with my body, or what I wanted or what brought me pleasure. It was personal, and I wanted it to stay that way. People can be so cruel. And in my business, believe me . . . it's not like Hollywood or something. It's brutal."

"But I'm not brutal. What did *you* think? That I would judge you? That I was some kind of prejudiced small-minded . . ." He drew a long breath, momentarily overcome by the thought of me—or anyone—thinking so poorly of him.

But what had happened to the "everyone" in his question? Even the "us" was gone. He wanted to know why I thought *he* wasn't trustworthy. He wanted to know why *his* impeccable liberal credentials were being questioned. It was about him, as was so much of what passed between us. It didn't bother me but it didn't escape me, either.

"You could have figured it out, if you'd wanted to," I said. "It was pretty much hidden in plain sight."

"No, it wasn't."

"Okay. Then it wasn't. Whatever. I was stuck in it."

He retrieved the last of the little bottles of booze. A gin for himself and vodka for me.

"I'm sorry I lied," I said. "But the truth is I love you. I didn't know how to say one without the other."

"I love you, too, Kip," he said, far too quickly for it to have much meaning.

"No, you're not hearing me. I love you. I want to be with you all the time. Forsaking all others. It's overwhelming. It's always been there and it doesn't go away. I love you and I love you and I love you." I was making the fatal mistake of repeating and restating, deluding myself into believing he didn't quite understand, or that he needed to be convinced of my sincerity.

He let out a breath, slowly. "Jesus."

"I really am sorry. I was always waiting for the right moment and now I've chosen the worst possible time."

"I get it," he said. "I know how it is. I mean with lies. Don't worry. Really. I don't want you to worry. Okay? You look so worried. You know what? Listen. It's like a writing problem." His eyes brightened. "You come to a crossroads on page five, does the baby live or die, do the brakes fail or do they hold, do they move to France or stay in Tuxedo Junction, does the guy buy a house he can't afford. You make the choice, you go left instead of right, the brakes fail, the house is bought, and before you know it you're on page one hundred and five and you're completely lost because you made the wrong choice and you've just piled one mistake on top of another mistake trying to make things right, but everything you've done to make things right has just made everything worse."

"In life, it's hard to get back to page five," I said.

He filled his glass and waited for me to fill mine.

"Next year on page five," he said, holding his glass aloft.

There was something else he wanted to say. He tilted his glass back and forth and the little bit of booze at the bottom coated one side and then the other.

"I have to ask you . . ." He finished his drink, glanced at the dresser, and saw all that had survived were two bottles, one of Campari, the other of Harveys Bristol Cream. "What did you see? I mean—in me? What did you see in me? All that time. What was it?"

Oh, the vanity, the vanity, and the infinite emptiness that could never be filled. How many times had I seen it? How many warnings did I need to gather up what was left of my pride and my life and head for the hills? Yet I did not and I could not. My attachment to Thaddeus was not *in spite* of his weaknesses.

I could not separate his weaknesses from the whole of him—they were as much *him* as his breath, his shadow, the sound of his voice, the scent of his scalp. His weaknesses were evidence that he was here, true and alive, like a curl of hair left at the bottom of the bathtub. His weaknesses were a secret revealed, and to perceive them brought you closer to him. And here is what I know. When you love what is most flawed and most troubling in someone there is no getting out. You are wrapped up. You are sunk. You are in for the duration. You have not only faced the worst, you have embraced it. It may be why stories about the gods are so filled with thunderbolt behavior, wrathful score settlings, pitiless punishments, perverse suggestions, irresistible temptations. We see the displays of indifference and animosity, and we sing songs of praise through floods and famine, through Hiroshima and the Holocaust, louder and louder, our faith a point of no return.

"How can these things be known?" I said. "What draws one person to another? There's no checklist."

"You didn't even think I was a good writer," he said. "Even in college you had your doubts. I think you could at least admit that."

"What did I care if you were a good writer or not? I knew what it felt like to be you. I knew when your laughter was real and when you were hiding behind it. I knew what your fingers felt like when you drummed them on the table. And year after year I watched you hold it together. . . ."

"Wait, wait," he said, laughing. "You're admitting that you don't think I'm a good writer."

"How could I know?" I said. "You never really had a chance."

His eyes moistened for a moment and he looked away, before turning toward me again with a smile as bright and tight as a brand-new zipper. "I don't even care any longer. At this point . . ." He raised his right hand and rubbed his pointer and middle finger against his thumb, the universal sign of surrender masquerading as common sense. "You know what?" he said. "I fucking hate gin. I'm going to raid the minibar back in my room and bring stuff over here."

I nodded, quite sure he only wanted to get away from me. In the countless times I had imagined telling Thaddeus how I felt about him, I had nearly as often imagined him dismissing me, not only as a lover but as a friend. He turned. He left. He didn't leave the door ajar. I pressed my ear to the wall separating his room from mine. What did I expect to hear? A desperate phone call to Grace? Peals of laughter? What I in fact heard was nothing, save my pulse pounding in my ears.

I went to the window and rested my forehead against the cool glass. My reflection was obscured by the warmth of my exhalations, and then the mist would disappear and there I was again only to be enshrouded by my next breath. The moment I had so often imagined and hoped for had already passed but I had still not caught up to it. I felt harmed, unmasked and small. How in the world was the next day or the next hour or even the next minute supposed to occur? I had said and done what I had wanted to do for so long, but wanting something and having it are very different matters. Desire fulfilled becomes a referendum on itself. Was this really what I had wanted and if it was: now what?

But the truth was in the end not really what I had longed for. Not really. The truth had no particular value. The truth was a means to an end. What I wanted was for him to choose me and for that to happen the truth was the only way in. What I had wanted was to make love to him, to travel together, to waste time with each other, to pass sections of the Sunday paper over the breakfast table, to push a cart up and down the aisles of a supermarket, or maybe to run away from this country and every wrong turn I'd ever made and every wrong turn he'd ever made and everyone we knew who it turned out didn't really know us at all and to take my money and buy a house in Crete or Tuscany or somewhere else bright and healthy and we would hammer a nail into the thick stone wall and hang a calendar from that nail and circle in red the day of our move-in and declare, This is when time begins, here, now, today, nothing else mattered before today, and nothing will be ordinary after. We would leave our former lives behind. People would be appalled. They would note that we were not exactly *good* for each other, as if that mattered, as if love was ever sensible. Sensible was a pose, moderate was a huge mistake. We would devour each other. We would be horrible company, you'd be making a mistake to share a meal with us, you'd end up either hating us or regretting your own life.

At the sound of the doorbell—a stately little two-note chime—joy and terror erupted in me like thousands of birds taking flight at once. St. Mark's Square, Venice. I can testify to this: I was not in my so-called right mind. And once that happens it takes a long while to get back.

"You all right?" he asked, as I opened the door. He carried a wastebasket filled with what he had taken out of his minibar. Without waiting for a reply, he stepped past me and began setting up our refreshment area on the dresser, first the booze, then the fruit juices, the nuts, the candy bars, even a deck of cards. Clearly, he wanted to be absorbed in a task. Clearly, he was as nervous and lost as I was.

I stood behind him. I put my hands on his shoulders. Disguised my intentions for a moment by massaging his muscles.

"That feels good," he said. He fussed with the little dollhouse bottles, putting them in a neat row, as if a great deal depended upon their looking a certain way. And also shifting that ever important center of gravity, giving me easier access to his trapezius, the aptly named trap muscle.

A word about self-control. If you are over and done with the self you have carefully constructed over the years, if you have mercy-killed it in its own bed of nails and are now some nascent, untested person, blinking, dizzy, and afraid, and up for grabs, then what chance is there for self-control? You can rely on some core values, some innate sense of right and wrong, some instinct for decorum, some hand-me-down checklist of dos and don'ts—but these sign posts of self-governance can be suspect and unpersuasive once you consider that they have been there all along, guiding your actions while your old self was cowering and making all the wrong decisions, that they were, in fact, collaborating with the enemy.

So here's what I did. I tightened my grip on his shoulders. He said *Ah* and I turned him around and kissed him more or less on the mouth. In my state of mind, I couldn't really gauge if he was accepting this kiss passively, if he was frozen with surprise and embarrassment, or if he was kind of kissing me back.

"Is this okay?" I asked.

"No one has ever felt that way about me," he answered. "The way you feel. The way you say you feel. I guess it's real."

"I think everyone has someone who feels that way about him. I think some people die without knowing how much they were loved."

"It's just that I've never had that," he said.

"But is it okay?"

He nodded. Silence. Then: "It's amazing," he said.

"You don't think I'm . . ."

"I think you're amazing," he said. "All these years. Did you really honestly feel this way about me the whole time?"

"'True love is a durable fire,'" I said. "'In the mind ever burning; never sick, never old, never dead, from itself never turning.'"

"Hey, Sir Walter Scott. Mr. Orkney himself."

"Close. Sir Walter Raleigh."

"Oh. At least I got the Sir right. I'm a solid B student."

"You're okay. You've come far, you've done more than you were built to do."

He opened his mouth to say something but thought better of it and nodded.

"Let's have one more drink," I said.

"Are we really going to do this?" he said. "Is this really going to happen?"

"Is it up to me?"

"I've had kind-of sex with guys," he said. "A long time ago. Just horny . . . nothing. But I've never actually gone to bed with a man."

"In most ways, we're in the same boat," I said.

"I'll probably bore the hell out of you," he said. "In the sack. I've become a bit vanilla."

Ah, of course: Grace's complaint. And he was a bit vanilla, I suppose. And a bit further along, he wasn't. He was spirited, game, but would ask me for encouragement, instruction. Ever auditioning, ever accommodating, ever eager to please: I could not shake him loose of that.

Yet for all of that, being with him was very close to what I had always envisioned. A kind of innocent, old-fashioned honeymoon, with a soupçon of porn. We were awkward, we were elbows knees foreheads toenails, were oops and Is this okay, we were wait wait that hurts, we were trying to slow things down and we were heedlessly charging forward. Had something gone awry with the air conditioning? We were coated in sweat like racehorses.

———

Alas, I fell asleep. I hadn't meant to even close my eyes—I knew sleep was a risk. But the day, the drink, and then the sex had finished me off and as my eyelids fluttered and closed, Thaddeus whispered into my ear, "Sleep, sleep, yeah . . ."

And so I did. And the world went on without me, as it always did and always will. In the meantime—how could I know this and, yet, how could I not have guessed?—Thaddeus's family was rallying, getting ready to be at his side.

Not only Grace, but David and Emma, too. And not only them, but Jennings as well, and not only Jennings, but Muriel, too. The five of them had driven up to Albany and taken the first flight to O'Hare. It was Grace who had organized it, chosen the flight, bought the tickets, but all of them wanted to be there for Thaddeus. Husband, father, benefactor: he was all these things but in their minds he was mainly a grieving son, and they were sure he needed them, and they wanted to show him what he meant to them.

I imagine them on the plane, a regional jet. They are half the passengers. Emma sits alone in the second row, with her knees drawn up, dozing with her head against the window.

David is a nervous flier, which he tries to hide, making matters worse for himself. David, if you ever read this: what you keep hidden inside devours you. Of the five of them flying to Chicago, Muriel is the most outwardly emotional. It may be her gentle nature but it's possible that the initial wonder she felt when Thaddeus gave them all the yellow house for a dollar will never fade. In her mind, he had parted the waters. She does not forget. Nothing is lost on Muriel. The things she cares about do not get buried in the cluttering onrush of events—daily life rarely intrudes on her. She is next to Jennings with her arms folded over her chest, staring straight ahead, silently crying. When Jennings takes her hand, she leans her head against him and says, "All he ever wanted was for everyone to be happy."

"Like that's going to happen," Jennings says, but luck is with him because either his wife doesn't hear his remark or she chooses to ignore it.

Grace sits alone, careful to keep her gaze away from Muriel, whose tears offend her. Grace is certain that Thaddeus will—at the very least—be grateful they have all showed up for him, and there is a good chance that seeing them all in Chicago, and knowing they have made an effort to remind him how much he is liked and loved might soften this brutal loss, the abandonment. Yet she cannot keep her eyes off Jennings, until her body suddenly has a memory of how it felt when he twisted and pushed his way into her, and she looks away.

I was awake for a few minutes, well before they boarded the plane in Albany. I'd awakened to that quick grab of panic and confusion—the *where am I* moment I'd gone through innumerable times over the years of business travel, shifting time zones, unfamiliar beds. Thaddeus was asleep on his back, with his left arm flung and his hand resting on top of his head, while his right hand rested on his chest, like a school kid about to recite the Pledge of Allegiance. That earthen, appley scent. Those deep breaths, just a notch below a snore. I was next to him. The sheets were heavy, like curtains that had been rained on. I marveled at the eucharistic intimacy of sex. To consume the fluids of another. To have the body of another within your own.

I didn't want to sleep. My life was three hours old. I fought sleep as one fights the sea. I squeezed my eyes shut and then opened them to their fullest aperture. I reached for my phone to check the time. It was 5:15 A.M. I lifted the sheet and used the light of the phone to see his body. Soft, its glory days well behind it. He was flaccid now, and there was something youthful and insouciant about his dick—collegiate, too—the ruffled skin of the circumcised foreskin encircling the head of it like a turtleneck sweater. He had drunk me, entered me, without fear of contagion. No questions asked, no precautions taken. *Don't leave me,* I thought. But he was gone, a citizen now of the other world, the world of night, and phantoms. My eyelids were fluttering. I was losing my purchase on staying awake. I thought of Wallace Stevens . . . of the two dreams, what dreamer, what lover would choose the one obscured by sleep. But my body had its own agenda. I left the world in which I had finally found my rightful place and entered a dark one full of fantasy, stored memories, symbols, and nonsense. At one point, I was back on Hydrangea Court having just used the bathroom and I was flapping a towel to dispel my scent while my sisters rapped frantically on the door. *Let us in,* they shouted.

I woke up.

Alone. I swept my hand across the sheets.

Thaddeus had slipped out of our bed. I felt a moment's panic, but then I saw him. He had gone to the closet.

He was on his haunches. He was undoing the clasps of my briefcase.

I was so tired and so drunk on the afterburn of sex that my first thought was *Oh good, he's still here.* He was being as quiet as possible. He opened the briefcase, its wide maw, exposing the accordion section within. All my PhoneClad notes were in there. The handwritten draft of my email to Ken. Yet that did not occur to me, not right away. *What is he looking for? What is he doing?* I wondered if perhaps Thaddeus was under the mistaken impression that I had Libby's will in my briefcase. Yet my body knew the truth even as I proposed one lame and improbable excuse after another. My body knew. I put my hand over my mouth.

To my sisters, to my friends, to the Court, and to every lonely, heartsick, memory-mad, desire-driven, sidelined person in the world: do not do as I have done. Give your unrequited love six months to make its way into reality; if it's not there by then, it's not going to happen. She does not feel what you feel, he can never reciprocate, and you are destroying yourself. Tell them the truth and move on, and if you can't reveal your feelings then kill your feelings, and if they resist murder redirect them and give that love to someone else and if that's not possible then march for peace or rescue animals or learn how to play the cello and if none of those things reduces the agony then toughen the fuck up and learn to live with agony. Don't be afraid of agony. Human beings are designed to absorb vast quantities of agony. Just look around you! But stop believing, stop hoping for the moment when unrequited love is given its just rewards. If only someone had told me this, I might have had a different life. But, in all honesty, Morris said as much. He told me! Even I said as much. I told me! But I did not listen to Morris and I did not listen to me. And no one else will listen to me. Am I the only person in the world who carried a torch for so long, watched it burn slowly down to the nub, and the next thing that burned was the hand that carried it, and when that was scorched it was my arm that burned and then my torso, my face, my life. I can't be the only one. We're irrational creatures. Not all that smart about matters of love and desire. We'll be traveling to other planets long before we have any real chance of self-control.

But I'm getting ahead of myself.

Here is what happened.

It was ten in the morning, though the room was still for the most part dark. I got out of bed. I walked across the room. He was so engrossed in his snooping that even though I was walking toward him he didn't know I was awake. He was reading my memo to Ken by the closet light.

"Hey," I said, "what are you doing?"

He was startled, but not embarrassed. "I'm on a treasure hunt," he said. He stood up. "So PhoneClad, huh. You could have told me. You know?" He put the memo back into the folder and the folder back into the briefcase, his movements very fastidious, especially for a naked man. He closed the clasps, but held on to the briefcase while looking up at me, the other naked man.

"You really have no right to do that," I said.

"I guess," he said, as if it were a matter of infinitesimal importance. When he saw my expression, however, he changed tack. "I think we're a little past that, aren't we? What happened to the love, man? You know? Where is it? Where's the love? Everyone talks about love but no one lifts a fucking finger for me. I'm in a fix. And you can help me out and you won't do it. Has working with money all these years hardened your heart, is that what happened?"

I pointed to the bed. "What was that? A tactical move? So you could steal from me?" I took the briefcase away from him—he resisted a moment but relinquished it. He made a sound, a kind of puff, as if I were acting like a fool.

"You're so suspicious."

"Suspicious? I was watching you do it."

"Kip," he said, in what was meant to be a calming voice, but which further enraged me, "you can't make a big deal out of everything."

Had a life of grinning and bearing it led him to believe I could grin and bear it, too? His attempt to diminish the insult came out all wrong. Similarly, I had meant only to swat him with my briefcase, but that came out all wrong, too. My body told my mind: step aside and let us take it from here. I surrendered control. I hit him with such tremendous force. The leather, the brass, the weight of my private papers.

He made a sound, half a cough and half a cry. He pressed his hand against his nose and checked it for blood. "Look what you did!" There was a wisp of pale red on his palm and a small dark red bubble trembled at the rim of his nostril.

I swung the briefcase at him again. He put up his arms to protect his face, but he was too slow. He was lagging behind the events. I may have missed out on the radiant history of my time, but I was dead center in the moment right now. The world was different, the world inside this room, and Thaddeus had not caught up to it. My captain's instincts were slack.

Despite a dead sister, a dead father and mother, despite a ruined career, and despite raising another man's child, he still
operated on the assumption that people would love him, and
that smiles and jokes and birthday cards and plenty of room
for guests and giving away a few extra acres and being a friend
to all would get him through. The brass clasp on my briefcase
struck him in the mouth and the whomp of it obscured the
damage being done—the porcelain, pulp, and nerves of his
two front teeth, dazzling and white with a little hairline space
between them, the crown jewels of his smile: ruined. In pain
and its retinue of fear and confusion, he crossed his arms in
front of his face. His nose was bleeding, and in the darkness of
that room the flow was black. My briefcase struck his crossed
arms and he stumbled and struck the back of his head against
the steel rod from which hung a few clothes hangers kitted out
in satin. The blow to his skull made a deep wet sound, like a
melon hit with a baseball bat.

"Oh shit," I said. "Are you all right?"

The hand that was covering his mouth went to the back of
his head. He made an agonized expression and I saw the emptiness where his teeth were once stationed. He closed his eyes,
groaned, bent forward.

"I'm sorry, I'm sorry," I said.

"I'm going to be sick," he said, and a moment later began
to vomit—a foul, alcohol-infused flannel, the color of oatmeal.
He pushed past me and staggered into the bathroom, and
slammed the door.

As I hurriedly dressed, the house phone rang—loud, rau-
cous, demanding, and I picked it up before the second ring.

"Mr. Woods. We have . . ." He paused.

"Grace, David, and Emma," Grace said, her voice cheerful

and loud from the other side of the front desk. "And Jennings and Muriel, too!"

"Have her wait a moment, if you would," I said to the desk clerk. "I'll call right back."

I rapped on the bathroom door. The water was running both in the sink and the tub. Thaddeus did not answer. I quickly made up the bed, swept the empty bottles into the trash basket. I checked the mirror over the desk. Why did I look so pleased?

I rang the front desk back, and asked to speak to Grace. I'd only kept her waiting a couple of minutes but she sounded put out.

"Kip? What's going on?"

"Welcome to Chicago," I said nonsensically.

"Where's Thaddeus? We called his room over and over but there's no answer."

"Yes," I said. "He's up here. Room fifteen twenty-two. He's with me."

"He's with you?"

"Yes. He's here."

"Okay, we're coming up."

"Grace?"

"Yes."

"Don't bring the kids. Okay? Come alone."

CHAPTER 40

The Ransom

If you have to be arrested, being an affluent Caucasian is the way to go. It wasn't exactly valet parking, but no guns were drawn, no voices were raised. They waited patiently while I shut down my desktop and my laptop and locked the bottom drawer of my desk. The only iffy moment was when I reached for the jacket draped on the back of my chair. The younger cop, Hawaiian by the looks of him, quickly squeezed my Paul Stuart from hem to collar looking for a weapon before allowing me to put it on. I was not handcuffed, but simply read my rights and guided delicately through the Adler Associates open-concept California Street office with no more than a finger on my elbow, just to remind me that for the next while my life was not my own. *Fine, take it, maybe you can do more with it that I've been able to.* My co-workers looked on, making no attempt to hide their dismay.

"It has nothing to do with my job," I called out, though that wasn't exactly true. It was felony assault and battery, yes, but if I hadn't seen Thaddeus trying to read the PhoneClad notes, things would have probably gone in a different direction. My fellow Midwesterner Stephanie Buchsbaum called out in her husky alto to ask if I wanted her to call one of our lawyers and I said, "Good idea," in a voice brimming with false bravado. She followed me out to the elevators. The elevators in that building were notoriously inefficient, though today the wait was not too bad. Stephanie got as close to me as the two officers would allow. She looked me up and down and made a rah-rah gesture with her fist and told me I was looking good and not to worry. "Thanks," I said again, my eyes suddenly stinging. I realized at that moment just how terrified I was. But it was a strange, truncated fear, like a dud firework that smokes and fizzles and then it's over. What did I care about this cop's finger on my elbow, or the inquiring eyes of the people from work, or going to jail, or having a record. I'd told Thaddeus the truth. The thing I most dreaded was already behind me.

Bail was easily taken care of. I was in the precinct for all of two hours and was home by the afternoon. No one—except, of course, for Thaddeus and Grace, and, a bit later, their lawyers—wanted to cause me any undo inconvenience. The San Francisco lawyers passed my case along to criminal attorneys in Chicago. I was not even required to appear in court, but I made the trip anyhow, behaving as much as possible like the innocent man I more or less felt myself to be. I wondered if Thaddeus was going to be there, too. I was quite sure he would be, but I was wrong.

The case was before a judge named Sidney Orloff, elderly, dapper, and caustic, and with a reputation for speedy work. He had already seen Thaddeus's videotaped deposition and he'd seen mine. There was no question in his mind as to who hit whom with what and where and when. The why really didn't interest him.

"You're making my life very easy, gentlemen," Orloff said, ignoring the fact that of the four attorneys two were women. Rather than pound his gavel against the sound block, he pinged it with his fingernail, and pronounced me guilty. "I'm going to cogitate on this before sentencing," he said. "And I will look at all supporting materials, statements, and whatever other nonsense you want to bring to the Court's attention. Is there anything you would like to add to my storehouse of knowledge before we adjourn?" He lifted his long chin and scanned the courtroom through the bottoms of his half-glasses. "Is either the plaintiff or the defendant present?"

I was seated on the left side, two rows behind my lawyers. There were twenty or so other spectators scattered about, folks coming in from the cold, others who probably alternated between courtrooms, libraries, churches, and homeless shelters. I whispered to one of my lawyers, asking if I should say something here, and she shook her head emphatically, like a swimmer trying to dislodge water from her ear. I sat back, wised up to the fact that in most legal proceedings the actual defendant was peripheral, and justice was hammered out by the people getting paid.

The lawyers on both sides gathered their papers, filled their briefcases, exchanged pleasantries. My team and I were going to meet in an hour at their offices on North LaSalle. I grabbed my topcoat and I hurried out. A few uniformed cops were standing on the steps in front of the criminal courthouse—an ugly, obdurate block of a building, a cross between a Roman ruin and a radiator.

A light snow was drifting through the gray air. Off to one side—I almost missed seeing her—stood Emma, wearing a blue trench coat and dark glasses. Her hair was cut short and parted on the side. She held an unlit cigarette in one hand and her phone in the other.

"Hi, Uncle Kip," she said, her voice soft and effortful.

"Emma! What are you doing here?"

"Dad asked me to let him know what happened," she said. "I'm in school at the University of Chicago."

"Okay."

"Are you going to jail?"

"I don't think so, Emma. We'll see. So . . . University of Chicago?"

"I got early admittance."

"I'm not surprised."

People streamed in and out of the courthouse. Mothers with children in tow, lawyers sipping take-away coffees, young guys on their way to prison, dressed defiantly. Emma glanced at her phone and tossed it in her shoulder bag. The snow fell with increasing force and the temperature seemed to drop.

"I better get going," Emma said.

"It's good to see you, Emma. You look great, by the way. I guess college really agrees with you." I wished she wasn't wearing dark glasses.

We were silent for a few moments.

"My dorm's really close to Dad's old apartment, you know, where Grandma and Grandpa lived."

"That's good."

"I guess."

"Your dad's a good guy, Emma. And boy, does he ever adore you. I'm sorry I hit him."

"Then why did you do it?"

"Oh, honey, it's never the right thing to do."

She took off her glasses. Her eyes were full of anguish. Maybe she wanted me to see that, to know. The wind was picking up and the snow was swirling. She must have been freezing in that trench coat.

"Can I give you a hug, Uncle Kip?"

"I would like that so much."

She put her arms around me and I lightly touched her shoulders.

"You were always my favorite," she said, and before I could say another word, she turned and stepped quickly away. A cluster of lawyers were just approaching the entrance, some in three-piece suits, some in high heels, a couple of them carrying tan and white boxes of documents. I wondered with a searing twist of grief if I would ever see her again.

I was sentenced to eighteen months' parole, with mandatory anger management classes—will someone please look into what I suspect is the cozy relationship between courts and the scammers who run these worthless anger management classes? Though I hoped they were wrong, my lawyers warned me that the main reason Thaddeus filed assault and battery charges against me was to bolster a civil case. That he would want to sue me seemed unlikely, but I wasn't able to put it completely out of my mind. In the meantime I could travel with permission between San Francisco and New York if my job required it. I could actually travel anywhere, for the job, even out of the country. The law treated my job at Adler Associates as if the fate of the nation were at stake, as if I were actually doing something necessary that could benefit others, like a surgeon or a teacher, instead of something with less social value than dog grooming, which a parole officer in New York told me was what she did to pay her way through Fordham.

I couldn't resign from Adler until my eighteen months suspended sentence was served. I went through the motions and did my best. Ken and the others were pretty damn decent and treated me no differently than they ever had. Perhaps they even treated me a bit better now that some of the blanks in my personality had been filled in. They all knew I'd struck a man with whom I was naked in a hotel room. I don't know what they made of that; I did a decent job of not really caring. All that time fretting about what people would say, do, how they'd look at me. I'd been a fool. Not even getting to live in a fool's paradise. Where had I been? A fool's purgatory?

Two months after the court date in Chicago, my lawyers heard from Thaddeus's lawyers. They supplied us with an angry little inventory of the damage I'd done. The broken front teeth, which had to be removed, resulting in an infection that lasted for three weeks. The scarring of the philtrum. The fractured cheekbone. And a new addition, not mentioned in the criminal case, the partial loss of vision in the left eye. Meetings missed, opportunities slipping by, incalculable (well, almost) loss of income, and, naturally, pain and suffering. They were willing—that's right, *willing*—to shake hands and call it a day for two million dollars.

Never mind that I did not have two million dollars. What antagonized me the most was his willingness to dismantle me, his hunger for revenge. Yes, I had harmed him in a frenzy, and it was my bad luck that what had enraged me was not persuasive in a court of law. We could have argued that he was snooping in my briefcase, but in order to make that case we would have had to prove he was looking for privileged information about a business deal I was involved in, and in order to make that case I would have had to reveal that it was not the first time he had come to me for insider information, which was something I could not do, or at least I *chose* not to do. So, yes, I whomped him a good one, pow right in the kisser as they used to say, but I was not in my right mind. Thirty years of exclusion mixed with three hours of sex makes a potent cocktail and I'd drunk it down to the dregs. Thaddeus's reprisal was another matter altogether. It was done calmly, with plenty of forethought and plenty of opportunities to change his mind. It was as far from a rash act as you can get. It was well thought out with charts and tables and calculations, and it was right there in black and white.

I composed furious letters to him, in which I sunk into the toxicity of revenge. I threatened to sell my Orkney acres to ExxonMobil, or to the Windsor County Gun Club. I threatened to build a house on those acres myself, a monstrosity with a tall tower he would have to see whenever he gazed eastward. I even threatened to clear-cut the land. Sinking still lower, I wrote that I knew where Emma was living in Chicago and I was perfectly capable of letting her know who her real father was. It's often been said that revenge is a dish best served cold. And maybe for some it is a kind of emotional delicacy, something to be savored by the psychologically refined. But like several of this life's so-called delicacies—sadism, fertilized eggs—it was not really to my taste. I found revenge, in fact, repulsive. Before long, I deleted the whole cache of unsent letters, every last syllable.

A year after the civil case was initiated, with a court date yet to be scheduled, I wrote him another letter, and this one I sent.

> *Dear Thaddeus.*
>
>   *I'm sorry I hit you with the briefcase. I am sorry I took it out of your hands and used it as a weapon against you. I am sorry your front teeth were ruined and you had to get implants. Sorry for the scar. Sorry most of all for the eye damage. You can bring this letter to your horrible lawyers and they can use it any way they like. However, I believe we can settle this matter without lawyers. Whatever lies were told and what buried truths remain unearthed, you and I have a long history. We both know that the two million dollars is never going to happen. Whether it was put out there as a bargaining tactic or if you were unconsciously aping our government's wartime policy of shock and awe, I don't know. But I don't want to haggle, I won't do that, and I've already had enough shock and awe to last a lifetime. So here is what I can do.*
>
>   *I will sell you the Orkney acres that I purchased. The purchase price I am asking—nonnegotiable—is one U.S. dollar, which is, if memory serves, the price you asked from Jennings's father after he fell out of one of your trees and you wanted to make it right by giving him the yellow house. Unlike that old transaction, this purchase will not cause you any trouble. The land will be yours again and I will not step foot upon it. Maybe this is what you wanted all along, to restore that missing piece of your property, which you can click into place like the missing piece of a jigsaw puzzle. Though you do know, I hope, Orkney will never be brought back to its original acreage. Now that the yellow house is off the tax rolls, they'll never give it up. And when they've shuffled off their mortal*

coils, their children will have the place, and their children after them. At any rate, getting those ten acres I bought will be a partial restoration of the original property. I imagine you'll take some comfort in that. You're someone who believes half a loaf is better than none. I think your marriage to Grace reflects that, too, an admirable, self-preserving capacity to compromise and protect yourself from the worst possible outcomes. I myself don't have that capacity for compromise, at least not in matters of the heart. And nowhere is that inability more apparent than in my feelings about you. What can I do about it? I've tried everything from analysis to Zoloft, which takes us from A to Z. We're all of us just who we are, and the essence of us is as indelible as our thumbprints. You were my darling boy and when I first "fell in love" with you the impact was so stunning and so brilliant I knew nothing would ever match it and I held fast to it with very little thought of any ultimate reward. It was its own reward, and the longing was more satisfying than anything that could ever be achieved by moving on, and the pain was preferable to the emptiness of renouncing my feelings. That's what I believed. And still do, alas. I put quotation marks around fell in love but I did that so as to not embarrass myself or you. In the privacy of my own being, those words are as real to me as hunger or thirst. I was fascinated and moved by everything and, frankly, anything about you. I loved to watch your fingers as you tied your shoes and waited for the moment when you gave the bow an extra tightening tug to make certain it was secure. I loved to watch you chew your food with that thoughtful expression on your face as if you were hearing distant music. I played the videotape of Hostages countless times, listening carefully to the actors say lines you had written.

I knew you would never love me. But that didn't stop me from coming up with all kinds of self-beguiling hypotheses that allowed me to carry on. And on and on. The main one was this: if I were keeping my sexual preferences a secret from you, there was a chance that you were keeping yours a secret, too. Yes you were married, yes you had children, but lots of gay people have done that, and continue to do so despite all the rainbow flags flapping in the breeze. And as long as I kept my secret I could imagine you were keeping yours, too. That night in Chicago, I struck you when it suddenly seemed you had gone to bed with me to create an opportunity to find out about that deal I was working on—by the way, if you'd put money into PhoneClad you would have lost eighty cents on the dollar. Now I no longer wonder what your motive was. Like a pearl pried loose from its sticky home, I possess that time in bed with you and it no longer matters to me if you were just after the payday or if you were curious or if you were moved by my ardor and drunk enough to get swept along or if you loved me, too, at least in that room.

I'm seeing someone. The father of one of your uncle's patients, by the way, which makes him a little too close to Planet Thaddeus for anything big to happen, but he's a great guy and we enjoy our time together. One day I imagine I will partner up with someone. I want to. But it will be something that happened after. What I felt for you? I won't feel that again, and I don't think I want to. But someone to pass a section of the Sunday paper to over breakfast? I can do that, and I want to, and I will. The hell of loving you all those years, my dear Thaddeus, when every moment was spent in longing, and every disappointment had buried in its nucleus a kind of promise, that hell was also a kind of paradise, and *you don't get to live in paradise. It's not fit for humans. We weren't cast out of Eden by an angry God—we escaped. We don't need Paradise. We'll do better in New York, or Chicago, or Detroit, or London, or Rome, or Scarsdale. I'd rather live in Scarsdale than Paradise and I'd rather spend the rest of my life with someone who does not make me tremble with lust and longing, someone whose happiness and well-being does not mean twice as much to me as my own. Goodbye, Thaddeus. If you pull out of this spiral and become the good man I always felt you almost were, I won't be there to see it. I won't see you grow old. I won't hear you laugh. I won't feel your touch. I won't hear your voice at the other end of the line. And you won't hear mine. To make sure this happens, I can sweeten the pot. The land is yours and I will add $100,000 to the settlement. It's the price of my freedom. Kidnapped Kip is paying his own ransom. Take the money, take the land, the trees, take the waiting and the yearning, take the hunger and the hope. Our fearful trip is done.*